The Twilight Obelisk

a novel

by Alexey Osadchuk

To my Dear Reader, with gratitude,
Alexey Osadchuk.

Mirror World
Book#4

Magic Dome Books

The Twilight Obelisk
Mirror World, Book #4
Second Edition
Published by Magic Dome Books, 2017
Copyright © A. Osadchuk 2017
Cover Art © V. Manyukhin 2017
English Translation Copyright ©
Irene and Neil P. Woodhead 2017
All Rights Reserved
ISBN: 978-80-88231-51-6

Table of Contents:

Chapter One

IT'S QUARTER PAST FOUR in the morning. The dawn is nearing. The snowstorm has died down; the stars twinkle yellow in the distant sky.

"Wouldn't it be nice to have some sunshine for a change?" I ask Prankster.

My pet is curled up at my feet, sniffing in his sleep. His ear twitches, betraying his eavesdropping. I already unsummoned Boris but let this lazy sonovabitch lounge around for a bit.

"I could use some peace," I tell him. "At least for a few days. Let's hope Laosh and his gang get here soon."

We have set up camp by the collapsed wall of the very same house where we met the Nocteans' attack. The crackling of the fire sounds so soothing. My hands reach out toward its warmth. Heaven!

The Caltean warriors are fast asleep. The city ruins reverberate from their heroic snoring.

I should add some wood to the fire. The others need to get warm.

Seet and Horm are making a remarkable recovery. No wonder: this new legendary order that we've received does indeed work miracles.

The Grace of the Earth, what a strange name. Its effects are even stranger, adding +25% to my group's regeneration times. By regeneration the system means both Life and Energy. Excellent, what can I say? Just when we needed it, too.

"And that's not all!" I whisper to Prankie as I open the characteristics tab. "We've received two more legendary orders! Shadow of a Giant and Friend of the Breeze. Both are very powerful spells. Cool, eh?"

Prankie twitches his hind leg in his sleep by way of reply.

"Okay, let's take a look," I tell him.

For some time, I study the new stats in silence. "Aha. I see. The Shadow of a Giant adds 30% to Life. Which means if I now have about 10,000 hp, this buff brings it up to 13,000."

I knead my beard as I try to work it out. "And that's not all. I can cast it on all fellow raid members."

Prankie sniffs his content in his sleep. He

doesn't seem to care.

"Not impressed, are you? Very well. How about Friend of the Breeze? Don't you like the sound of it? Here, listen to what it says," I puff my chest and recite in a low voice, "The spell adds 45% to Speed to all raid members."

I cast a meaningful stare first at Prankie, then at my comrades in arms. All of them are dead to the world.

I suppress a smile. We must look a sight! "You've no idea guys who you've got involved with."

I glance over the next line. "Wait a sec. So stupid of me. I have another spell, don't I? The Hand of the Outcast? That's what I received with the legendary achievement for maxing out the clan's Reputation. Plus 30 pt. to all clan members' Morale, wasn't it? Whatever that's supposed to mean. Never mind. I'll work it out, I'm sure."

The gifts weren't without their drawbacks. All the new magic tricks I'd just received had a cooldown of 24 hours. Too long, but that was a negligible inconvenience compared to all the perks.

"I really can't complain, buddy, don't you think? First the late-night scuffle with the Nocteans, and then the meeting with the ancient NPCs! I have less than twenty levels left till 100. My Control skill is at 5 now. That's five scarabs, can you imagine? That's one hell of a force. Don't even ask how I'm going to pay for all the metal, but it's worth it."

I rub my hands, realizing I probably look like a nutcase. What can I say? It's not normal for me, I know. I never thought I could get to love fighting so much.

"And that's not all!" I whisper in excitement. "We had scarabs and fleas, and now we have a new blueprint: a Scorpion! Call me the Lord of Insects if you want!"

Prankie still plays dead — but his cunning moist nose twitches in synch with his rising belly, signaling for me to go on.

"Okay, if you insist. The Scorpion's specs say that it's mainly metal plus 15% toxins. Originally designed by Master Brolgerd in order to deter predators from attacking the shepherds' flocks, later it was adapted for military purposes. Oh. Now why am I not surprised? Humans! Sentient beings, yeah right. They just have to wage war on each other."

I mechanically readjust the non-existent glasses. "Now let's check out the stats of our new six-legged team member. A poisoned blow... what else can he do? Aha, he can also grab an enemy with his pincers, immobilizing them for a few seconds. Useful thing, especially against physical classes."

I pause for a second, mentally comparing the Scarab to the Scorpion. "Just as I thought. One is a tank who's already excelled in action, the other is sneaky with excellent speed and agility."

I close the insects tab and move over to the pets.

Both have grown a lot, almost reaching level 100. That's good news. The bad news is, if I want my little menagerie to continue advancing, I'll have to travel all the way back to Master Rotim in order to level up Riding.

The problem is leveling up my beasties' respective skills. Both Boris the Hugger and Prankster the Black Grison seem to lag behind. And I never got the chance to read the warning messages because I've been so insanely busy just lately.

I could level up Boris' Flight up to level 3 and his Triumphant Crow to 2. Same for Prankster. So it looks like I'll be obliged to fly Boris to the village of Tikos in the Tallian Prairie.

There's just no other way of doing it. Pretty predictable, if you think about it. The game developers have to have their profits. I have a funny feeling this is going to cost. A lot.

More expenses. I just hope Rrhorgus likes the loot. Werewolf fangs, stone clubs and animal pelts — that was all the loot the Nocteans had offered. Which wasn't a lot to begin with: we didn't get any loot or XP for those killed by the Forbidden City guards.

"Talking about loot," I murmur. "Isn't it time to open the remaining chest?"

Are you sure you want to open the Precious Wrought Iron Chest?
Accept/Decline

"Absolutely," I say, pressing Accept.

Congratulations! You've just opened the Precious Wrought Iron Chest!

Reward: The Magic Mirror of Ishood, 1.

That's interesting.

The Magic Mirror of Ishood is an ancient artifact, the work of an anonymous Master of the Divine Era. There is a theory that the Master had once endowed the item with part of his own soul. Until today, the item was considered lost.
Part of the legendary collection The Five Masterpieces of the Divine Era.

The item's characteristics:
The Mirror's owner can use it to summon his own reflection to his or her aid.

Warning from the item's designer:
Beware! The summoned entity is but a mirrored reflection of your own soul! It's a fake — a phantom!

Restrictions:
The reflection's life span: 2 hrs
Cooldown: 2 hrs

More system messages start pinging in my interface,

Congratulations! You've received Achievement: A Self-Professed Collector
Reward: +1% to your chances of receiving Knowledge in battle

Congratulations! You've received Achievement: A Beginner Collector
Reward: +3% to your chances of receiving Knowledge in battle

Congratulations! You've received Achievement: An Advanced Collector of Relics
Reward: +5% to your chances of receiving Knowledge in battle

Congratulations! You've received Achievement: A Treasure Owner.
Reward: +10% to your chances of receiving Knowledge in battle

Congratulations! You've just found an item from

---

the legendary collection: The Five Masterpieces of the Divine Era.

Collect all five items to receive a bonus!

Puzzled, I scratch the back of my head. I've heard about collections before, of course. There're tons of them in Mirror World: you are supposed to collect sets of figurines, tableware and even pieces of mosaic.

In this case, however, I've been lucky enough to lay my hands on a legendary — and hopefully very useful — amulet. Its effects are still a bit unclear but the description sounds rather promising.

I turn the small and rather plain mirror around in my hands, studying it, then place it in my backpack. In any case, collectibles are always in high demand at auctions, and relics like these are expensive. My old friend Rrhorgus will be ecstatic about it.

"Ah! Prankie, I completely forgot," I say, rummaging through my bag. "I've got one more item, haven't I? Where is it now... Aha, found it."

The buckle of the Wings of Death combat belt.
Effect: +150 pt. Strength
Effect: +100 pt. Defense
Effect: +250 pt. Endurance
Effect: +150 pt. Stamina
Restriction: Only Ennan race

Level: 50
Warning! This item is non-transferrable!

"Just look at this, buddy! This is also almost a collectable, isn't it? Look at these stats! It suits my level, too. Only how am I supposed to wear it? I need a belt to put it on, don't I? That's another thing to add to my to-do list: visit a leatherworker."

After some careful studying, the buckle too goes into my bag, replaced by the last masters' gifts.

"Now the main part," I say, unraveling the yellowed parchment scroll. "Let's take a look. According to Master Satis, the scroll holds the answers to many important questions."

... I've never seen anything as majestic in my life — and let me tell you, I've seen a lot. The Emerald Palace of the Alven Prince; The Brown Deserts of the Narches; The boundless moors of the Dwandes... all these places pale in comparison with the Brutville Halls located at the very heart of the Twilight Castle...
(The Notes of Arwein, page 12)

It takes all of my self-control not to explode with laughter. "What, is that it? Answers, yeah right! This sounds like even more questions! You guys have a really sick sense of humor..."

Shaking my head in disbelief, I throw the

scroll back into my bag. After a brief inspection, the bunch of keys I received from Master Axe follows in the same way.

"Why would I need keys in a city without a single door left standing?" I grumble while studying the magic sphere. "Can you even call this a city? You can't even find an outhouse here!"

I struggle to concentrate on the artifact's stats. Oh well. I force a sarcastic grin. We've just received two weeks of absolute immunity.

With a sigh, I close my eyes. "Congratulations, Olgerd, my boy. You've just become the new guardian of this tip. The Lord of the Ruins."

I can understand the game developers. They need a sensation; a war to end all wars. A mega scuffle. The more clans that go at each other's throats and try to lay their claim to this city, the more profits there are for the Glasshouse owners.

For some reason, mundane obelisk activation isn't good enough for them. In any case, it's too early to even think about it. I've only been here for a few hours, and I've already begun to overcomplicate things.

In any case, what did I expect? They used me as a bait. And they told me as much. I was their whipping boy. I knew what I'd been getting myself into. With a handful of NPC warriors, a useless bunch of keys and a protection sphere I was meant to be a red flag to motivate other players into action. As in, *"if this useless noob activates the obelisk, he's going to get all the rewards that come with it!"*

I was pretty sure that Twilight Castle was already being discussed in every chat and forum. Auction prices for the few fragments of old maps mentioning No-Man's Lands must have rocketed. Very soon, the strongest armies in Mirror World would arrive here, possibly wiping us off the face of this earth like the wind wipes away the dust.

That's why Tanor must have stopped messaging me. Why would he? This was the end of the line. The cards were on the table. Now everything depended on the other clans' quick reactions and how well they prepare for the raid. Or, as a certain Julius Caesar once put it, "I came, I saw, I conquered".

Very well. The clans' agendas as well as those of the Reflex Bank owners were pretty clear to me now. Now what would my next steps be?

At first sight, my affairs seemed to be in a sorry state. That's putting it mildly. But if you tried to look at the problem from a different angle — or even better, from several — they offered a very interesting view of the picture. Naturally, my lack of gaming experience didn't allow me to grasp it all, but even I could see that not all was lost.

What's more, I too was in the mood for a big scuffle. Anyone who'd attempt to arrive here in order to "see and conquer" would be in for a truly unforgettable experience. I'd take care of that. I knew I could do it.

"I can and I will! Honest to God I will!"

"Olgerd? Whatcha mumbling there?"

Droy's sleepy voice distracted me from my musings. He levered himself up with his elbow, his half-opened left eye staring ironically at me. "Are you casting your magic?"

I chuckled. "You could say that, I suppose."

He beamed. "That's good. Keep going. Your witchcraft is helping the boys, I can see that."

I glanced at the sleeping Seet and Horm. They kept regenerating.

"Yes, leader," I replied. "Soon both will be back on their feet. They will need some rest and care though."

Droy nodded. "Good. When the others arrive, Orman's wife Carina will soon put them right. She's the tribe's medicine woman."

"A medicine woman?" I asked curiously. "That's interesting. Do you have many of them around here?"

Droy craned his neck to make sure Orman was still sleeping, then turned back to me, "Olgerd, you amaze me sometimes. You're such a smart guy. But some of the things you say..."

"Why, what did I say?"

Droy shook his head in amazement. "You're lucky Orman can't hear us. He would have told you a thing or two... He might have even punched your lights out despite you being the tribe's friend and all that."

"But why? What have I done?"

"Don't you understand? His wife is *unique*. There's nobody else like her in the whole world. Every woman is equally unique. And you're talking about them as if they're a bunch of rag dolls. Please, next time watch what you're saying."

"I see..." I mumbled, open-mouthed.

What was that now? Had this NPC just made it clear that I needed to change my attitude to them if I wanted to keep my Rep points? This piece of binary code actually supported the illusion of this world's perfect authenticity?

How interesting.

"Droy, my friend, I'm very sorry," I began cautiously. "I'm afraid you misunderstood me. No, it's not that. I just failed to formulate my question correctly."

"I know what you wanted to fro...fom...formulate," Droy shrugged my apology away. "You wanted to know whether there were other healers in the tribe. Of course there are."

Was he kidding me?

Droy frowned. "Don't look at me like that. I'm

a smart man — it's because I know you for quite a while. But other Calteans might not understand you as well as I do. We're all different. Some are smarter than others; or should I say dumber? It's just a lesson for you for the future. Make sure you don't say something you might later regret. It would be a shame."

Jesus Christ. Was it my imagination or was the relationship between the NPCs and players gradually evolving, rising to a totally new level? Every time I looked at this black-bearded Caltean tribe leader, I began to wonder if he was indeed controlled by the invisible puppeteer — or had all the AI controllers been fired?

"I can see that got you thinking," Droy said with a sarcastic grin. "That's good. They say that thinking is a healthy habit."

I shrugged. "What can I say? You're dead right there, my friend. Thanks for the tip."

"That's all right," Droy grinned good-naturedly. "As long as you learn from my words. Like I learned from yours that day when we battled the Darks by the River Quiet."

We both heaved a sigh, staring at the dancing flames.

Personally, I couldn't tell whether that slaughter had been beneficial for me or detrimental. All I knew was that without it, we'd now have had fifty more warriors. Plus a shaman. Which is a power to be reckoned with.

"Very well, soldier," Droy said. "Carry on with your watch. I'll get some more sleep."

Judging by his Energy bar, it would take him another couple of hours to fully restore. Same for all the others — except for the wounded warriors, of course.

Now was a convenient moment to do what I'd planned to do all along but never had the time. I needed to study their stats.

Let's start with Droy.

Level: no problem. Another battle might bring him up to 300.

How about his characteristics?

Oh wow. That was in fact quite complicated! A combat class. Abilities. Skills.

Class: Warrior. Sub-class: Lancer. Why lancer? Droy was good with all sorts of weapons, wasn't he? He was an excellent archer and could brandish his sword with the best of them. What was the catch?

Aha. Found it.

An NPC's sub-class depends on the skill level of a particular weapon. In its turn, the skill level of a weapon depends on how frequently it is used in combat.

That made sense. Indeed, the spear seemed to be Droy's weapon of choice. He was good with it, too. How he'd skewered the Nocteans with it!

Droy took a great deal of pride in his spear: a strong, well-made shaft topped with a long iron head. Still, a closer inspection of the weapon's stats proved less than impressive. Its level corresponded to that of his own, but its icon... it was "gray". Ditto for all of Droy's gear: his knife, his sword, his bow and his clothes.

Same applied to all the other warriors. They didn't have a single "green" or "blue" item between them.

Oh wow. Once again I caught myself rubbing my hands like some... some nutcase?

No wonder! A whole Klondike of opportunities was opening up before me.

Thoughts began thrashing about in my mind like a flock of scared birds. What if I was wrong? What if NPCs couldn't change their pre-programmed weapons? Then my discovery wasn't worth jack.

On the other hand, why would they color the icons at all? Why would they allow NPCs to level up their skills and abilities?

I couldn't remember NPCs ever picking up loot — but that didn't mean anything. Everything in Mirror World happened for a reason. For instance, Nocteans' stone weapons were of a different class and therefore not suitable for the Calteans who in turn didn't seem to be able to see certain types of players' weapons. Was there a pattern there somewhere?

"Never mind," I murmured. "We'll tackle that problem when we come to it. What next?"

Apart from his military skills, Droy also boasted other more peaceful abilities. Apparently, he was a passionate hunter and fisherman; he could cook you a mean meal; etc. etc. The numbers against each skill said nothing to me. Once I compared his stats to those of his warriors, I might draw some conclusions. But even that wasn't that important. The main thing was, they did have skills which could be leveled.

I'd been so busy studying Droy's potential I was oblivious to everything around me. In the meantime, it had started snowing.

Oh, well. So much for the sun. At least it wasn't windy. I suppose that was good news.

I had to climb to my feet and go fetch a new helping of firewood. There was plenty of it lying around, anyway.

The fire accepted my offering and began to grow, reluctantly at first, its circle of warmth widening. Now the snowflakes melted in mid-air just out of our reach.

"Excellent," I sat back down and made myself comfortable. "Who's next?"

Seet the Burly and Horm the Turtle were both

archers. But as for Orman the Bear and Crym the Hammer, both were light infantrymen.

How interesting. Seet was only three levels away from becoming a lancer. And Horm must have used his sword a lot in the recent skirmishing: it looked like he might soon swell the ranks of our infantry.

As for their more peaceful skills, Orman was an excellent cook (with which I agreed wholeheartedly) while Crym the Hammer was a budding mason — a colleague of mine, to a degree.

Each of them had a good couple of dozen other skills in various degrees of arrested development.

Never mind. We had a lot of work to do. Plenty of opportunity to level up every warrior's skill and ability.

Talking about stat comparing... what was that little app I'd received? The one with all the graphs? I'd forgotten all about it.

Very well. I pressed Raid Control.

Active raid members:
6/296

What was that supposed to mean? Aha... Number six was our little group. The other 290 were still on their way here. So apparently, I only had access to the stats of those NPCs who were currently with me.

Very well. That little was clear. What next?

Jesus. They didn't make it easy for you, did they? Tabs and more tabs, at least fifty in total, packed with charts, graphs and diagrams...

Aha. The Morale tab! Wasn't it the one I could improve with the Hand of the Outcast? Let's have a look.

Wow. Judging by the numbers and the icons' intense green hue, my clan members could take on the world. Which was normal, really. They'd defeated the Nocteans; they'd found a seat for their clan; they'd even managed to stay in one piece. Apart from a few wounded, we had no casualties. No wonder their morale was sky-high.

Even though the developers had skimped on information, this characteristic was pretty much self-explanatory. A drop in Morale could have had some potentially unpleasant consequences, especially for me as the raid leader.

The interface was pretty clumsy, I could see that. Still, it did simplify the task of raid control. I wouldn't be surprised if at some point the game developers asked for my feedback.

Next tab: Life Support. So many stats! Satiety, Fatigue, Physical Health... and so on and so forth, at least twenty of them. Now I didn't have to peer at every warrior to find out how he was feeling. All I had to do

---

was to open the chart.

Actually, judging by the sagging graph, my men were hungry as hell. Also, I could see that our food supplies were running low.

How strange. I'd never looked at it that way. To me, the Calteans had always been pretty self-sufficient. They used to cook their own meals on the fire, they drank their own drinks and mended their own clothes. They had managed very well without me. But now that I could see the whole picture, I could on one hand monitor it all but on the other, it added to my already quite hefty responsibilities.

I spent some more time studying the interface until I located another very useful little app: Coordinator. From now on, it was going to report all instances of level drops for each and every one of my raiders' stats. I could monitor each person individually or control the raid's combined characteristics.

I tried it out, setting it to 80%. Immediately I was flooded with hundreds of alerts. I brought the number down to 60%, then to 40%. In any case, it looked like food was a priority.

When the others woke up, I should really watch Droy issuing orders. According to the app, we had enough food left for two more meals. Hunting was the only way we could restock our supplies. And now that I knew each person's Hunting levels, I was curious which of them Droy would choose for the job.

I just hoped I wouldn't have to interfere with what I used to consider an automated process. Because if I did, I might end up being buried under an avalanche of petty problems. Then I could kiss my big plans goodbye, that's for sure.

Chapter Two

"CRYM, I WANT YOU to check the area for any game," Droy said, dishing out lumps of cooked meat out of the cauldron. "See if you can catch something."

Crym the Hummer nodded. "Will do."

Bugger. So much for my not interfering.

Everything had seemed to go smoothly once the raiders had woken up. Orman — who'd been the first on his feet — got busy making breakfast which looked more like an oversized dinner. So far, so good. Apparently, the system worked well without me.

But once Droy had started allocating daily tasks, I got worried.

Okay, both Seet and Horm needed to heal and

couldn't be disturbed. But why had Droy left Orman behind to keep camp while sending Crym out hunting? Crym was hopelessly behind in Hunting: in fact, he had 50 pt. less than Orman. Shouldn't Droy have left Crym to keep camp instead?

I waited patiently for both to get on with their tasks, then took a seat next to Droy. "Mind if I ask you something?"

"Fire away," Droy said, warming his hands over the embers.

"I just wonder, why did you send Crym out hunting? Isn't Orman a better hunter?"

I very nearly told him about the stats but bit my tongue just in time.

My friend arched a surprised eyebrow. "Funny you ask me."

"Why?"

"Well, think about it. You were never interested in these things before."

I nodded. "I wasn't. I'm just curious."

"Very well. It's quite simple, really. Your mistake is you only look at the problem from one angle. What you need to do is see the entire picture."

"Sorry, I don't get it," I said.

"I'll explain," Droy said, still smiling. "You're absolutely right in saying that Orman is the better man for the job. But!" he raised a meaningful finger. "You only thought about hunting. You seem to forget that Orman is also an excellent cook. So I want him to stay in the camp and set up his own kitchen. This is something only a cook can do. And if I asked Crym to do it instead — and you probably know what kind of 'cook' he is..."

"How can I ever forget," I winced, remembering the dinner Crym had helpfully cooked for us once.

Droy chuckled. "Exactly. And you shouldn't doubt Crym's hunting skills. He'll be back with something, that's for sure. He's a Caltean, after all."

"You think?" I asked, still unsure.

"Of course. When I took a leak this morning, I saw some boar tracks real close. They've never seen man in this part of the world. They've probably never been hunted before. I don't think the ancient Gods were into hunting that much. So I gave Crym a tip. You shouldn't think I'm going to hang around doing nothing. I'll help Orman a bit, then I'll keep an eye on Seet and Horm."

He paused, thinking. "There's something you can do, too. The snowstorm is over. Now is the time for you to summon your flying beast and take a flight around our new territory."

I nodded, deep in thought, digesting yet another lesson I'd just learned from this NPC.

He was right again. Embarrassing, really. On the other hand, it was great news. It meant I wouldn't have to concentrate on petty stuff.

And as for taking a flight... What a good idea!

Boris materialized out of nowhere full of life and energy, his eyes shiny, impatient to take to the sky. What was I waiting for?

I unsummoned Prankie and leaped into the saddle. With a joyful cry, Boris the Hugger shot into the sky.

Immediately the wintry air froze my facial muscles solid. My eyes watered. The speed! Well done, Boris! He's come a long way.

I allowed him to frolic about for a bit. After a few loops, I told him to level out.

We soared over the ancient city ruins. You couldn't make anything out among the heaps of collapsed stonework and banks of age-old snow. Not a single building was left standing. What had happened here? A tornado? An earthquake?

Only an occasional glimpse of the remaining foundations gave you some idea of the city's layout.

So what did I see? The city's main landmark was a mountain which had offered its foothills to the Ennan builders. I could clearly see the outline of the five city walls which had encircled it: it was a bit like looking at a slice of a layered cake.

The lowest wall — or rather, its ruins which served as a base for our camp — was also the longest. If we wanted to restore it by the deadline, we would probably need to enroll all of Mirror World's builders.

And even then I wasn't too sure that they'd make it.

Restoring the wall was only part of the problem, though. We also needed to defend it. I dreaded to even think how many warriors I might need just to post on the city walls.

Never mind. This structure was way out of my league at the moment. Ditto for the next three walls. But the highest and the shortest one... I just might make it.

If the maps were to be believed, that's where the Brutville Halls used to stand. Almost on top of the mountain. You could indeed call it the heart of the Twilight Castle.

I needed to take a closer look.

Obeying my order, Boris landed on top of the tallest fragment of the wall.

"So! It's not that bad at all!" I exclaimed, surveying our future campsite.

Boris sniffed his contempt. I could understand him. Here, the tallest of the wall fragments were about seven foot high, not even. Considering the nature of our enemy, these so-called fortifications weren't going to stop anyone. Some of our future opponents might not even need to jump: they'd simply step over them.

Now, what else... According to the map, I was now standing at the very center of the Brutville Halls so eloquently praised by Arwein.

I suppressed a bitter chuckle. I'd done so

much in order to get here; I'd traveled so far — and finally I'd arrived.

"What now?" I shouted at the empty, wintry sky.

Silence. As if! Even Boris had ignored my outburst of frustration.

Then again, who said it was going to be easy?

I spent some more time walking about the ruins. This place seemed perfect for our little gang.

How ironic. This part of the city used to be the grandest. This is where their elite used to live. Or even their kings. And here we were, barging in like some barbarian tribe into Rome, settling down here with all our caboodle. The only thing that excused our presence was the fact that unlike the Vandals and such, we hadn't come here to destroy.

I gave the gloomy ruins one last look. They seemed okay. There were only a few minor points left to check out. Once that done, I could go back and report.

I told Boris to take off. "Let's circle the mountain one last time, then we can go back to the camp."

Silently he obeyed.

* * *

My recon flight lasted until midday. We could have stayed longer had it not been for the snowstorm. Still, what I'd already seen was plenty. Time to return to base.

As we flew over the mountain summit, I noticed a rather wide rocky ledge. I could almost bet that it hadn't been there when I'd first passed. Someone must have taken great care to keep this part of the cliff as inconspicuous as possible. You could only see it from the air, and even then only at a certain angle. Even so I had a funny feeling that discovering it must have had something to do with my Survival Instinct.

Boris banked into a smooth turn and landed on a flat rectangular surface at least fifty paces wide. Its outer part was completely snowed in. Closer to the wall was a black rocky platform. Someone must have invested a lot of TLC into this hideout.

"So that's what it is, then," I whispered, staring at an enormous door hiding under a rocky outcrop. "Not all is ruined, apparently."

Calling it a door was actually an understatement. A gate, rather, big enough for a smallish truck to drive through.

Slowly I looked around me. To my left was a descending staircase cut into the rock, wide enough for two people to pass each other. Three even, if they're someone my size.

Okay. Now, the door. Without leaving the saddle, I told Boris to get closer.

He'd barely took two paces when a new system message popped up,

The gate to the West Grotto
Would you like to enter?
Yes/No

My body erupted in a cold sweat. So this place wasn't all ruins and desolation?

My heart missed a beat as I pressed *Yes*.

Warning! In order to open the gate, you will need the key.

I reached into my bag and began rummaging inside with a shaking hand as my gaze searched for a keyhole.

A bunch of keys appeared with a sonorous clink. One key was highlighted blue: a heavy rectangular lump of steel two inches wide and at least two hands long. Its sides were machined with a jagged pattern of square teeth.

I sprang softly down onto the stone tiles. The keyhole was now level with my chest. No wonder: this

---

place had been built by and for fellow Ennans!

The key struggled a little, squeaking its way into the lock. Now I had to press it. My shoulder muscles tensed.

The lock clicked, triggering some invisible process. The door's recesses began to clank and rattle. Then the key sprang slightly backwards as if letting me know it had completed its job.

I pulled it out with ease. That must have been the signal for a transformation. The heavy slab of rock shuddered with a crunching sound. Emitting little clouds of stone dust, the door began to slide upward, showering the tiles below with sand and small pebbles. The gaping dark entryway behind it oozed cold and damp.

Finally, the stone door disappeared into the cliff's innards.

Congratulations! You've unlocked the gate to the West Grotto!

Boris and I looked at each other. His eyes glittered with enthusiastic curiosity. So did mine, I suppose.

I leaped back into the saddle. Better that way. "So, kiddo? How about we take a look at this grotto of theirs?"

Boris flowed gracefully in. A new warning

appeared before my eyes,

Warning! The West Grotto had remained unclaimed for many a century. Finally, it became home to a colony of Thorn Rats.

Warning! This location can be too dangerous for players under level 290. Please turn back.

Aha! I mentally rubbed my hands as I stepped back. There it is, the first instance we'd found in the Forbidden City! Excellent. I needed to wait for Laosh and the others. We needed to discuss this properly.

Thorn Rats, oh well. As I had no access to the bestiary, I couldn't look them up. I inserted the key in the lock and closed the door. Better safe than sorry. I didn't want those beasties to escape and prowl the area. We had enough on our plate as it was.

When I was already up in the air circling the cliff one last time, a new thought struck me. A West Grotto. Did that mean there might be an East one somewhere? Or, who knows, one more in the South and another one in the North? That would make sense, wouldn't it?

I spent another hour circling the mountain slopes but to no avail. I hadn't noticed anything. I got the funny feeling that the 55 pt. of Survival Instinct I'd received with the Fort Guardian Kit wasn't enough to detect any other grottos. It was already a good thing that it had allowed me to discover the West one.

"Never mind," I told Boris. "Let's go back to the camp."

* * *

The results of my little recon sortie produced quite a stir in the camp. Everybody grew restless. I too felt pretty much on edge. Apparently, not all had been lost. There were still some places left in this ancient Ennan city which didn't resemble the ruins of a Roman circus.

The only person who'd kept his head about him was Droy. Had it not been for him, we'd have already been on our way to the grotto to genocide the Thorn Rats. I wouldn't say he was less excited than the others but he kept his cool as a commander should, insisting we waited for Laosh to arrive.

So we had lunch instead. The hot meal and the warmth of the fire seemed to have had a soothing effect on our nerves. We began to wind down.

Indeed, what was the point in going there now? There were only four of us. This was the worst moment to die a stupid death. Me, I could always resurrect but my friends couldn't. So we decided to wait for Laosh, call up a raid and purge the instance properly.

Even though their first bout of enthusiasm had already expired, the warriors hurried to finish their meal and immediately began preparing their weapons.

As I watched their practiced actions, a new idea struck me. Why not? I could try, couldn't I?

What a shame I didn't have anything on me I could experiment on. Never mind.

I heaved a theatrical sigh and reached into my bag. The Noctean stone axe felt as heavy as a ton of bricks. I tried to take a swing with it but failed miserably, receiving a shower of penalty messages which brought each and every one of my characteristics deep into negative numbers.

I closed the messages, then studied the primitive weapon, pointedly ignoring everyone around.

Oh. It wasn't even an axe really but more of a club. I even got some idea of how it had been fashioned out of a young tree: someone had bashed a flat stone into its roots and cut the trunk to about five foot long. Nothing was strapped down. I could even see the bits of earth still stuck to the roots. This was stone age in all its prehistoric glory.

The axe's stats, however, came as a surprise. This was one hell of a lethal weapon. Its damage was impressive. Its durability, however, left a lot to be desired.

The Calteans had ceased talking and were now

watching me, disgust and animosity in their glares.

Sorry, guys. It's either this or the slingshot. I had nothing else to use for my experiment.

Crym spoke first. "Just get rid of it, Olgerd," he said, frowning. "Filthy thing."

Well, he'd have to grin and bear it, wouldn't he? I didn't say so in his face, though.

"In a moment," I replied. "I just want to have a look at it."

"There's nothing to look at," he insisted. "Useless stick."

"That's what you think," I said. "Even a stick like this can tell a lot about its owner."

"I can tell you all you need to know about its owner," Droy said calmly.

"Which is what?"

Droy grinned. "He's dead, isn't he?"

The others guffawed. Orman slapped their leader on the shoulder.

I wasn't going to give up so easily. "Anything else?" I asked once they stopped laughing. I sat down next to Droy and offered him the axe.

He looked at it with disgust and shook his head.

"And you, what can *you* see?" Orman asked with a cunning smile on his bearded face.

I pursed my lips and turned the axe in my hands, doing my best Sherlock Holmes impersonation.

"Firstly, our enemies don't know tanning yet. The stone isn't strapped up," I ignored their sarcastic smiles and continued, "Secondly, it is an axe, not a club. The stone is covered in tree sap which means they used it to cut down trees. And thirdly, the axe's owner was quite intelligent for a Noctean."

"What makes you think so?" Orman asked.

Droy replied, joining in my little Baker Street game, "Think for yourself. He had enough brains to break down a tree and stick a stone between its roots. And not just any stone but a flat one to make it easier to cut things down with."

The others stared at me, waiting for more. I didn't play hard to get. "The type of stone and the kind of tree can tell us where they came from. The fact that the earth still sticks to the roots means it was made recently. There's little blood on the blade which also means its owner didn't use it in combat a lot."

The Calteans fell silent, staring pensively at the item.

I continued, "The handle is covered in dark red spots. Its owner must have rubbed his hands raw which means he's not used to handling this sort of tool. It looks like this was his first weapon — and probably also his last."

"Anything else?" Droy asked. His eyes glowed with respect.

"Actually, yes," I said. "He was left-handed."

Seeing the amazement on their faces, I explained, "Look at the handle. You can still see the handprint. It's a left hand, isn't it?

Now the moment of truth. I offered the weapon to Droy. Would he accept it? Fingers crossed.

After a moment's hesitation, Droy took the axe from me and began studying the handle.

Yes! He did it!

Shaking with triumph, I hurried to open Droy's stats.

Oh wow. He'd received more or less the same penalties as I had. But that was irrelevant. I've just managed to prove that the Calteans weren't tied to their own weapon types!

How cool was that? It opened up some truly promising horizons!

The axe was already changing hands. The Calteans were busy discussing it as they studied it closely, looking for some signs known only to them.

I leaned back, staring at the fire and trying to calculate how much my future re-armament race might ultimately cost me.

Chapter Three

EARLY NEXT MORNING we grabbed a quick bite to eat and set off for the Upper City as I'd christened it. We'd broken camp, planning to set it up anew on the mountain top — the tribe's future home.

To show some team spirit, I chose to walk on my own two feet, especially seeing as the two wounded raid members couldn't walk at all. They were dragged along in makeshift sledges that Crym had fashioned the night before. I was helping Orman to drag Horm while Droy and Crym took turns pulling Seet along. Judging by their stats, the wounded guys were about to come round. With all its fabled authenticity, Mirror World was still a computer game.

The sledges slid effortlessly over the snow,

allowing us to reach the summit before midday. We had to thread our way around many a collapsed building which was actually for the better: this didn't make it any easier for any potential enemy.

Actually, I needed to check the hunters' stats to see whether they could make traps and snares. If they could, then this trek was begging to be turned into a deadly gauntlet for any trespassers.

The Calteans loved the spot. They even began discussing how they were going to set up tents and things. Yeah, dream on, guys. I had my own ideas regarding our future camp's planning. Some of them might not like it but one thing was for sure: I wasn't going to tolerate the chaotic mess that passed for a Caltean camp.

Orman started the fire. We were already making ourselves comfortable around it, about to discuss everything we'd seen, when a strange noise alerted us.

The Calteans froze momentarily, then leapt to their feet and ran toward the wall which offered a good view of the valley.

While I was getting my act together, the sound repeated, again and again, louder and stronger every time, until finally I realized what it was I was hearing.

It was a Caltean bugle.

The snowstorm had stopped already an hour ago. The valley lay before us in a dull cloudy half-light, revealing the black dots of our fellow tribesmen on the white snow below.

Something wasn't right there, definitely.

But of course. How stupid of me. This was the rest of the tribe approaching. And if they signaled with their bugle, it meant they were in trouble. Our clan was under attack!

I had to act fast, before my team awoke from their stupor and did something they would later regret.

"Droy," I said, investing as much authority in my voice as I could muster.

The Caltean leader startled and looked at me.

"Wait for me here," I said. "Do you hear me? You can't do anything there. At least the enemy can't get here. The ancient magic of this place won't let them in."

After last night's battle, I'd already explained to them this place was actually a mixed blessing.

"Make sure the guys keep their emotions in check. They're not in a position to help the tribe. If they try, they'll only get themselves killed. I'm going to fly there. My little mechanical friends will be of more use there. You know that yourself."

Droy's gaze cleared. He must have remembered my scarabs and their defeat of the Nocteans. "Go," he wheezed.

Good. Droy seemed to take it seriously. Now I

could leave them. I could only imagine what it was going to cost him. His own son was with the tribe, as well as the other guys' families.

The moment Boris appeared, I sprang into the saddle. With a sharp jolt, we were already airborne.

The air screamed in my ears. My eyes were running. Sensing my state of mind, Boris was doing his best.

We crossed the valley as if it wasn't even there. As we approached, I could see the tribesmen waving their hands to me. The carts and sledges, the animal noises, the shouting of the children and women...

The bugle sang its melody again. What a powerful instrument.

I was already flying above the traveling group when I finally understood the reason for their anxiety. They were surrounded by Nocteans on three sides who drove them like a herd of bison from a safe distance of about two hundred paces. They probably didn't dare come any closer for fear of Caltean arrows.

How many of them were there? At least three hundred. They walked unhurriedly; their ugly faces betrayed no sign of fatigue.

The Calteans, however, looked exhausted. Their numbers seemed to have gone down.

I ran a quick check. I was right, dammit! The system showered me with warnings and alerts.

The Calteans were at the end of their tether.

Most of their stats had dropped at least 40%. We were 260 now: minus 26 clan members. Damn those Nocteans!

Why weren't they attacking? I double-checked their positioning. Aha. From what I could see, the Nocteans seemed to be thinking they were herding their quarry to the slaughter. They were sure that the Calteans wouldn't dare enter the Forbidden City, so they'd be forced to stop and fight.

The cannibals' ugly mugs betrayed their impatience. This group didn't seem to have anything in common with the Nocteans killed by the city's ancient guards.

One of them stood out even among his hairy tribesmen. He towered at least two heads above the rest, his body covered in shaggy dark fur which looked almost black. Definitely the leader of the pack, judging by how the others were running around him.

A werewolf, for sure.

A group of about fifty more Nocteans armed with stone axes surrounded him as some prehistoric analog of bodyguards.

I flew up closer. Shaggy had noticed me a long time ago and was looking at me with curiosity now.

Our eyes met. So! This one seemed to be marginally smarter than the rest. His black eyes glinted with all the superiority of a wild beast — and maybe just a tad of discomfort. Normal, really. A

---

midget flying a magic animal can discomfort anyone.

Boris banked into a steep turn, heading back toward the Caltean group. I made out Laosh' gaunt frame at the center of their ranks. He was looking up, waving his hand to me.

Soon I was already standing before him. The old man was in a bad way, his eyes red from lack of sleep. Apparently, the Nocteans prevented their prisoners from stopping for the night.

The Calteans' rough voices cheered my arrival. Laosh gave me an unembarrassed hug. Hands kept slapping my back and shoulders.

"You've made it," I said when they finally left me alone.

"Not all of us, unfortunately," the shaman replied. "Still, we're here. And you?"

"We're fine," I reassured him. "The city belongs to us. What about those?" I nodded at the Nocteans.

"They attacked us in the dead of night," Laosh replied curtly. "We lost almost thirty warriors in that battle. It's been three days they've been following us."

I clenched my teeth to suppress my anger. "They're driving you like game beaters. Never mind. As long as we make it to the city, they'll never get you."

Laosh' eyes focused watchfully on me. "I can sense some powerful witchcraft."

I produced the sphere from my bag by way of answer.

Laosh closed his eyes. "Two weeks' protection," he whispered with relief.

I climbed back into the saddle. "Laosh!" I turned to the shaman as Boris took off, "I'll try and buy you some time. But be quick!"

The old man nodded and began barking orders. As Boris headed toward the Noctean ranks, I noticed a few smiles on the Calteans' faces. I checked their stats. Indeed, their Morale numbers seemed to have improved ever so slightly.

And what if...

Would you like to activate the Hand of the Outcast?

Absolutely.

Congratulations! You've received +30 pt. to all your clan members' Morale!
Duration: 5 hrs.

By now, the entire tribe had already heard the good news. The Forbidden City was safe and off limits for Nocteans!

That, in combination with the Hand of the Outcast, had produced the desired effect. The Calteans picked up the pace; even the women and children fell quiet. Men strengthened their grips on

---

their weapons, their faces glowing with determination. Even the animals seemed to realize the importance of the moment.

I seemed to be feeling different too. How weird. My emotions seemed to have intensified, my blood boiling with adrenaline. What's that? Had the VR capsule staff injected my lifeless frame with amphetamines after I'd activated the Hand of the Outcast? I absolutely needed to find that out once I resurfaced back in the real world.

The change in their quarry's mood hadn't gone completely unnoticed by the Nocteans. They grew restless. Their leader emitted a powerful growl, encouraging the others.

Bad timing, dammit! That bastard was too smart for his own good. Never mind. We'd give him something to do in a minute.

Actually... easier said than done. What was I supposed to do, step in their horde's way with my insect squad? But this wasn't a couple dozen werewolves! These guys would just trample right over us, end of story. I'd waste the remaining metal in vain.

Still, I had to put my money where my mouth was. Especially because I already had the first inklings of a very simple plan. I decided to attack Shaggy, the leader. Why not? I would fly over to him and set a few fleas on him, how about that? Maybe loose a few slugs from my slingshot, just to keep him on his toes. He's

---

not gonna like it. And when the others see their leader's humiliation, they'd be reluctant to continue their pursuit.

That's settled, then. The Noctean leader was already directly below me. He scowled. Level 350! Not too shabby at all!

The other Nocteans bared their teeth at me. I was at least fifty feet above them and still they jumped high in the air, trying to get to me. Those creatures could jump, that's for sure.

Shaggy abstained from their impromptu pogo jumping competition. He could see he wouldn't make it, so what was the point in looking stupid in his own warriors' eyes?

I kept a watchful eye on my clan. They were making good speed. I'd managed to distract the Nocteans: they were too busy now trying to catch me.

I met Shaggy's eye. What a bastard! He too could see the Calteans' escape so he promptly switched his priorities, losing all interest in me.

The leader emitted a threatening roar. The gray hairy mass of Nocteans shifted as one man, about to follow their fleeing quarry. That made sense. I hadn't aggroed them, had I?

Never mind. I'd do it — now.

You've built the simplest mechanical creature: a Swarm of Fleas!

Level: 120

Number of swarm members: 5

The first swarm came as a complete surprise to Shaggy. They even managed to bite him at least once each before being struck by his bodyguards' stone axes.

Shaggy howled in pain. The Nocteans froze, then hurried to his rescue.

All hell broke lose. All of them were jumping, trying to get to me and Boris. While they were thus engaged in this admittedly useless exercise, the Venom of Swamp Monk began to work, sending Shaggy shrieking to the ground.

Then a strange thing happened. A giant gray Noctean slid like a shadow out of the crowd and went growling for their leader. Soon the two Nocteans were at each other's throats.

"Oh wow. It looks like we've triggered a local power struggle," I whispered, watching this battle of the titans.

Soon the two Nocteans transformed to their werewolf shapes. Now they were twice their original size. The venom couldn't kill the leader whose level and regeneration were now considerably higher. It looked like his opponent realized it, too. Shifty-eyed, he lowered his ears, apparently regretting his impulse but not enough to surrender.

I could see he'd decided to fight to the last. Even if he'd wanted to escape, he couldn't: the Nocteans surrounded the two fighters, encouraging them in this prehistoric version of gladiatorial fights.

They were too busy now to worry about us.

The leader's gray opponent couldn't have chosen a better moment to claim power. Unfortunately, he was no match for Shaggy who was ten levels above him.

Still, that wasn't my problem. As long as he managed to distract the leader for a while, that was fine with me. Should I send in a few more fleas? Pointless, really. Everything was working out just fine without me. The two were ripping each other apart.

The Calteans had crossed the valley remarkably quickly. Their first sledges reached the town walls just as Shaggy finally dealt the decisive blow to his opponent. He tilted his head up to the skies and howled, informing the world of his victory. His hapless rival lay at his feet with his throat ripped out.

Shaggy gave his tribe a long, almost insane look as if challenging the next contender to come forth. Predictably, there were none. Heads lowered in a mass act of subordination. Wheezing, the leader turned the still-warm body on its back, then ripped his heart out in one strong, practiced motion.

Yuk. Blood and gore had never been my thing.

Time for me to go. Especially as most of the Calteans had already entered the city.

As Boris whisked me away, I sensed a hateful glare focused on my back. I turned round.

Shaggy watched me leave, munching on his rival's twitching heart.

Oh. It looked like the Nocteans were here to stay.

Chapter Four

I CAST A PRACTICED GLANCE at the clock in the right upper corner of my interface. 2 a.m.

How funny. I seemed to be developing new habits, reflexes even. If you had to check both the time and your own stats thirty times a day, that could be quite habit-forming.

In real life, too, I seemed to be constantly searching for those pale-blue buttons hindering my view. This was actually one of the giveaway signs that you were speaking to a gamer: the person's eyes would constantly wander as they habitually checked his or her stats.

The camp was asleep. All but the guards on duty, of course. I'd just finished talking to Laosh. First

I'd had to tell him all about our travels, then listen to his tale of their own trials and tribulations. It had taken me a lot of effort to talk him into getting some sleep.

The old man's eyes had glistened with boyish curiosity. He wanted to know everything. He made me recount my conversation with the city Keepers word by word. He studied the bunch of keys the ancient masters had given me; he'd reread the scroll several times and inspected the magic sphere, leaving his greasy fingerprints all over its surface.

How I understood him. He was now standing in the sacred and terrible place his own parents used to scare him with when he was little. No wonder he was all shaking.

Admittedly, the Calteans were a highly adaptable bunch. At first they too had appeared wary — scared even — but soon they thawed out. They got busy making fires, cooking food and setting up camp which must have distracted them somewhat. Also, the rapid succession of several stressful situations must have played their part: after the hasty exodus across the snowed-in valley followed by the Noctean attack and their close escape to the Forbidden City, the Calteans felt like little could surprise them. They were safe now, and that was the most important thing.

The Nocteans hadn't followed us into the city after all. They stopped by the walls, venting their disappointment with some theatrical howling and growling, then turned back toward the hills. Still, I didn't think they were gone for good. Judging by the meaningful stare their shaggy leader had given me, we would hear from them pretty soon.

I didn't mind. Why not? With one correction: our next meeting was to be on my own terms.

If the truth were known, I hadn't been at all sure whether the magic sphere would work. It had. Which was good news. What a shame we didn't have enough time to prepare properly. As it was, time kept slipping through my fingers like the desert sand.

The crackling of wood in the fire felt soothing — while also putting me in a working mode.

I opened my control panel. Now that everybody was present and correct, I had full information about my new clan members.

Let's start with the worst. Casualties. Six warriors and twenty civilians. And I had barely begun my leadership!

Then again, had it not been for me, the clan might have already ceased to exist. The route chosen by Laosh was fatal. They would have all been killed, either by mobs or by players. In this respect, my conscience was clear... and still I felt uncomfortable.

The next bit of bad news: we were running out of food. Another week like this, and they might need to start slaughtering their livestock which I absolutely didn't want to happen. They had several dozen draught animals level 300+, not counting the young, the sheep, the poultry... I had a whole animal farm under my control. No idea how long my Reputation superiority might last but the opening opportunities were impressive.

If you took all the draught animals plus the carts and the drivers... it was a ready-made caravanning business. Why not? It was an option, surely. We could very easily compete with the Guiding Eyes.

I could almost see a banner announcing *"Olgerd and Co. Shipping and Logistics Services — Your Partner in No-Man's Lands!"* How awesome was that? I could lay a mean route through this part of the world. And as for the guards defending the convoys, a few dozen level 300+ NPCs were a force to be reckoned with.

Of course, if I failed to find the Twilight Obelisk, I could always take my tribe somewhere else. Not that I was going to give up, but if all my attempts to locate it failed, I wasn't going to make my clan confront a predictably overpowering enemy.

Talking about confrontation, today had been a moment of truth for me as well. Finally I'd realized I could do more than just dance to somebody else's tune. I knew of course that the Reflex Bank had been instrumental in my victory but then again, they

---

wouldn't have achieved much without me, either. And if I remembered rightly what Vicky had said, they'd had a lot of guys like myself in the past but I seemed to have been the only one who'd had something to show for it.

In this, too, preserving the Red Owls clan was my priority. They were my trump card.

And as for the city... well, if it didn't work out, we could always find some other place to live. There was plenty of space in No-Man's Lands for everyone. Admittedly, the ancient Ennan city seemed perfect for our development. I had a funny feeling these ruins would be full of surprises. Or at least I hoped they were.

The more I looked into clan control, the better I realized that caravanning wasn't the only option open to us. I had almost 300 NPCs at my disposal — warriors as well as regular workers. Their system and interface differed dramatically from those of the players, but it didn't change much, did it?

Now, the basics. We didn't have a single "green" item in the clan. Zilch, nada. All their tools, weapons, clothes, food, even animals were "gray" albeit high-level.

That gave me the impression that the Red Owls were literally one step away from a major development breakthrough.

Take their blacksmiths, for instance. They

only had two: the red-haired Zachary with giant fists and Prochorus, a sinewy guy with an ugly scar across his face. They had an apprentice each. That was the extent of it. All the other blacksmiths had died: some on their way, others by the River Quiet; some had been killed defending their tribal lands. So these two and their assistants were busy working 24/7 trying to meet all of the clan's needs.

Each of them had a mobile smithy and some tools — all of them low-quality "gray". They were quite efficient, though. The items they made may have been simple but were sturdy and reliable: nails, needles, horseshoes, arrowheads, knives, etc. etc.

But that wasn't the point. The thing was, I noticed that NPCs didn't seem to have the same professional ranking system as players did. There was no such thing as a Master or Expert NPC. They only had a skill bar — or rather several, each for every skill. If you looked at them, you'd see that Zachary excelled at weapon making while Prochorus was good at forging agricultural tools.

I needed to look into it further. The camp was asleep, anyway. According to Laosh, as long as we had the sphere we were safe. Apparently, even wild animals were supposed to give us a wide berth. Still, Droy being Droy had set up patrols on the city walls. As in, better safe than sorry. Which was a good thing.

Now, the blacksmiths. The first thing I'd

noticed was that the quality of their work didn't improve one iota. It seemed perma-frozen.

I knew why, too. The blueprints were the problem. Each blacksmith had an impressive list of the blueprints he'd studied. All of them were "gray" too. Ditto for the materials they used: iron ore, charcoal, etc.

What did that mean? It meant that just bringing them a "green", "blue" or "purple" material wasn't enough. The two blacksmiths would then have to study the relevant recipes they could apply to the new materials.

In any case, it was worth a try. I'd have to do it first thing tomorrow morning.

As for the levels of the resulting items, they depended on the blacksmith's own level. Prochorus was level 270 and Zachary, 290. That's if I understood correctly.

Both were also decent lancers. Not as good as Droy and his gang, but if they wanted to abandon their tools and become warriors, they could easily do so. The NPC class and profession system seemed to be much more supple than that of players... probably because they didn't have to pay for their account upgrades.

Prochorus — the one who made agricultural tools — was actually a Red Owl himself while Zachary was an ex-Black Axe.

Which offered another very interesting insight. The Black Axes were mountain dwellers good at everything to do with mining or masonry. In view of the upcoming events those skills would be a Godsend. The Red Owls in turn specialized in livestock farming and agriculture. Perfect symbiosis.

The six military engineers mentioned by the game engine especially interested me. I was already dreaming of all the things we could do together. No such luck. By 'military engineers' the game meant siege vehicle staff. Which was already a good thing, I suppose.

We even had our own trebuchet now. Which was a mixed blessing, really. Firstly, this useful machine had suffered a lot in the last battle. Secondly, it required not six but ten men to operate it. And thirdly, judging by the materials it was made of, I shouldn't hold my breath.

But even that wasn't so important. The main thing was, we had a powerful weapon which just might become a weighty argument in any future confrontations.

Apart from these professions, we also had a Master Crossbow Maker and a Master Fletcher. Plus a guy who made nothing but arrows and crossbow bolts. Plus two female healers. Not that it was a lot. The kids didn't boast any particular skills: they were mainly gatherers who could be used to run errands, I suppose.

I didn't bother to study the tribe's young. All their skills were still in the bud. The kids had a lot to grow and learn. I checked out a couple of the older ones, then closed the tab.

I wish I hadn't.

* * *

Early at dawn, the camp awoke to a new busy day. The air rang with shouting, singing and laughter. It was amazing how little time it had taken the Calteans to recover from the shock. Which was excellent.

I checked the control panel. It seemed to function like clockwork. The best thing was, the system was perfectly autonomous. I didn't even need to interfere. Laosh and Droy were more than capable of any decision making.

Remembering Laosh' clingy nature, I hurried to blend into the crowd. I already had a plan of action.

First thing, I visited the engineers.

"Finally!" Pritus met me by the entrance to his tent. "Please come in!"

His intelligent pale blue eyes studied me curiously from behind his pince-nez. His short red beard was peppered with gray. An old burn scar marred his large forehead.

So I'd been right that night by the fire. Pritus

was an intellectual. A fellow nerd.

"Thank you, Master Pritus!" I smiled back. "How could I have forgotten about you? It's not in my nature to ignore fellow clan members who are worth an entire army!"

Pritus suppressed a smile. Strangely enough, he felt flattered by my clumsy praise. "Please take a seat. Would you like some herbal tea?"

"Yes, please," I said absent-mindedly as I sat down at the table, trying to take in my surroundings.

No wonder: the engineer's humble tent looked more like an antique design office. It was busy with piled-up books and scrolls, plank tripods holding makeshift drawing boards, and all kinds of rulers, compasses, quills, inkwells and tons of other items whose purpose I could only guess.

Pritus noticed my interest. "We're settling down, bit by bit," he made a sweeping gesture around the tent. "Your tea."

A silent pause hung in the air as we savored our hot perfumed drinks, casting studying glances at each other. Even buffless, the tea still tasted great.

"So," Pritus broke the silence first. "What brought you to my humble abode?"

"Firstly, I wanted to get to know you better," I said, earning an encouraging nod from him. "Secondly, I did mean it when I said that your engineering crew was worth an entire army. Artillery is an important argument in any battle."

He looked up at me in surprise. "How do you know these words? 'Artillery', 'engineering crew' — have you heard them before?"

I nodded. "I have. I'll tell you more: I'm an engineer myself, although in a different field."

You wouldn't expect me to tell him I didn't yet know myself which field it was, would you?

He seemed to be completely floored by this last revelation. As he was busy picking up his dropped jaw, I decided to capitalize on the effect,

"I've come to you in order to find out what you might need in order to fix the trebuchet and get it running."

* * *

An hour later, I left the engineer's tent carrying the list of all the materials he needed. As it had turned out, he'd already found four new assistants for himself to replace those killed. Now he needed to ask the clan leader's permission to recruit them. And seeing as I was the aforementioned clan leader, I'd given him my permission on the spot.

Also, I entitled him to use my name whenever he heeded to seek help from any other craftsmen. And once Pritus found out I could get him any materials he could possibly need, he hurried to compile a lengthy list.

Once that was out of the way, we'd spent some time talking over tea. The red-bearded engineer told me the sad tale of their failed storming of the Citadel. About Laosh' useless command. About the death of his friends. And about the loss of ten machines out of eleven, the last one only salvaged by his colleagues' heroic efforts. I ended up soothing him and calming him down.

If the blueprints he'd shown me were any indicator, the machine in question did resemble a medieval trebuchet. It seemed to work well even though, according to Pritus, it could use a few improvements.

Despite his "gray" gear and tools, I could see that this individual was long ready to advance to the next level. And of all people, I could help him with that.

As I walked back, I noticed the orderly layout of all the tents and marquees. Droy must have taken my advice to heart and made sure that the camp didn't resemble an illogical maze anymore.

The sounds of hammered steel were coming from Zachary's mobile smithy. I was just about to go and see him when my gaze alighted on one of the carts.

How interesting. This was a traditional

Caltean cart which looked no different from the rest, with one exception. All of its parts were covered in a fancy vine-like pattern.

I walked over to it. On closer inspection, the patterns turned out to have been made with ordinary green paint. Still, the artistry of them was incredible.

I walked around the cart several times, tracing the vine pattern. The more I looked at it, the more details I noticed. Not a single identical leaf or twig. Each of them seemed to have its own meaning and purpose.

This was amazing.

Curious, I decided to check the item's stats. Imagine my amazement when I realized that the anonymous artist had considerably improved both the cart's protection and its durability.

I opened the clan control panel and looked for the Transportation tab, then searched through items by durability. The painted cart was at the top of the list well ahead of all the others.

"Nice, eh?" a wheezing old voice asked behind me.

I promptly closed the windows and turned round.

An old Caltean stood not five paces away from me, his hair snow white, his broad face furrowed. His bushy white eyebrows stood on end like the wings of a bird. Despite his old age, his shoulders were broad and strong.

I hurried to check his stats. Aha. This was Crunch. His most advanced skill was Cart Maker, with Cart Driving and Draught Animal Care just behind it. I'd been expecting something like that.

I checked the blueprints he'd studied. This was a very, very useful senior citizen.

"This is awesome," I agreed. "And the durability it adds!"

The old man kneaded his beard, then cast me a suspicious look. "We *are* talking about the cart, aren't we?"

I smiled amicably. "Not exactly. I was talking about your drawings."

He stared at me, uncomprehending.

Then it dawned on me. This old NPC couldn't see all the advantages of his own work. How was it possible? Judging by his large rough hands that resembled two digger shovels, how could he have even managed to create something this beautiful?

"Haven't you noticed that your cart became sturdier after you'd decorated it?" I asked him.

The cart maker gave his creation another look, as if seeing it for the first time. He crouched and studied the bottom of the cart, then yanked at the wheels.

"I think you're right," he finally said. "I couldn't understand why the shaft had lasted so long.

Normally, it should have broken several times already. And the wheels are still in one piece. Actually, it's lasted me for ages without a single accident," he ran his hand lovingly over the painted designs. "Thanks for telling me what it was, Olgerd. I heard people say that you can see things nobody else can. Now I've witnessed that myself."

Oh. I'd love to know what else they were saying about me. Still, I couldn't wrap my head around the man's behavior.

He must have read it in my face because he dissolved in a smile. "You must be thinking, 'How's that possible? How come a master can't see the results of his work?' Am I right?"

I shrugged. I had nothing to say to that.

His next phrase confused me even more. "I'll tell you something. You're probably right. *The master* can see the results of his or her work. But *I* can't," he smiled dreamily, thinking about something.

Oh, great. An NPC with a split personality disorder.

"Dear Master Crunch," I said, slowly backing away, "thank you very much for your time. I really enjoyed talking to you. Unfortunately, I have too many things to-"

"You wait," he said. "I'm not crazy, if that's what you think. I told you that the master could see the results of her work. I think she did. She did tell me the cart would drive much better."

"Wait a sec," I said. "Now I'm totally confused. Who is she? What's with the master?"

"My granddaughter! My little one! She is the master! She painted the cart for me. And she did tell me it might not need repairs for a while. I didn't believe her, did I? I just let her paint my cart, why not? There's no harm in that, is there? She's my only flesh and blood... Her parents died two winters ago from the sweating sickness. And now this... Oh no!"

I jumped from his sudden change of temper. The old man grabbed at his head, his eyes wide open. "She's painted everything we have, hasn't she? The tent, the kitchen pots, even my tools... She wanted to paint my clothes too but I didn't let her. Our neighbors were laughing at us as it was. How strange..."

Curiouser and curiouser. His oversight was quite understandable, but me? How could I have missed a girl capable of improving items' protection and durability? Very clever, Sir Olgerd.

Oh well. I had to correct my mistake now, didn't I?

"Dear Master," I said, "You don't need to worry. I suggest we both calm down and talk about it. None of this is your fault..."

"No, but-"

I didn't let him finish. "You don't have

anything to do with magic, by any chance?"

The question completely floored him. "Who, me?" he mouthed, voiceless.

"Yes, you."

"I don't think so..."

"So you see," I raised a didactic finger. "If you and your neighbors didn't have an aptitude for magic, how could you have noticed your granddaughter's skills?"

He stared at me, uncomprehending. Before he could get his wits together, I continued, "You couldn't. Only a shaman or a shaman's apprentice is capable of that. But as you well understand, they've had their hands full with other things just lately..."

He nodded. "You could say that."

"So you shouldn't worry about it. I suggest we rectify this slight oversight on our part."

"Excuse me?"

"Well, how about we meet your little Master for a start?"

"Yes, yes, of course!" the old man swung around, drawing me along. "Of course! Please come this way!"

He was quite fast and agile for his age. As we approached his neat tent, I came across plenty of evidence of the young artist's work. Everything around me was covered in fine intricately drawn patterns. The fence poles that served as tethering posts for the large, slow buffaloes munching on their grass, were decorated all over. Ditto for all the spades and pitchforks, hoes and buckets and clay pots. Each item sported durability and protection bonuses. Cool!

I peered closer at the vine-like patterns. They were identical. Even the paint was the same hue of green. Having said that... not really. The girl had also used black and white paints.

Three colors. A single pattern, masterfully drawn. What did that mean? It meant that the girl was ready to advance to the next level but couldn't. She had neither the knowledge nor the right materials. Nor the tools, most likely.

"So what did I say?" Crunch made a sweeping gesture around his household. "You can see for yourself, can't you?"

"You bet," I replied with a smile. "I'll tell you more: I like it a lot. Your granddaughter is a very precious asset to the clan. A craftswoman like her should be treasured and cherished."

His surprised eyes filled with tears of joy. I could understand him. He'd been living all those years suffering his neighbors' ridicule about the weird child he'd sheltered under his roof.

We found the heroine of all the commotion sleeping soundly inside. Unhesitantly I opened the girl's stats.

Name: Lia. Ten years old. A tiny little thing. A

fragile frame; a head of raven-black hair. Her plump little fingers were clutching a thin paintbrush. There was paint all over her face.

My heart clenched. She was so like my Christa. Was she okay?

A hand touched my shoulder.

"Go in," Crunch whispered. "No point in standing in the doorway."

"Sorry. Of course," I shook off the memory and returned to Lia's stats.

Skills: a standard set. The girl was a gatherer and a housekeeper. I scrolled through the list.

Aha. There it was! *Magic Painting.* The numbers were good: much better compared to her other skills.

"Cheeky devil!" the old man whispered. "Look at my tools! She just couldn't help it, could she?"

Indeed, the familiar vine pattern coiled around the wooden handles of his modest tools.

"This is a very good thing," I told him. "Now this hammer, chisel and saw will last you a lifetime. I suggest you ask her to paint everything else you have in your house. The sooner you do it, the better. What your granddaughter does, she adds magic bind lines to the objects she paints."

At the words "magic bind lines" he cast a reverential look at the sleeping girl. "Why such a rush?" he asked me.

"Because, dear Master," I replied in a whisper, "very soon Lia might have lots of work to do. With your permission, of course."

Chapter Five

I SPENT THE REST OF THE DAY walking around the camp talking to workers. Blacksmiths, saddlers, shepherds, miners, stonemasons — I hadn't missed anyone. I spoke to each and every one of them, asking questions and listening to their requests. By the time I got back to Droy's tent I was dead on my feet. I had a splitting headache. Still, the result was worth it.

I'd been right all along. The Red Owls clan was balancing on the edge of a small local revolution. All the Calteans needed was a tiny nudge to send them to stage two of their social and cultural development. All I had to provide was a scientific base — that is to say, new recipes, new blueprints and sketched designs for my future masters.

Unfortunately, the expensive materials I'd so generously provided them with didn't work at all. You can't fool the system. The clan's development had to run its course. What a shame.

The heat from the fire felt soothing. The embers crackled, sending sparks into the night sky. A meat stew bubbled in the pot, whetting my appetite. My nostrils welcomed the amazing aromas.

Droy grinned at me. "Tired?"

I sighed. "You can't imagine. Still, it's all gonna work out in the end. You'll see."

"Don't take their complaints too close to heart," Droy said, stirring the stew. "They love moaning. It'll take you an entire lifetime just to look into it all. Have you learned anything about the city?"

I shook my head. "Nothing new. The Black Axes keep rehashing the same old legends which you already know. Crym is still the only person who's seen the place from afar. All the others are already dead. Some were killed at the Citadel walls, others by the River Quiet."

"It's all right," Droy reassured me. "Tomorrow we'll call up a council. We need to decide how to purge the dungeons you found."

"I'd like to strongly discourage you from that idea," I said.

Droy stared at me in surprise, forgetting his stew. "Pardon me? I thought you guys couldn't wait to go back there. And now you *strongly discourage* the idea..."

I ran a tired hand over my forehead. "I have a funny feeling we might not come out of it alive. It's just a hunch. A foreboding, if you like."

How else could I explain it to him? The dungeons were crawling with high-level mobs. How was I supposed to tell him that Caltean weapons and gear were just not up to the task? He wouldn't understand me. He might even take offence.

"A foreboding? That's serious," Droy agreed, returning his attention to the pot. "You should never disregard a bad foreboding."

"I'm not going to," I said. "We need some time. Once we settle down a bit, then we can start worrying about these things."

"I like your way of thinking," Droy nodded, bringing a steaming spoon to his mouth.

He smacked his lips several times, then paused, apparently thinking what else he could add to his brew. Still, the result seemed to have pleased him.

"Ready," he lowered the ladle into the steaming, bubbling thick stew. "Let's eat."

I offered him my bowl. Life was good. My stomach growled its agreement.

"Tim," Droy called his son. "Come and eat before it gets cold."

The boy ran out of the tent. Grinning to me, he

plopped onto a rock by the fire. His bowl was even bigger than mine. No wonder. He'd been seriously sick, almost dead, for God knows how long, and then he'd had to hike along with the rest of the tribe all across No-Man's Lands. And he was only thirteen years old. His body needed nutrition to grow.

Actually, judging by his stats, this boy was mere points away from becoming a Warrior. He had a healthy Hunting skill plus some introduction-level sword and spear work. His father must have been training him. Add to that whatever quarry the boy had managed to shoot on his way here, and that could explain why his level was not very far from my own.

"What about Pritus?" Droy asked. "Can't he tell you anything?"

"I don't think so," I said, setting my empty bowl aside. "I don't think he knows anything."

"Well, he wasn't the best the Axes had," Droy said with a hearty burp. "The Lighties slaughtered their leading techs in the first minutes of the fighting. At least that's what Crym told me. Apparently, the Lighties started by destroying the trebuchets, and only then did they turn on the foot soldiers. Yeah... The Axes used to have the best army. But after what happened by the River Quiet, nothing can surprise me. And that was only an avant-garde! I can only imagine what's gonna happen if the Lighties bring their main army here."

I heaved a sigh, staring at the fire. What could I say? Droy's words had cut me to the quick.

Still, our enemy had its weaker points, too. "Droy, you know what? I don't think our enemy even has an army. There's a Citadel garrison and also one in the capital but an army? I doubt."

"Yes, but what about-"

"What about what? Look at yourselves. Can you honestly call Calteans a united nation? All you have is a few clans who failed to unite even in the face of a common enemy. The powers of Light — or Dark, for that matter — are no different. And if — or should I say *when* — they come here, they'll arrive as a military union of several clans. Not as a single army under one sole command. And that gives us a definite advantage."

"What kind of advantage is that, Uncle Olgerd?" the boy — who until then had been listening to us with bated breath — voiced his curiosity.

"Well, think for yourself," I told him. "A united army under the authority of a single commander can be compared to a human body. It acts in synch. Each one of the troops knows their own job. There're archers, footmen, the cavalry, the artillery and the service corps. There's a strict hierarchy when everybody knows their place and their direct commander. The troops are well trained and maintain a strict discipline. Luckily for us, that's not the kind of army we're about to confront."

"Why not?" Tim ventured.

"Because an army like that doesn't exist in this world. Not yet. The powers of both Light and Dark have some very strong warriors. When they group up together, they're a power to be reckoned with. And still they're not a proper regular army like I've just described to you."

I paused, trying to focus. How was I supposed to explain to an NPC that all those super warriors were nothing but fancy avatars concealing ordinary human beings inside? They weren't professional soldiers: they were teachers, doctors, programmers, builders or even translators like myself. Trying to organize them was a job and a half. They only obeyed clan leaders if they felt like it and only if it was worth their while.

The moment players sensed that a commander's order contradicted their interests, you could forget discipline. Each of them expected a return on what they'd invested in the game. Not necessarily a monetary one: some were after an adrenaline rush while others were looking for cool loot; yet others just needed a break from the real world. And above all this loomed the admins with their Rules and Regulations, of which the most important one was a player's freedom to do what he wanted to as long as it didn't hinder the gameplay.

The boy's eyes betrayed his incomprehension. Okay, let's do it again.

"You see, Tim, the warriors of both Light and Dark are very freedom-loving. They don't like being told what to do. Not to even mention their great heroes and wizards. No one can make them do something against their will. They can question a commander's orders or even refuse to obey them."

"Uncle Olgerd's right," Droy agreed. "I saw it myself. There was that big guy by the River Quiet who was arguing with his own commander like you can't imagine while his brothers in arms were busy fending our warriors off. He may be a great hero and all that, but I don't need the likes of them, not when my soldiers' lives are at stake. If everyone starts questioning my orders in the heat of the battle... oh no, thank you very much! Even though he *was* a great hero... many a Caltean warrior met their deaths by his terrible mace."

"You're absolutely right," I added. "A wise commander would know how to talk such divas around but an obedient, well-trained soldier makes up the backbone of a victorious army. And luckily, warriors like that aren't our enemy's forte."

"What Uncle Olgerd wants to say, son, is that we need to make sure that no one can weed us out of this city at the first try."

"That's right," I said. "I can bet anything you

want that our enemy won't be able to sustain a lengthy siege."

"Good," Droy said. "Isn't it time you go to bed, boy? Tomorrow will be a tough day. Go get some sleep. Uncle Olgerd and I will stay here for a while."

Tim heaved a sad sigh, rose and went reluctantly back into the tent.

For a while, we just sat there, thinking each our own thoughts. Finally, Droy broke the silence,

"Methinks, the first attack will be dreadful," he said, frowning. "But if we don't buckle, the rest might be easier. Do you think they might agree to negotiate?"

"Eventually yes," I replied. "My granddad fought in a terrible war. He used to say that at first, the enemy wanted to see what we were made of. But if, as you rightly said, we hold our own ground, then they just might negotiate. Because whoever comes here first, their main objective will be to take the city before the next bunch arrives."

Droy guffawed. "The Lights battling the Darks under our city walls! Never thought I'd live to see that!"

I smiled at the idea. "Also, don't forget the Nocteans prowling around. At the very least, they'll spoil the visitors' party."

We fell silent. No idea what Droy was thinking of but his face took on a dreamy expression. Me, I couldn't help contemplating the forces of Light and

---

Dark, imagining them going at each other's throats by the city gates while we stood leisurely on the walls watching them smoking each other.

Having said that, "city walls" was an overstatement: we were yet to build them. All in all, I didn't think Mr. Random would go that far just to accommodate us.

Oh well. There's no harm in hoping. Still, we shouldn't walk with our heads in the clouds, otherwise our return to reality might be a bit traumatic.

Droy's voice disturbed my disjointed thoughts,

"So, how about we start rebuilding the wall tomorrow?"

"Good idea. I've already spoken to the masons. They have some thoughts on the project."

"Masons? How many of them are there?"

"Three, if you only count those who actually know their trade."

"That's not a lot," Droy said moodily.

"It's not. Still, they have an apprentice each. Also, I gave them my permission to look for more assistants."

In actual fact, I'd consulted the clan's stats, then told the masons exactly who they needed to hire.

Droy shook his head. "Still not enough."

"Well," I shrugged, "we have to work with what we've got."

"I was told, Pritus was running around the

camp like a headless chicken all morning. Did you say something to him?"

I nodded. "They'll start building a trebuchet tomorrow morning."

"That's good. It'll take them some time to build and test it. Then they'll need to train new operators. And you, what are you going to do?"

"Well, once I'm finished shooting the breeze with you, I might go out on another recon trip."

"You should get some sleep," Droy made an unenthusiastic attempt to stop me.

"As my granddad used to say, 'plenty of time to sleep when I'm dead'."

* * *

The moon was especially bright today, large and full, hanging so low in the sky I could almost touch it. Not a trace of wind or snow. Perfect weather for flying.

Boris spread his wings wide, soaring on the air currents visible only to him. His ashen gray feathers quivered in the wind, appearing almost silver in the moonlight.

We'd spent some quality time studying the surrounding area and nearby locations. Not good. Judging by the sheer numbers of Noctean tribes prowling around, human players weren't our problem. It may have been my imagination but I had a funny feeling that all these creatures had arrived here solely because of us. You never knew with the admins. They seemed to love surprises.

Having finished my air inspection of the Icy Woods, I told Boris to head for the lands of Light. It was time for me to take an in-depth look at the auctions.

* * *

After all the snow, frozen mountains and gloomy forests I desperately needed to get to the sea. I needed a change of scenery, otherwise I might simply go nuts.

We were flying over the ocean now. The continent was barely discernible on the horizon to our left. To our right lay the boundless expanses of water which I still didn't have access to. For the moment, I was perfectly happy with this strip of sea offering me some of the most amazing views in Mirror World.

The ocean was calm today, gentle even. The fresh breeze sprayed me with brine lifted from the countless frothing crests of clear blue waves. So good.

I could inhale the fresh sea air forever, celebrating the ocean, the warm sun and the clear skies. The place made you feel alive again.

A small island appeared at a distance: Lone Isle, according to the map. I'd set my sights on it during Boris' first test flights. At the time, we'd only

---

flown at night, taking every precaution possible — but now that both he and I were bigger and braver, I was dying to see what was there.

The moment we reached the island's small but cozy bay, the wind died down as if by magic. The roaring of the surf echoing from the cliffs was the only sound disturbing the surrounding tranquility.

The flat beach was deserted. No system messages. Peace and quiet everywhere.

With a crunching of pebbles, Boris landed by the water's edge. I activated the summoning charm. Prankie jumped down on the sand and immediately headed for a small copse nearby on a makeshift recon mission.

In the meantime, Boris and I inspected the beach, looking for any footprints. The place was admittedly awesome but you shouldn't let your guard down.

Having discovered nothing that could set any alarm bells off, I decided to give myself a well-deserved break. I could use a walk and a sightseeing tour. I needed to unwind.

According to the map, there was a small lake at the center of the island.

I patted Boris' powerful neck. "Let's walk over there."

After having ploughed my way through snowbanks for so long, walking on green grass was a strange albeit pleasant experience. The ground seemed to spring underfoot. I was so happy to find myself away from the freezing wind and the snow-bound ruins, even if only for a few hours.

We entered the woods and took a trail uphill toward a rocky plateau. I walked gingerly on the stones overgrown with tufts of low grass, avoiding the gnarly little pine trees that poked out of the undergrowth.

The trail brought us out onto a tall cliff about sixty foot high which offered a breathtaking view of the sun setting into the sea.

Finally, I tore my eyes away from the vista and concentrated on the island lying below.

It was shaped as an irregular ellipse of about 500 acres. Most of its surface was overgrown with pine trees and tufts of grass. Nearby, the lake's surface glistened in the rays of the setting sun.

"What a place," I told my two pets. "It would be so nice to build a house here, don't you think? My girls would love it."

Boris stretched out on the grass and laid his massive head on his front paws, his eyes closed, his wings spread wide, chilling out. He seemed to be loving it.

Prankie was too busy studying the undergrowth. He didn't give a damn about me getting all sentimental. He had more important things to do with his time.

I lingered some more till I'd seen everything I needed to see, then began descending toward the lake.

It was surprisingly clear. An occasional fish resurfacing for a gulp of air left small circles in the mirrored expanse of the lake. Peace and quiet, indeed.

"That's it, I'm gonna build me a house here," I mumbled, ambling along the water's edge.

I walked the entire island in under an hour without coming across a single mob. The lake fish seemed to be the only local dwellers.

How strange. Then again, not really. The admins had more important things to worry about at the moment than a tiny desert island in the sea. They'd incorporated it and even added some vegetation and animal life to the script, gentrifying it as best they could. And seeing as no player apart from me could yet reach it, they probably decided not to go overboard with the worldbuilding. The island was still a work in progress.

Which was fine by me. The island had turned out sufficiently lifelike.

"We really should come back here one day," I promised myself as I clung to Boris' broad back, watching Lone Isle disappear on the horizon.

Where to next?

The second half of my trip wasn't as enjoyable as the first one but it wasn't too bad. About an hour after we'd left Lone Isle we came across another little island, nameless this time. It further confirmed my "work in progress theory", the only difference being that this isle didn't have much to show for itself at all. Some gnarly little trees dried out by the sea breeze and a bunch of prickly gray bushes: the island was basically just an ugly rock poking out of the ocean.

Ah-ha... and this here must have been the cause of the islands' deserted status. Remember the monstrous fish I'd seen in the river in No-Man's Lands? It was tiny compared to the monster I was looking at now. It seemed to have been pieced together from several sea dwellers. It had a powerful shark's body ending in four fins and a long flat eel-like tail. Its head on a long powerful neck resembled that of a crocodile, replete with jaws full of sharp triangular teeth.

The creature swam unhurriedly, circling the island, then disappeared into the depths, splashing a cascade of spray. It was probably its dinner time.

Oh well. That was scary.

Today of all days I felt especially exposed. Judging by Boris' raised hackles, he too was duly impressed by the encounter.

* * *

...It looks like all the buzz around your name is blowing over. I got the impression I'm not under surveillance anymore. Freakin' Sherlocks! Still, I'm not in a hurry to get rid of some of the more expensive stock you sent me. Better safe than sorry, if you know what I mean. Those items are quite conspicuous.

In any case, I've already sold all the pettier ones. I think this was the right decision. If you're reading this letter, you must have already checked the auction. They have everything you need for a DIY Noctean Warrior kit. The fangs, the hide, the clubs. The items dropped by Noctean werewolves are especially sought after. Get my drill? LOL.

I sent the money to your account. Plus the materials for your insects: the best metals and toxins I could buy. I think I've bought up Mirror World's entire stock of steel scales.

Also, at your request I invested into some jewelry with bonuses to Alertness, Detection, Vigilance, etc. What are you going to do, go treasure hunting? Good idea. I'm all for that!

So I suggest you check the attachment. I'm sure you're going to like it.

Ah, one other thing. I might be AFK for a while. The doctors are sending me to the seaside for some

---

occupational therapy. My health isn't what it used to be.

Max can't wait to join you but I told him to give it a break until it cools down a bit. I don't want him to get killed. You understand, don't you?

Don't hesitate to auction some of the petty loot. Currently there's a steady flow of items coming from No-Man's Lands so yours might easily go unnoticed. And keep the more interesting stuff for me, will you?

What else did I want to tell you... Oh, yes. The updates. I suggest you study them. You might find some very useful info there.

That's it, man. Talk to you soon!

We sat on the hill by the seashore, enjoying the warmth of the night, the smell of brine and the soft sounds of the tide. I was more than happy to have shed the armor and the fur coat, offering my body to the breeze.

Good location. Calm and warm. Sheer heaven after the barren and freezing expanses of No-Man's Lands.

My two pets were lounging on the grass nearby, snoring away. What a bliss.

The moment we'd crossed the border back into the lands of Light, my inbox had kicked back in, showering me with messages. However, one-liners like *Where did u get that gear* and *I want me a pet like yours* were now few and far between. Good.

Tanor too seemed to have stopped inundating me with messages. Admittedly, it felt a bit unsettling. On the other hand, it was quite predictable.

Nothing from my friends, either, not to mention my old friend Rrhorgus whose letter I'd just finished reading. I just hoped he didn't have anything serious healthwise. I had big plans for him in the future.

And as for the updates he'd mentioned... true, I'd received a whole lot of them. Some of them indeed dealt with No-Man's Lands; one had even sparked a public outcry at forums, especially from high level players. No wonder. When did game developers ever have players' interests in mind?

The update had affected me too. On one hand, I could understand the players' resentment and rooted for their cause, but on the other, I was happy as the proverbial pig.

In a nutshell, it went like this. The update regarded the resurrection protocol. From the moment it went live, players would lose their right to set up their own resurrection points in No-Man's Lands. Whenever they died, they were redirected to an obelisk of their choice situated on the territory of their corresponding side. Those who'd already set up their own respawn points, could only use them once.

In other words, I could only resurrect in my

secret little cave once. After that, whenever I was killed, I'd be sent back to the lands of Light.

What could I say? At first I resented the news too. The admins' brazen liberty-taking was annoying to say the least. They'd managed to completely undo the peace which I'd found in the knowledge of having a safe remote resurrection spot. Now I felt exposed, which admittedly drove me up the wall.

But once I'd cooled down and given it some thought, I decided it wasn't that important in my case. I even benefited from it in a way. Why, might you ask?

Firstly, I didn't have to walk. It took me minutes to fly the hundreds of miles that other players would have to travel on foot. Strangely as it might sound, I could afford to die in No-Man's Lands only to promptly resurrect in a nice warm spot like this island because I could get back in no time.

Other players, however, would have it tough. In the case of their character's death, they'd be back to square one, having wasted weeks of a complex and very challenging journey.

And that was not all.

After the update, a player wouldn't be able to resurrect immediately anymore. He or she would be subject to a time penalty whose duration depended on the mobs' aggro levels in the location where one had been killed.

As an example, this island location was

marked a safe green on the map. If, by any chance, I got killed here, I'd be able to respawn within an hour. But as for the unsafe "red" zones, there the duration of the time penalty could vary from twelve to twenty-four hours depending on the mobs' aggro levels.

The forums were absolutely seething. Surprisingly, the admins — who normally suffer players' critique in silence — actually posted a reply, saying that they'd been forced to do so by pressure from the general public. Apparently, there had been a lot of protests from social groups condemning them for allowing people to spend weeks in VR capsules. That way at least they could take breaks from playing.

Indeed, what was the point lying flat in a virtual coffin for twenty-four hours if you could spend that time IRL?

The world was changing. Virtual reality had entered our lives, adapting them to suit its own demands. I had a funny feeling that Mirror World was only the first harbinger of the changes to come. New virtual projects were about to sprout up everywhere, sucking in millions of human lives.

On one hand, having to live through such gigantic changes was admittedly exciting. On the other hand, it felt pretty scary.

I was quite sure governments wouldn't stop at gaming. Nothing prevented them from creating virtual prisons, mental clinics and retirement homes. Just to de-escalate social tensions in the world, you know.

The question was, would they be able to pull it off? Difficult to say. Such forecasts rarely come true. Too many things depend on too many tiny and easily overlooked details.

At the moment, it was all academic, anyway. Never mind. Back to the upgrade. Despite the pressure from the mysterious "general public" (whose intervention I very much doubted), the game developers left one potential loophole for the players.

Field altars.

I'd already come across that particular artifact during our battle with Sub Zero. According to the update, although you couldn't use field altars on friendly territories, you were more than welcome to do so on enemy turf. Each Altar opened a portal you could then use to travel elsewhere.

Still, even this little gap in the rules had strings attached. Field altars came with energy restrictions. They took ten to twenty-four hours to recharge, depending on their capacity.

Also, you couldn't use them while they were on charge, either. You could only activate them once the energy was back to 100%.

In any case, how were you supposed to lay your hands on one?

According to the Wiki entry, it was a piece of cake. Every Altar consisted of five parts. You had to find all five, then press "build". Easy peasy. In theory, at least.

As everything else in Mirror World, Altar portals came in various types from "gray" to "red". Should I even mention that prices both for Altars and their parts had skyrocketed?

Acquiring Altar parts was a whole new story. The devs had had a ball coming up with all the new rules. The parts could drop from any mob, from a level-1 rabbit to a Cave Dragon. The higher the mob's level, the higher a player's chances of laying their hands on a more advanced kind of the same part. That is to say, a rabbit and a dragon could both drop the same part, the only difference being its color.

I did a quick bit of market research at the auction. Oh wow. A single Altar part could buy you a small car IRL. Fair enough. Rare loot called for higher prices. Especially in the light of the upcoming colonization of No-Man's Lands.

I chuckled as I read a report about some level-3 players killing a level-5 Brown Bear only to discover he'd dropped a "gray" altar part. Lucky people. They had a reason to celebrate. I could imagine their unbridled joy when they'd realized what it was.

Undoubtedly, every clan's sales department must have been on the lookout for items like those.

Never mind. Let them have their fun. Lady Luck is a fickle enough lady. Trust her to strip fellow players of their well-deserved moment of good fortune.

Admittedly, the latest updates worked very well for us. If you took that guy, what's his name... yes, Dimax, the giant Horrud who'd decimated the Caltean ranks back at the river — imagine him getting killed while his field altar was discharged? When he resurrected, he'd find himself back where he'd come from. The twenty-four hour penalty plus the daunting week-long hike back to our castle walls... he'd be out of circulation for quite a while.

Seriously, I just loved this update. It improved our chances a hundredfold. Now players would have to think twice before launching suicidal attacks on us: they'd have to be more economical both with their time and with their altars.

Judging by his message, Rrhorgus had it all under control already. He must have been laughing as he wrote the letter, imagining the look on my face. For sure! He just couldn't help passing along the good news.

"Right, Sir Olgerd," I said, opening the auction. "Time to get down to business."

I scrolled down to *Blueprints, Sketches and Recipes* and did a search for "green" items.

Not bad at all. The variety and the items' sheer number — and especially their low prices — pleased the eye. Which was logical, really: "green" blueprints and recipes were standard loot dropped by low-level

---

mobs.

I checked the profession list of my new clan members. Even better! I could easily supply each of them with ten to fifteen items.

I hurried to fill my shopping basket. It wasn't even that expensive.

Next. Crafting materials. I ran a new search. Metals, wood, leather, parchment, paints and sewing supplies — not a problem. They cost nothing.

I bought a little of each material. I shouldn't be too greedy or I might not be able to fit it all in my bag.

Now, tools. Aha. It wasn't as easy as I'd thought. Most of the items had runes installed. Some were even charmed. I saw a pick almost identical to the one I used to have at the beginning of my Mirror World career.

The tools weren't cheap. Still, it was worth it. This was an investment into my clan's future. I had the money, anyway.

Strangely enough, Lia's tools turned out to be the most expensive of all. The vendor offered them as a single lot. You could tell that he took his profession seriously. Each item came with a rune and a few magic extras.

I spent more time choosing gifts for the little painter girl than for all the other clan members. I can't tell you why. She so reminded me of my little Christa,

---

that's for sure.

Five brushes and a palette made of Alven oak. A spatula, a scraper and three palette knives in various shapes and sizes, all of the finest Dwarven steel. Finally, seven tubes of charmed paints.

Unfortunately, I only managed to locate five "green" sketches for her. Apparently, her profession was quite rare. According to the sketches' stats, she could only use seven colors. Never mind. Once Rrhorgus was back, I'd have to ask him to get her some more. The man was a market genius.

That was it profession wise. Now all I had to do was get some foodstuffs.

That's when the bad news hit me. It wasn't about prices even: they were okay. The problem was, I simply didn't have enough space in my backpack. In order to transport just one sack of flour, I'd have to empty my entire bag first.

That was clever, in a way. They simply made sure that freight drivers could earn a living too.

Never mind. It wasn't as if we were starving. Droy had even promised me to create a special team of hunters and fishermen. Still, we'd have to address the problem as soon as possible, if only to provide fodder for the livestock.

Who would have thought that I, a sworn townie who'd only seen cows on TV, would have to create an animal farm from scratch?

Talking about animals... I checked the clock. Almost 4 a.m. I had to move. I had one last problem to address.

Chapter Six

THE VILLAGE OF TIKOS was conveniently located by the foothills of the mountain I'd landed on a few hours ago. The Great Ocean spread before me. The Tallian Prairie lay behind me. That's where I'd taken my first Mount Riding lessons.

Despite the early hour, the village was bustling with life. No wonder: it may be night in Europe but across the Atlantic the day was still in full swing.

This time I'd decided not to bother with any disguise. I simply kept a low profile, attracting occasional curious glances. A level-50 Alven lady lingered by the door of a magic shop, her amazed gaze filled with recognition.

That felt admittedly funny. They probably

---

viewed me as some sort of legendary high-level player. On my way to the riding hall, I hadn't met a single player whose level was higher than mine. In a way, this was flattering but still I shouldn't give in to the illusion. They could look at me all they wanted but none of them had yet attempted to speak to me.

Which suited me just fine. All I wanted was to reach the riding hall without any more surprises.

I saw a tavern and hurried to cross to the other side of the road. It was dimly lit; two of the streetlamps weren't working. Excellent. I took a shortcut through a dark side street stinking of rotten vegetables and cat piss.

Where to next? In front of me lay a public garden. Good. I hurried toward it. Quality gear was a great thing. It gave you this invincible feeling.

I moved through the garden in short bursts, lurking in the shade of the trees. My heart was about to jump out of my chest.

Finally, I forced my way through the garden hedge and stopped, facing a small square. The gate of the riding grounds was visible at its far side.

I lingered in the shadows, watching. Someone short and stocky — could be a dwarf or a Dwand — sneaked through the gate. A tall blond Alven archer with a quiverful of arrows slung on his back followed him.

That seemed to be it. All was quiet. Off we go.

I crossed the square in two heartbeats.

Now the gate. I hurried to enter.

Finally I could catch my breath. No one had attacked me yet. And I knew that all fighting was off limits in the riding school.

"Ah-ha," a familiar voice said behind me. "Look who's here!"

I turned round.

Master Rotim hadn't changed. Same bronzed skin and clean shaven chin, his slanted eyes watching me closely from under his closely cropped hair.

"Greetings, Master," I said. "I'm so happy to see you. I feel flattered you remembered me."

"How could I ever forget! A Miner wishing to learn mount riding!" he curved his mouth in a sarcastic smile. "Or should I say, a renegade warrior wanted by the Mellenville authorities?"

I was speechless. That's what the absence of Reputation can do for you.

Master Rotim must have noticed my hesitation. He waved a nonchalant hand, "I shouldn't take it too seriously. I don't care if you have problems with those paper-pushers. I can tell you everything about them myself. They don't know what they want, the bastards!"

That was an oversight on my part. I really should have checked his story out in Wiki. He sounded like someone with a bit of a past.

I nodded my understanding. "I bet. Today they shower us with privileges, and tomorrow-"

"And tomorrow they give us the boot and send us to some God-forsaken prairie to teach wannabe cowboys how to tell a horse's head from its backside," he ended my sentence for me.

Aha. He wasn't too happy with the powers that be, was he?

Actually, he was one of the very few NPCs I'd seen outside Mellenville or the Citadel. In a way, he too was an outcast. Just like myself.

"Never mind," he waved a dismissive hand. "You'd better tell me what brought you here this time. Will I be able to finally see your mount?" his suntanned face dissolved into a cunning smile.

He must have known I'd had a mount all along, he'd just been too tactful to press the subject. Then again, what was I saying? Of course he knew. He was only a computer code. He was part of the Mirror World system.

By way of an answer, I activated both summoning charms. First Prankster's, then Boris'.

Rotim's previously slanted eyes took on the shape of two saucers. I thought he'd stopped breathing. He just stood there like a salt pillar.

Ignoring the transfixed riding instructor, Prankie set off to inspect the new territory. He was now the size of a young panther clad in armor from head to toe. No wonder Rotim looked impressed.

A few players beelined for us. I didn't mind. Let them look.

Sensing my frame of mind, Boris reared up, showing off the ashen gray span of his wings. His gorgeous armor glistened in the moonlight. He looked good even if I say so myself.

The players surrounding us studied him in admiration. A dark-haired girl opposite me covered her mouth in awe in a funny childish gesture. Heh. These weren't your regular common-or-garden pets. These were relic animals. I still couldn't believe my own luck.

Master Rotim was the first to come round. With a gulp, he took his eyes off Boris and looked around him. He didn't look too pleased.

"What are you staring at?" he shouted at the players. "I thought you had a job to do? Or do you think manure will disappear on its own while you're fooling around?"

The players promptly made themselves scarce. What remarkable obedience. He must have issued them some really important quests. That was the answer to my question of how they managed to keep the place so clean.

My chat box started pinging. Someone was desperately trying to contact me — one of the players I'd just seen, most likely. Sorry, guys. I'd have to deal with you later.

"Olgerd," Master Rotim's voice shook with emotion. "Am I seeing what I think I'm seeing? This is a Night Hunter! And a Black Grison! How is it possible?"

Oh. How interesting. "You're full of surprises, Master Rotim," I said. "I had no idea you were familiar with these breeds. Your erudition is impressive."

"Thank you," he said with a small bow.

I could see in his face he was pleased with my flattery.

"May I touch him?" he asked in a voice filled with reverential awe.

He *was* impressed, wasn't he? "Absolutely," I said, sending Boris a mental command to approach.

Boris obediently froze a couple of feet away from the riding teacher.

Rotim's shaking hand lay on the beast's neck, his fingers stroking the silvery feathers.

"You've no idea what seeing him means to me," his voice rang with regret. "I grew up on legends about the great Night Hunters and their riders. My grandfather used to tell them to me as bedtime stories."

"And now you discover that one of those riders is your own student," I added, smiling.

Rotim laughed softly, trying not to scare the motionless animal. Finally, he wiped his tears and said, "I know it's none of my business but would you care to answer a question?"

"Depends what it is."

"Are you a descendant of the Der Swyor clan?

I froze in place, flabbergasted. "How do you-

He chuckled. "You too are full of surprises. You don't have to answer my question. I already know. And as for my, as you put it, *erudition*... That too is my granddad's influence."

I couldn't believe it. It looked like I'd finally stumbled across a clue, after all. And in Rotim's stables, of all places!

"Would you care to listen to one of my granddad's tales?" Rotim asked.

"Honestly, I was just going to ask you the same thing. Please do," I coughed, clearing my suddenly tense throat.

"It's not very long," Rotim reassured me, then began his tale,

> *"Deep in the mountains in days of yore*
> *Amid all the stones and layers of ore*
> *A master craftsman finished in his lair*
> *His last most amazing ware.*
>
> *In awe he stood before his great work,*
> *The marriage of magic and steel,*
> *But then the Mountain King went berserk*
> *And the treasure he planned to steal.*

To the craftsman's house his guards would go
On the orders of the king
For to seize the fruits of the master's work
And forth the capital to bring.

Then all the workers laid down their tools
And took up arms to a man
In order to save the master's great work
And thwart the king's scheming plan..."

He paused, whispering something with his eyes closed as if trying to remember what came next. He didn't look as if he'd succeeded, though.

"Shame," he sighed. "I used to know the entire ballad by heart. I must be getting old..."

"Can you just tell me what happened next?" I asked.

"Well, to cut a long story short, the master's apprentices weren't the only ones who took his side. The leader of the Der Swyor clan offered the old man their protection. His warriors were known as the Wings of Death. They used to ride Night Hunters."

I gulped. The belt buckle in my bag! Apparently, it had a fine history.

"...Unfortunately," Rotim continued, "the Der Swyor troops suffered a resounding defeat. The King under the Mountain was so furious that he ordered his men to kill each and every one of the Der Swyor.

There was something else I couldn't understand as a child. According to my granddad, the king was so furious he even had all the Grisons exterminated. Why would he do that? They're such beautiful animals!"

"You're lucky," I said. "But I can tell you why. They killed Grisons — although as you can see, they failed to eliminate them completely — because they served as a silent reminder of the crime they'd committed."

"I still don't understand. Why Grisons?"

"They had the misfortune of being part of the Der Swyor emblem."

"I see," Rotim said darkly. "You know, sometimes I ask myself why animals can't live on their own without the interference of humans? The world would have been a much better place..."

He heaved a sigh, then continued in a more cheerful tone, "Never mind! Enough sadness. You never told me why you came. Having said that... don't. I think I know."

He gave my pets a quick once-over and pronounced his verdict,

"Your Hugger has grown a lot. His magic abilities need fine-tuning. I think I could raise his Flight to level 3. That way his range would double. He'll also be able to carry four more items. And most importantly, he's now strong enough to carry two riders."

"Excellent!" I stroked Boris on the head, unable to suppress my excitement.

Rotim smiled. "That's not all. His ability to temporarily stun the enemy..."

"Yes, the Triumphant Crow!"

"I think I can bring it up to level 2. That would double the stun times."

"Excellent."

"Now, your Grison. This beast is born to defend his master. His ability to repel part of the damage dealt to his owner deserves to be doubled. His healing ability can be trebled. There's something else I could do: I could make him heal any other person of your choice. I can offer you all this at the discounted price of four hundred gold. What would you say to that?"

"Oh yes, please!"

For the next quarter of an hour, Rotim was busy exercising his magic on my pets, running his hands over their heads and whispering something. The two creatures suffered the weird ritual in silence; even the restless Prankie didn't show any attempts to run off.

I read the system messages reporting their progress. When the last one of them appeared, informing me of Prankie's Reflection ability reaching level 3, Rotim finally opened his eyes.

We spent a few more minutes discussing my

pets' future transformations. This, however, seemed to be the standard pitch he delivered to every customer. He just sounded too stilted, just like he had on my first day in his stables.

Compared to his initial emotional reaction to my menagerie, the rest of our conversation seemed too dry and mundane. Admittedly I was taken aback by his change of attitude. Then again, what could I expect from an NPC?

And still, if you took Droy and his stone-age gang, they seemed perfectly real. With them, I tended to completely forget I was in a game.

Having paid Rotim for his services, I headed unhurriedly for the exit. I lay my hand on the door handle when I realized I'd been followed by a very annoying sound.

That was the chat box again. Someone was insistently trying to PM me.

Okay, let's take a look. Who might that be?

As I pushed the front door open and stepped outside, I opened the chat window. Several identical lines were typed one under another in ALL CAPS:

WATCH OUT! THEYRE WAITIN 4 U!

I didn't get the chance to see the sender's name.

Someone attacked me.

Warning! Player Regron (112) has cast Gust of Ice on you!

Congratulations! You've successfully dodged your opponent's attack!

Had I? How had I done that? The guy wasn't a necro, was he?

But wait a sec... How about that achievement I'd received for defeating the lich? Didn't it say something about improving my chances of dodging magic attacks?

All these thoughts had flashed through my mind in an instant. I'd never been known for my quick thinking under stress. This was a recent improvement. That's exactly what constant interactions with mobs and high-level players can do to you.

Mechanically — blindly even — I set a swarm of fleas onto my attacker.

You've built the simplest mechanical creature: a Swarm of Fleas!

Level: 170

Number of swarm members: 8

There were eight of them this time! Level 170! I felt sorry for this Regron or whatever his name was. He was only level 112.

The wizard cussed, investing all his

amazement in a few choice words. And that was only the beginning. Trust me.

I rolled over to the wall and froze in a crouching position, taking in the situation.

There were five of them, levels 100 to 130. I couldn't make out their nicknames from this distance. Two wizards, judging by their outfits, the other three swordsmen. Their gear was "blue" but not top level.

The Alven player at the center was especially picturesque. His suit of armor glinted in the rays of the setting sun. His greaves and gauntlets were "purple". He was quite a handsome sight. I had a funny feeling I'd already seen something very similar... somewhere.

I clenched the teleport crystal in my right hand, activating it, then scrolled through the impressive list of potential destinations. Yes! The Ennans' city.

Would you like to teleport to your chosen destination: Yes/No

I was just about to press *Yes* when a nasty little voice disrupted my thoughts,

"Get that bastard! Don't let him escape!"

How could I ever forget that voice! Talk about bad luck. It was Shantarsky Jr, a.k.a. Lord Melwas, as large as life and twice as ugly.

What was it his millionaire banker daddy had said about his precious son? *"He's too young and too quick off the mark; for him, you're nothing."*

What else had he said? *"Power is the only language he understands... You might say you're a human being — but that's not enough for him. I've been raising him to be a leader, proud and strong. I've taught him never to bow his head to any Tom, Dick or Harry..."*

Very well. I might be a regular Dick but I wasn't going to run from him this time. I wasn't their quarry anymore.

Only now had I realized that I'd been waiting for this moment all this time.

I looked around me. Idle players started arriving at the scene. Rotim's front door opened again, letting out a whole crowd of them. They weren't in a hurry to interfere, though, too curious to see how this show might end for me.

I returned the teleport crystal to the bag but kept the summoning charms close at hand. Then I stepped back toward the wall to safeguard myself against any overzealous onlookers who might decide to stand up for Shantarsky Jr.

I found it strange I didn't see any of the local clan's members. This was happening on their territory and they didn't seem to care. What was the name again — was it the Steel Fists? Oh well. They must have decided to turn a blind eye. Apparently, a neutral clan is supposed to remain neutral even on their own turf.

I heard screaming as the fleas had finally got to Regron. That was quick! Less than fifteen seconds.

The other wizard actually tried to help his colleague. He began shooting some sort of fireballs at the fleas while the swordsmen were trying to outflank me, brandishing their weapons.

Unfortunately, all the wizzy had achieved was to attract the swarm's attention: some of the fleas left their victim and went after him with a vengeance.

A new system message promptly informed me of all the details. The other wizzy's name was Zarlog. Level 104. His chances were even worse.

Melwas was full of surprises, however. He bared his sword and rushed to the wizards' rescue.

He was actually quite good. He very nearly killed one of the fleas — no wonder, with his level 130. With a bit more durability, my little beauties would be priceless.

Right. While those three were tied down doing some pest control, I could turn my attention to the swordsmen.

They were almost upon me. The one to the right was a Rhoggh. Name: Armadan. Level: 128. The one to my left was a level-100 human called Ridd. They moved swiftly but cautiously. Their faces betrayed their anxiety about the strange behavior of the other three.

I wasn't surprised. I would have been anxious too. It hadn't gone exactly as their underage leader had planned, had it?

They tensed, preparing to attack me. Sorry guys.

You've built the simplest mechanical creature: a Scorpion!
Level: 150

None of them expected a steely level-150 insect the size of an SUV which had appeared completely out of the blue. Even I stood speechless, staring at his massive pincers and his long tail tipped with a sting.

The crowd gasped as one, recoiling. The swordsmen's faces lost some of their enthusiasm.

Zarlog screamed, apparently expressing his displeasure with the venom of the Swamp Monk. That was my last vial, what a shame. This was a perfect psychological weapon.

My little babies had suffered some losses too. Shantarsky Jr. had managed to smoke two of the fleas. He seemed to be getting the hang of it. Not that it was going to last, though. Very soon the fleas were obliged to notice the new target.

The swordsmen began gulping down elixirs,

changing their tactics. They stood shoulder to shoulder, preparing to defend themselves — or should I say to play for time?

I couldn't help smiling. I could read them like an open book. They must have contacted some top-level colleagues who in turn must have asked them to hold the fort until they arrived.

I didn't like the idea. At the moment, I was a cut above my enemies. Until now, I'd been a passive onlooker. But that might not last. Judging by the two swordsmen's gleefully expectant faces, they were awaiting some heavy cavalry. And I couldn't afford to face it quite yet.

Never mind. Impatient as I was to get to their "magnificent Lord Melwas", I might have to leave it till some other time. Honestly, after what I'd just seen, it didn't seem to be such a good idea anymore. If anything, I felt slightly ashamed of myself. Had I really wanted to wreak my revenge on this kid?

I activated both summoning charms.

The audience gasped their admiration at the sight of my two beasts. I leapt into the saddle as Melwas strained his voice over the melee,

"My clan guarantees protection and a fair reward to anyone who stops him!"

The crowd stirred. Exactly what I hadn't wanted to happen. I hurried to issue orders, telling Boris to take off, Prankie to cast his shield, and the

Scorpion, to cover our retreat.

Hissing and snapping his pincers, the Scorpion began to back off. I sensed Boris' body tense up as he prepared to take to the sky.

That's when a fiery spindle shot out of the crowd. Not the fastest of spells but then again, nothing seemed fast enough to me after Furius and his arrows.

The spindle barely grazed us as we took off and was completely absorbed by Prankie's shield. I didn't bother to strike back, afraid of hurting our supporters in the crowd. Still, I remembered the caster's name. Just in case.

Chapter Seven

WE WERE ABOUT to drop into the clouds when the system informed me of the two wizards' death. Despite the penalty I'd received for fleeing the battlefield, I'd managed to make level 98. Excellent. Me and my team kept growing.

Below, Shantarsky Jr. kept cussing and raging, promising to "stuff me" and "make mincemeat out of me". Yeah yeah. The fleas must have turned their attention to him already. He probably had more important things to do with his time than chasing after me. Somehow I didn't think his cavalry would make it here in time to help him.

The chat window flashed with new messages. I opened it.

That was cool dude
Totally awesome!
I luved it!

There were at least thirty more messages in the same vein, as well as a few friend requests. Naturally, I'd also received a few threats from today's opponents and a long epistle in ALL-CAPS from Shantarsky Jr.

I shoved everything into the Recycle Bin. Having said that... wait a sec. One nickname seemed familiar. It was she who'd warned me about the ambush to begin with.

She'd left a brief description of her character in the letterhead. Normally, I never used that option. My friends already knew everything they needed to know about me. Still, it was a nice gesture.

I glanced over the information she'd so helpfully provided.

Name: Elrica. Level 37. Race: Human.

That was the extent of it. Not that I needed to know anything else.

Actually, there was something else: a screenshot depicting a beaming blue-haired girl astride a pink panther. Judging by her light armor and the fancy staff behind her back, she belonged to one of the magic classes.

She merited a reply.

Hi Elrica,

Thanks a lot for the tip. Shame I read it too late.

I pressed *Send*. For a while, nothing happened. I was about to close the chat window when she finally replied,

Hi,

You replied to my message! I must be dreaming!

The letter was peppered with a variety of cheerful emoticons. I just couldn't understand her. Then again, why not? For most people, this was a game. Unlike myself, they were in it simply for a good time.

Of course I replied to your message! I had to thank you. You were the only one who warned me.

You're welcome! It was awesome! What a fight! A giant scorpion! Your pets are out of this world! And your fleas! Oh those fleas! You know what they now call those Gold Guild idiots in the forum? 'Flea bags' and 'mangy dogs'! LOL!!!

She was something else. My eyes flickered with all the grinning little faces.

Then it must have dawned on her. *Wait a sec. What do you mean, I was the only one? Do you mean to say that no one else had warned you?*

That's exactly what I'm saying, I wrote back. *You were the only one who did.*

But that's not possible! she added a dozen of her bug-eyed dropped-jaw emoticons. *I heard some guys in my group discuss the arrival of the Gold Guild warriors. It was Drox who tipped them off, apparently. I can't believe they didn't warn you!*

Drox... wait a sec... I definitely heard that name before.

But of course. He cast that fire thing on us, didn't he? Still, I had a funny feeling I'd heard the name before.

Drox is the one who attacked you with a Fire Twister! Wretched shaman! A sorry excuse for a Dwand!

Yes, of course! Drox! That was the funny guy hung with charms and ribbons who'd pestered me with questions last time I was here.

Is he a Gold Guild spy? I typed.

Yeah, I think so. Sort of. He's basically a major brownnose who sucks up to Melwas. Our rich daddy's boy Melwas, aka the flea bag! I just love it! You know your fleas took him apart, don't you? Armadan and Ridd were really lucky. The Nerzul group saved them just in time. It's a good thing you left when you did. Nerzul's warriors are all level 200-plus. They're the top.

Are they? How interesting. *How long did it take them to kill my scorpion?*

Not very long. But it did give them a good run for their money, LOL. A lot of people have got a bit more respect for you now.

Do they? Why?

Don't you understand? You're not a top level player and still you managed to defeat a whole group! They had to request help from a top level group because they couldn't handle a single player! You're a hero!

I winced. Oh, great. A hero! That was the last thing I needed.

Can I ask you a question?

Dammit. Here we go. Now she'll want to know

---

everything about me. All the 'hows' and 'whys'. *Of course. On one condition.*

Which is?

Promise not to get angry with me if I choose not to answer it.

Of course! I mean, no I won't! I understand!

Okay, I typed. *Fire away.*

You see, I study journalism.

Excellent. I'm very happy for you.

Thank you! The thing is, I have this vlog on the side...

How interesting. What's it all about?

Basically, it's about everything that happens here in the Glasshouse. I call it Elrica *and her Little Mirror. I just update my subscribers on all the local news...*

I'd love to check it out sometime but unfortunately, I'm pretty busy...

Of course! I understand! I just wondered if you might find an hour or so whenever you're available...

To do what?

To allow me to interview you.

More emoticons, shy and embarrassed this time.

Interview me? Do I look like the President? Or a movie star?

I don't think you have any idea how popular you are.

I don't think I have. And what's more, I don't think I've ever been interviewed before. Not that I look forward to the experience.

In that case, let's do it this way. I won't insist if you promise not to say no. Let's just file this conversation for future reference, okay? If one day you reconsider, we'll discuss it further. Is that a deal?

Deal, I replied. I liked the fact that she was tactful and not pushy. She must have realized that my present situation was a bit sensitive.

Yes!! She showered me with another load of happy grinning faces. *Feel free to write to me any time. I'll add you to Favorites.*

And so will I. Thank you. You can write to me any time you want. There's one problem, though. I might not be in a position to reply promptly.

That's all right! I understand! Oh, and... if by any chance you get the opportunity to make a few short videos about No-Man's Lands, that would be fantastic. I could post them on my channel. That'll definitely boost my subscribers numbers! These videos are very few and they're crazy popular. And a battle video could guarantee millions of views!

Oh well. Why not? The girl seemed quite nice. The squeaky clean Doris Day type. And she'd been the only one who'd warned me of the danger...

At my wife's request, I'd actually been filming quite a lot. I used to send her the nicest videos to show to our little Christa. I could give Elrica one of them, I suppose. How about the one taken from Boris' back as we flew over the river, the one with all the giant fish jumping? She might like it.

I think I might have something you could use, I typed.

No way! Thank you!

Ignoring a new emoticon attack, I pressed "attach file", selected the 10-min river video and sent it to her. *There you go!*

More thank-yous and a new shower of emoticons grinning from ear to ear. Could she even speak without them?

On this friendly note we closed our exchange, with more promises from me to think about the interview. When I finally closed the chat window, I felt absolutely drained.

"That's it, kiddo. Let's go home."

Boris — who'd all this time been soaring regally above the clouds — banked into a smooth turn and alighted with a single stroke of his big wings.

We were already within a few minutes from No-Man's Lands when my inbox pinged. Who might that be?

Oh. Elrica again.

I braced myself for a new emo attack. That's right. The girl was true to herself, ending every sentence with grinning funny faces. So, what did she have to say?

Ah-ha... it looked like I'd just got myself a spy all of my own. Apparently, Shantarsky Sr. had just visited the battlefield. According to her, he wasn't happy at all. He'd yelled at the surviving swordsmen. The girl was standing too far to hear it all — but what he *had* heard was "a bunch of idiots", "that wretched noob!" and "you missed him!" She seemed quite offended by him calling me a noob. Apparently, so were lots of other people, according to her. *No noob would ever be able to do what you did today*, she wrote.

I just loved her pro-newb enthusiasm. Then again, I wasn't the clueless klutz that had first entered the Glasshouse trying to walk to the nearest town on a few Energy points.

In a brief postscript, she praised my video, promising to upload it to her channel later that same night.

Whatever. As long as it kept her happy.

Chapter Eight

"WE'VE GOT VISITORS," Droy announced the moment I touched the ground.

I could see he was struggling to suppress his agitation. Orman and Crym stood next to him, both equally on edge. What visitors were they talking about?

The sun was about to set. I hadn't headed home straight away as I'd decided to check out the nearby locations. To tell you the truth, I hadn't liked what I saw there at all. Now I was really hacked off. The last thing I needed were mysterious guests whose arrival had already made the usually impassive Droy nervous.

"Who do you mean?" I asked, jumping off

Boris' back.

"The wolves," the three men replied in unison.

I frowned. "Which wolves? Animals, you mean?"

"You could say that," Orman replied grimly.

The others nodded. Jesus. What was that now?

"The Northern Wolves," Droy explained. "A Caltean clan."

"Wolves? They're coyotes!" Crym growled his indignation.

The others nodded.

"You're right."

"They are."

"Traitors!"

"It was them who warned us about the Noctean hordes arriving to claim Silver Mountain Valley," Droy explained. "But when they attacked, the Wolves chose to leave for the Ryan Steppe. They refused to fight."

"They fled the battlefield with their tails between their legs," Orman butted in. "They're horse dealers, what do you want? Cowards."

"They're nomads," Crym agreed. "They roam from place to place without settling down. How can you trust them?"

"Are they friends or foes?" I asked.

"Neither," Droy replied, scratching his beard.

~ The Twilight Obelisk ~

"We don't consider them our brothers. They're Calteans, yes, but still they're different. We were never enemies but we were never friends, either."

I nodded. "Very well. That much is clear. But how did they find us?"

"We told them," Droy replied calmly.

I couldn't believe what I'd just heard. It's one thing to be accidentally discovered by another clan's scouts who'd just happened to wander too far off to the North, chancing on the Forbidden City. But to basically invite them here was something totally different.

Also, how had they communicated? It's not as if the Calteans had their own postal system in place.

"How did you do that?" I asked.

"They followed my magic marks," Laosh said behind my back.

I turned around.

"I can see it in your eyes that you're worried," the old man walked over to us. "You don't need to be. Only Caltean shamans know how to read their secret signs. The Wolves' scouts had Amai with them. He's their young shaman and the clan leader. He may be a bit hotheaded but he's not as headstrong as their previous chief."

"Do you mean to say," I began, "that you kept leaving magic messages marking your journey?"

He nodded. "I did."

~ 125 ~

"What did you say in those messages?"

"The Forbidden City belongs to the Red Owls."

He had a freakin' cheek! Did that mean he'd left those messages behind even before we'd claimed the city? How were you even supposed to keep these guys in control?

"Are you sure that no one else can read those signs?" I asked, struggling to sound calm.

The old man smiled. "Absolutely."

I heaved a sigh, trying to take in the news philosophically. Before, I might have freaked out but by now I'd already gotten used to my new friends' antics. Still, there was no guarantee that some player might not be able to decipher those signs.

Then again, why should I worry myself sick about it? So they'd decipher the signs, big deal. They still wouldn't be able to use the information. The Calteans were the only ones who knew about the Forbidden City. Nobody else had any idea about its existence, let alone its whereabouts.

I had to get a grip. The men stood there waiting for my decision. "Very well. Take me to these Wolves of yours."

The Wolves' scouts had set up camp in the towering ruins of the collapsed city gate. They didn't start a fire for fear of attracting unwanted attention.

As we walked downhill, they were already expecting us. Their sentries knew what they were doing. But still I noticed them before they noticed me. I had this little trick up my sleeve... literally.

The Bracelet of Thai Kho — the thin strip of gold studded with tiny emeralds which was currently hugging my wrist — gave +30 pt. to Observation Skills. Rrhorgus had sent it to me together with two rings fashioned from Drukharm bone, whatever that was supposed to mean, which gave me another +25 pt. And finally, the Tamyan Necklace — an unpretentious chain with added +55 pt. to Gut Feeling. I could see all those stats as separate lines in my character's chart even though they performed the same functions as my Survival Instinct. If you summed them all up, they trebled my power of observation.

Which was why I immediately noticed the Wolves' sentries lurking behind the giant slabs of collapsed masonry.

Judging by Laosh' untroubled face, he too knew about them. How interesting. I really needed to give his stats a closer look. I'd never had the chance to do that.

I could see the scouts now, even though they were still too far away to make out their faces. They were the same height as the Red Owls. Their brown horses were rather bulky but short with large round bellies.

"Actually," I turned to Droy, "you don't have

many horses, do you?"

"We used to," Orman grumbled.

"Before the epidemic claimed them," Droy added. "And when the Nocteans came-"

"We never had too many," Seet butted in. "They're too fragile. Buffaloes are much better. They're hardy and strong. Easy to control, too. They can last a long time without food or water."

"They're not afraid of the cold," Laosh added.

Judging by their enthusiasm, the Red Owls seemed to like their pets a lot.

"How about my buffalo coat? I'm so happy I have it!" I joined in, earning myself a few nods of approval.

Talking in quiet voices, we finally approached our "visitors". They really looked a lot like the Red Owls, stocky and slant-eyed. Their hair and beards were black but their skin seemed slightly lighter than that of the Owls'.

They were armed with composite bows and scimitars dangling from their belts. Spears were strapped to their saddles. All of their weapons were "gray": I hadn't noticed a single "green" item.

The warriors stood with their arms spread wide palms up. Uneasy smiles froze on their tired faces.

"What does that mean?" I whispered to Laosh.

"Look at their hands," he hurried to explain in

a low voice. "Can you see the green ribbons tied around their wrists? This means they've come in peace."

Orman grinned. "Or that they're surrendering."

We stopped within a few yards of the newcomers. They stood without lowering their arms, their stares prickly.

The biggest and shaggiest one glared at me, his disheveled mane and beard peppered with gray. His furrowed face appeared mature but not old. There was something of the wild animal about him. His name was Pike, level 270. He had a massive bow behind his back as well as a quiver packed solid with fat arrows. Two scimitars graced his belt.

He looked over my gear, then cast a quick glance at Boris behind me and squinted, apparently impressed.

A young Caltean stood at the center of the group. He was just as stocky as the rest of them but his beard was somewhat thinner. This was Amai, the shaman and leader of the Northern Wolves. Despite his young age, he already boasted the highest level in the group: 293. This was one hell of a strong and dangerous NPC.

Unlike his clanmates, Amai looked relaxed, his eyes kind, his smile sincere.

Okay, time to break the uneasy silence.

"I am Olgerd, the Keeper of Twilight Castle," I said with calm dignity. "What has brought you to the land of my ancestors?"

Their faces betrayed surprise. Apparently, it wasn't me they'd expected to see as the city keeper.

The young shaman quickly recovered from his shock. "I am Amai, the leader of the Northern Wolves. When I saw the message left by honorable Laosh, I decided to summon my finest warriors and go visit our best friends."

Judging by my men's grim faces, they didn't share these professions of friendship. In any case, seeing as we weren't at war with each other, we were obliged to let them in. They were bound to have some news for us. We might even learn something useful, you never know. And in any case, we couldn't stand there all day, not with Noctean scouts prowling around.

"Very well," I said without a smile. "Old friends are always welcome."

My invitation received a mixed reaction. The Red Owls growled their discontent while Amai and his Wolves grinned triumphantly.

You can grin all you want, buddy.

The system wanted my confirmation to let in a group of ten riders. I pressed *Yes*.

Amai nodded to his men. They hurried to cross to the safe side, leading their horses by their reins. They must have had their fair share of unpleasant encounters along their journey.

With every step they took, their grins faded. These steppe nomads looked around themselves open-mouthed. No wonder! This place was the stuff of their childhood nightmares since time immemorial.

You'd think that the Red Owls were already used to it but they too cast wary glances around, peering into the gloom of the ancient ruins.

* * *

As Orman and Crym were trying to find accommodation for the Wolves warriors, Laosh, Droy, Amai and myself retired to Laosh' tent for the bread-sharing ritual. For the Calteans, eating bread together was a sign of friendship, so now our guests had no reason to worry for their lives.

Once we'd finished with all the formalities, Laosh got down to business, "So what has brought our valiant steppe brothers to our lands?"

Laosh was on a roll tonight. He managed to imbue the word "valiant" with a hefty dose of sarcasm — and the way he'd pronounced *"our* lands", you might think this place had belonged to the Red Owls since time immemorial.

If Amai had been hurt, he didn't show it. He might have even chosen to ignore the shaman's petty sarcasms. Why would a Wolves leader react to them, really? Unlike all the other Caltean clan leaders who'd wasted their precious time quarrelling, he'd left their council and saved his clan by retreating into the steppes. According to Crym, the Wolves still had almost four hundred warriors.

Despite all his experience, Laosh seemed to be naively thinking that this young leader who was wise beyond his years might take offence at his childish jabs. Why would he? Who was Laosh, anyway? A stubborn old fool who'd very nearly led his clan to its death? Not very likely!

I wasn't going to interfere quite yet. I wanted to keep a low profile for a while, keeping an eye on young Amai and his burly friend Pike who followed him everywhere like a bad smell. Now he too was sitting at a respectful distance from us, concealing a cunning smile within his shaggy beard, apparently amused at our old man's pompous antics.

"We followed your signs, O wise shaman," Amai replied calmly. "Please don't misinterpret our intentions. It's not every day we get word that one of the, ahem, *Caltean clans* is lording it up in the Forbidden City. I wanted to see it with my own eyes."

His "ahem" was pregnant with meaning, as if he'd been about to say something rather unflattering.

Laosh swallowed the hint, ignoring it entirely, then resumed his attack, "So how did you like our

---

land?"

"If the truth were known, I expected more from it," Amai replied with a crooked smile.

This time he'd overdone it. His reply sounded like a childish quip in a grownups' argument. Even Pike cringed. The Forbidden City was the Caltean version of Eldorado. Whoever said he wasn't duly impressed by it was either a pompous idiot or a liar.

Laosh suppressed a smile, apparently pleased with the result.

Amai's face didn't twitch. Still, his eyes betrayed his annoyance at losing the first round to a more experienced schemer. He squinted. "I can sense some powerful protection magic here."

"This is true," Laosh stuck out a proud chin. "The city's protected by great wizards."

"Aha," Amai pensively rubbed his scraggly beard. "My mentor always told me that magic is like a fire. If you want it to burn long and strong, you shouldn't throw all your firewood in it at once. You should add wood to it bit by bit."

"Your mentor must have been wise amongst Calteans," Laosh replied ceremoniously. "Still, there's no need to shiver next to a weak flame when you have plenty of firewood. It'd be much better to get warm by a powerful fire, wouldn't it?"

Oh. The old man was bluffing so masterfully you really couldn't feel a thing! He had to. No one else

---

should know about the magic sphere's two-week deadline. Even though the Wolves weren't exactly enemies, we shouldn't drive them to temptation.

"Well, if that's the case, then you don't need to worry," Amai smiled. "The ancient magic will protect you."

"Protect us?" I asked. "Against what? I know of course that these lands are fraught with danger. I just wondered if you might know something definite."

"How is it possible?" Amai exclaimed theatrically. "Don't you know yet?"

Laosh, Droy and I exchanged glances. My back erupted in a cold sweat. "Know what?"

Now it was Amai's turn to exchange glances with Pike. They seemed to be sincerely surprised.

"The Horde is coming."

* * *

That's what it was! This was the bugbear that hadn't left me alone all this time. All my recon sorties had finally pieced together into a finished picture. And not a very good one, either.

All this time I'd been watching small groups of Noctean scouts sneak about nearby locations. I thought it was the standard scenario because I'd seen similar things in Blackwood and other places. I thought it was normal for NPC mobs to stay in one place, respawning as they got smoked.

That was my mistake.

After some time in No-Man's Lands you can fall into the trap of thinking you're already a local. You think you know everything — until you receive a flick on the nose like a naughty puppy. It's a bit like seeing all the signs of the looming raincloud and still leaving the umbrella behind.

Did I tell you about Pyotr Alexandrovich, our sociology professor? We'd nicknamed him the Colonel. At fifty-six, he still preserved his ramrod-straight military bearing. He was always clean-shaven and well-dressed. His suits weren't expensive but they hung perfectly. This was a case of a man doing justice to his clothes and not the other way round.

My classmate Sergei used to live on the same block as him. He told us stories about the Colonel's morning jogs and exhausting athletic workouts.

The Colonel didn't smoke or drink nor did he eat fast food. As we later found out, he'd even written a few healthy lifestyle books. He was one of those health aficionados whose sole goal in life is to "die healthy", as we say in Russia.

I still remember the day when they told us that he'd actually died. It was a wet Tuesday in October. Sociology was our first class. We'd sensed something was wrong: the Colonel was a whopping five minutes late. Nothing like that had ever happened before — not in our year, at least. His punctuality was legendary: you could literally set your watch by the guy.

Five minutes' late! We were rubbing our hands in anticipation, thinking of all the jokes we could make. He had a good sense of humor, in fact. His frequent sarcasms were always funny and to the point.

Then the door opened and the principal walked in, looking grim. He told us that the Colonel had been knocked down by a car as he was crossing the street heading for the university.

The media picked up on the story. Very soon after, that particular pedestrian crossing was fitted with a speed bump — something that the Colonel had been campaigning for for several years prior to his death.

We all came and held a memorial service next to it. The promptly-built bump on the tarmac was covered in flowers. It made it look like a grave.

Oh. Now why would I be thinking about that? Probably because you can never be fully prepared. The man had led a healthy lifestyle, battling old age as best he could. But death has its own dirty tricks. It doesn't care about your best-laid plans.

I used to fear the upcoming war with the united powers of Light and Dark... but now it looks like that was the least of my problems.

* * *

"Are you sure they're heading this way?" Droy the Fang asked grimly.

"Unfortunately," Amai replied.

"How far are they?"

"They'll be here before the new Moon," Amai concluded.

That's three weeks from now. I had three weeks to find that wretched Twilight Obelisk, damn it.

And then what? Even if I managed to activate it, how would that save the Calteans? I might fulfil my obligations to the bank but what was going to happen to my clan?

What a predicament. I absolutely had to find the Obelisk but failing that, I might need to take my clan to a safer place.

But where?

My head buzzed with all the thoughts like an upturned beehive. In fact, I'd never stopped thinking about it in all the time I'd been here. Now my head was about to explode.

I shook off my thoughts and looked up with a startle. Amai was saying something, staring directly at me.

"... if the Keeper agrees with my suggestion..." I heard his last words.

All eyes turned on me.

I frowned as if making up my mind while I hurried to rewind the video I'd been making. My wife Sveta had asked me to document my every moment in Mirror World, so I had.

Where was it now... aha... found it! Let's take a look.

Ah, I see. Amai had suggested we simply loot the Forbidden City and get the hell out of here before the Noctean horde arrived.

This actually sounded quite reasonable. I had to admit that Amai's thinking was typical of a human gamer. Still, judging by the grim expressions on my clanmates' faces, they didn't like it.

In any case, what was there to loot? All we had to show for our trouble were piles of snow and heaps of collapsed stonework. That was the extent of the treasures left to me by the city's previous Keepers.

The warriors waited for my decision. I could see that my clanmates were prepared to stand their ground. The Wolves appeared calm, even though I could read in Pike's eyes his disapproval of his young leader's indiscretion.

Amai stared right in front of him. This must have been his usual manner of speech. He probably thought — and rightfully so — that they were stronger.

I'd already made some calculations. If Crym

were to be believed, the Wolves had twice as many regular clan members as they had warriors. Which brought their numbers to almost fifteen hundred.

Not a good ratio compared to our meager ranks. If these NPCs changed their status from neutral to enemy, they could create a lot of problems. We needed them as friends.

Never mind. Time to finish this discussion. Laosh was already at the end of his tether, I could see that. As shamans went, he was quite irascible. Just my luck. His diplomacy skills were non-existent. He'd rather call a spade a spade. Which was great if you wanted to start a war with someone but pretty useless if you hoped to strike an alliance with them.

The problem was, Laosh still viewed Amai as a green youngster who'd only ascended to the leadership thanks to his initial position as a shaman. Me, however, I could see the young man for what he truly was: a tough albeit slightly cantankerous leader, smart and cunning beyond his years. At least he had enough sense to listen to his advisor. I'd already taken a closer look at Pike and let me assure you, he seemed to be much more than he appeared to be. Whoever chose to view him as a shaggy ape were making a big mistake. I could bet all you want that the Wolves clan was in fact ruled not by one but by two heads.

Neither Droy nor Laosh seemed to realize that. No wonder the shaman's popularity ranking with his

---

clanmates was at its all-time lowest.

"I heard your words, O brave Amai!" I hurried to announce before Laosh got the chance to tell us everything he thought about the Wolves' leader. "I heard you and I understand your position."

My clanmates' faces betrayed their indignant incomprehension. Amai, however, grinned back at me while breathing an inconspicuous sigh of relief. No wonder: this wasn't his prairie home and he'd definitely overstepped the line. He didn't need a conflict any more than I did.

"Still, you need to understand me," I continued. "This city belonged to my ancestors. I'm its Keeper. Then a Caltean stranger comes along offering me to loot my ancient heritage."

The Wolves' smiles began to fade.

"I know where you're coming from, Amai, which is why I'm not angry with you," I added pointedly. "Being nomads, you can't understand our respect for the land bequeathed to us by our ancestors."

Amai gritted his teeth. Pike clenched his white-knuckled fists, his slanted eyes glistening under bushy eyebrows.

Ah, so you didn't like it, did you? Never mind. You'll have to grin and bear it, I'm afraid.

Droy appeared relaxed but I could see he was like a taut spring, prepared to jump upon the Wolves

---

at a moment's notice. Laosh bared the yellow stumps of his teeth in a smile, enjoying the show.

I paused. A heavy silence hung in the tent. The glares of Amai and Pike were literally boring a hole in me.

Right. Time to lighten up. "As you may well have noticed," I said, "we can't accept your suggestion."

Amai chuckled. Pike fidgeted in his place, and so did Droy — or so I thought. Laosh snapped his fingers as if saying, *that'll teach you!*

"But!" I raised a meaningful finger. "You're our guests. And as we well know, you can't let a guest leave with a heavy heart. If you do, he might never come back which will bring disgrace on his hosts."

It was funny to watch the change of atmosphere in the tent. Now both Wolves and Owls were staring at me open-mouthed.

I rose ceremoniously. "On behalf of my clan and in my own name, I offer our friendship to you and your people! Let us seal our union with a peace agreement! From now on, your clanmates are guaranteed shelter, food and protection in our ancestral lands! And to celebrate our alliance, I'd like to invite you and your warriors to take part in a raid on the ancient dungeons we discovered a few days ago."

There! A peace treaty to begin with, how about

that? And then we'll see. The dungeon loot would sugar-coat our refusal very nicely.

Now it was his turn.

Amai too rose from his seat, albeit slightly too hastily. Judging by Pike's unhappy expression, he must have noticed it too.

"I, the leader of the Northern Wolves, accept the friendship of the Red Owls! I swear to be a trusty friend and a good neighbor to you! And I accept your offer of hunting for your ancestors' treasures!"

A *good neighbor*, wow! That was lucky! And I'd thought we'd just part ways, end of story.

The realization of what had just happened must have finally dawned on Laosh who hurried to add,

"I suggest we seal our union with the magic oath created by our forefathers!"

Both Amai and Pike nodded. Excellent. No problems there.

The magic oathing procedure turned out to be rather simple and mundane. The system didn't offer any surprises. I received a standard message informing me of a peace alliance between the Red Owls and the Northern Wolves.

The next message, however, did surprise me. I'd received +50 pt. to my Reputation with the Wolves. How interesting.

We spent another hour celebrating our

agreement, then parted ways — mainly because Laosh had underestimated his drinking prowess and had fallen asleep right there by the fire.

Droy took Pike on a guided tour of our camp. Actually, it might have been a clever move on the part of Pike in order to leave Amai and myself alone with each other. I didn't mind. It would be a good idea to talk to him in private.

We walked out of the tent and stood by the collapsed city wall. Parts of it had already been restored. My masons didn't waste their time.

"I didn't know any Ennans had survived," Amai spoke, looking at the vast expanse of snow covering the foothills.

"Some say there's a drop of their ancient blood running in Caltean veins too," I said.

Amai chuckled. "Don't think we have much of it left in ours."

"Maybe not."

"Can I be honest with you?" Amai suddenly asked.

"That's probably the only way we can stay friends," I said.

"Then I'd like you to tell me something, Keeper. Do you really believe you can defend this place? With a handful of Caltean hunters? I don't think you're a match for those who're about to arrive here."

"Are you talking about the Nocteans?"

"Not necessarily. My brothers made some hasty decisions which got all their clans into trouble," Amai nodded at Laosh' tent. "First they failed to unite against the Noctean hordes. And then they stirred up a hornets' nest in the south, losing their best warriors in an unnecessary scuffle."

"Couldn't you have done something?"

"I tried," Amai replied sadly. "But as you surely know, Laosh is a pigheaded bastard. And he was the weakest among those who decided the fate of our clans. Me, I was the youngest. No one listened to me. They just said I was speaking out of turn. And when I took my clan out onto the steppes, they called me a coward!" he added through clenched teeth. Judging by his blushing cheeks, he still smarted from the memory.

"And where are they now?" I tried to cheer him up. "You turned out to be the wisest among all those gray-haired elders. You saved your clan. Or did they expect you to humbly obey their ridiculous orders?"

The young shaman chuckled. "You sound like Pike."

"And probably not just him. I can see it in your eyes that you've heard it before. You know what my granddad used to tell me? He said, if a friend tells you you're drunk you can disregard his words. But when five friends tell you the same thing you'd better go home and sleep it off."

"These are the words of a wise man. I need to remember that."

"Can I ask you something?"

He nodded. "Speak up."

"Do you know anything about the other clans?"

"I don't think so," he admitted. "We were the first to leave the valley when the Noctean horde had just arrived at the Crooked Ravine. That's two days' march from the Silver Mountains. Do you think they might discover the magic marks left by Laosh?"

"I've only just learned about them," I admitted. "But seeing as they're already there, they might help other Caltean refugees to find their way here. We could offer them food and shelter..."

"You're more worried about them than their own leaders," Amai said. "I'm not surprised the Owls obey you. The Black Axes must have joined them only because of you. Don't look at me like that. You really think that Crym or Pritus would listen to Laosh like they listen to you? I don't think so. I'm pretty sure that old Laosh didn't even know where he was supposed to be taking them."

He was quite astute, wasn't he? "You shouldn't exaggerate. If you take Droy..."

"Forgive me for interrupting you," Amai raised his hands in reconciliation, "I have nothing against

---

Droy. He's a powerful warrior and a strong commander. But he can't think several moves ahead. Let me be completely frank with you. I know about your battle with the Darks. Before you arrived on your flying beast, I took the chance to talk to some of the Owl warriors. I didn't like what I heard. At the beginning of the battle, they outnumbered the enemy ten to one, if you count both Owls and Black Axes. I expected to hear a glorious tale of their triumph. Imagine my disappointment when they told me that had it not been for your clever move involving the Erezes, it might have ended very badly for them..."

We talked well into the night, mainly discussing our future cooperation. As it turned out, the Wolves didn't have any problems with either food or cattle fodder. They even had some to spare. What they did need was tools, especially weapons: the tribe wasn't good at working steel. Normally, they bought everything they needed from the Caltean highlanders. But now that their habitat had been destroyed, they had to look for new solutions.

So this was the result of our conversation: we made an agreement to exchange tools and weapons for food and fodder.

Somebody might say this was a pittance. But personally, I think we'd made a very good start.

Chapter Nine

ONCE WE'D SEEN our guests on their way the next morning, I decided to distribute the items I'd bought for my clan members. If the truth were known, I was quite restless. What if it didn't work? It wasn't about the money even because I could always resell the items at auction. But my theory... was it right, after all? Because if it wasn't, we might just as well pack up and leave. Without having the option of leveling up, my NPCs were doomed: sooner or later, they'd be annihilated by either the players or mobs.

"Uncle Olgerd! Granddad said you had a present for me!"

Aha, here was my first test subject. Lia couldn't wait for her turn, could she?

Crunch stood behind her, shrugging in amazement at her childish impatience.

The girl's hands, face and even clothes were covered in paint. Her little turned-up nose seemed to live a life of its own. Her emerald green eyes beamed with hope and excitement.

I couldn't help it. My hands hurried to produce all my purchases from my bag.

"Your granddad is wrong," I grinned back to her. "I haven't got a present for you. I've got lots of them."

As I spoke, her face changed expression from hope to disappointment to unbridled joy. She was almost hopping with excitement.

"There you go!" I began pulling out all the art tools I'd bought for her.

As the pile of gifts in front of her grew, Lia's eye opened wider and wider. The box of paints and the packet of brushes were met with a happy squeak.

Finally, Lia calmed down a little. "Thank you so much, Uncle Olgerd!" she pressed the paints and brushes to her chest like the greatest of treasures.

Then she said something which held the promise of my plan's success. "What a shame I can't use any of this..."

Big sign of relief. "Why not?" I asked, second-guessing her reply.

She lowered her eyes. "Because I don't know

how to use these things yet... "

Crunch stood motionless, afraid of speaking. I could see he didn't understand what was going on — but still he seemed to know it was all going to work out fine.

"How did you paint before?" I asked.

"Well," the girl hurried to lay the presents onto the table, then reached into her own little pocket, "I had this."

"What is it?" I asked, peering at a tiny scrap of parchment.

"My mom showed me how to draw a vine. She also marked down which paints and brushes I should use. And here, the words I should be saying as I paint..."

That came as a surprise. "Words? Which words?"

Crunch decided to interfere, "This is ancient sorcery. My wife learned it from her grandmother. She taught it to her daughter who in turn passed it on to Lia..."

Aha, so that's what it was, then. How clever. This seemed to be a double-barreled profession. Just painting a pattern wasn't enough: you still had to cast a spell on it. I hadn't thought about it. Still, it was only understandable: all these professions were complicated to say the least.

Never mind. Next time I'd know what to look

for.

"Not to worry," I said. "The merchant who sold me the paints also gave me this," I produced five scrolls tied up with pale green ribbons.

The girl's hands shook as she unfolded the scrolls and began reading.

Now, the moment of truth. I was probably the more excited of the two of us.

After what seemed like an eternity, Lia looked up at me.

"What do you think?" I asked, trying to keep my cool.

"These are sketches," she replied. "They look very similar to the ones Mom made. Only they're prettier. And better. They're easy to copy. I can draw them now, no problem. The rhymes are easy to remember too."

Yesss! Yesss!! Yessss!!! I could scream and shout with joy. Still, I had to be careful not to scare the girl.

It worked! I did it! My NPCs will *evolve!*

Wait a sec. What had she just said?

"Which rhymes?" I asked.

"They're similar to the ones Mom taught me. When you say them, the drawing will make the object stronger."

Grrrrreat. So the sketches were sold complete with their respective spells. Excellent. One headache less. "So these sketches, what are they like?"

"This one," the girl pointed her little finger, "if I paint it on Granddad's cart, it'll make it run faster."

Crunch opened his eyes wide.

"If I paint those little leaves on his hammer, he won't miss when he hits nails anymore. And those flowers, if you paint them on a tent, they'll make it warmer on cold winter nights."

Oh. Beautiful. Excellent!

"Thank you so much, Uncle Olgerd!" laughing, the girl skipped out of the tent, hugging her armful of treasures.

I shouldn't forget to tell everyone not to interfere with her art activities. Let her paint what she wants and where she wants. She needed the practice.

With that out of the way, I turned to Crunch. He didn't take much time. I handed him some tools I'd bought for him, as well as a few blueprints and a small supply of materials. He thanked me profusely, both for himself and his little granddaughter. We shook hands, after which he hurried to his workshop to try out his newly-acquired knowledge.

There it was, the first droplet — which I hoped would spread, making very wide circles indeed.

I spent the whole evening walking around the camp distributing my wares. The whole place was buzzing with excitement.

Before going to bed later that night, I wrapped

myself in animal skins for warmth and opened my clan control panel. I think I fell asleep with a happy smile still glued to my face, watching the drab gray of my clanmates' possessions being replaced by the cheerful glow of a hopeful green.

* * *

"Now look here," Zachary the blacksmith rubbed his red beard. "This one is for archers. This one is for shield-bearers who are the first to fend off the enemy. And this one is for lancers!"

His large hands gingerly readjusted the weapons and suits of armor that he'd laid out on a large flat rock chosen by him to showcase his new collection. Droy, myself and all the warriors made up the panel of judges. You should have seen the amazement on their faces as they studied their new "green" equipment. The sight of them pleased the eye.

I looked over the group, "I have a suggestion to make."

They stopped talking and turned to me.

"On my request, these three suits have been custom-made for Droy, Crym and Seet. Why, might you ask? I'll tell you. Zachary, can you explain, please?"

"There's nothing to explain, really," the blacksmith began. "You all know how important it is to get the size right. And as I couldn't take everybody's measurements, I had to make do with these three. That's basically it."

None of them looked offended. They were warriors, not sissies.

"In which case I suggest they try them on and we'll take a look. We might find some ways to improve them."

The warriors hummed their agreement. The three "test subjects" went into the tent to don their armor.

Half an hour later, we were looking at a totally different kind of Caltean warrior. No wonder: they'd just made a leap from prehistory right into the Iron Age.

Admittedly, the game designers hadn't been too original. This was a rather impressive-looking Scandinavian-type suit of armor.

The warriors fell silent. Imagine a painting called *Vikings Landing in the Land of Savages*. All those helmets, chainmail shirts, bracers and greaves...

The gray-haired Crym looked especially impressive. Big and thickset, he towered over his brothers in arms like a cliff. A sword in a steel-decorated scabbard hung from his belt; his battle axe glinted predatorily behind his back, next to the massive limbs of a crossbow. The broad pauldrons made him appear even stronger and burlier than he was. In his left hand, he was holding a shield with a large steel boss at its center; in his right, a long poleaxe.

The armor's steel parts clinked as he stomped about. Jesus. The guy was a killing machine.

Droy's equipment was only marginally lighter. Still, unlike Crym who was more or less familiar with his type of armor, Droy's boasted some new features. His shield was broad; his new pike a couple of feet longer than his old spear. He had a chainmail shirt, a pair of pauldrons and greaves, and a brigandine covered in small steel plates. A Scandinavian helmet sat on his head, protecting the upper half of his face and leaving the lower half open.

Seet may have been an archer but he too looked suitably impressive with a new composite bow in his hand, a quiverful of arrows, a steel-plated vest and a leather helmet with a long steel nasel.

While the other Calteans surrounded them, chattering their excitement, I opened my new warriors' stats.

Oh wow. I couldn't have even dreamed about this. Both their defense and attacking stats had grown 40%!

Also, they seemed to belong to slightly different classes now. Crym used to be a Light Footman — but now he was a Heavy Soldier. Droy was now a Heavy Pikeman. Seet the Archer had now become a Crossbowman.

I squeezed my eyes shut with pleasure, visualizing my powerful future army. Talking about which...

I turned to the blacksmith who was beaming with pride and took him aside, "How much time do you think you'll need to equip all of our warriors?"

He must have given it some thought already because he replied without hesitation, "About four days, I think."

"And if we find you some assistants?"

"I've already found them," he replied. "Four days."

Okay. Four days was good enough. I shouldn't pressurize him. It was a game, after all: things happened insanely fast here as it was. I dreaded to even think how long it might have taken a real blacksmith in real life to single-handedly equip a bunch of warriors like this one. Months? Or even years?

Once the excitement around the blacksmith had calmed down a bit, Droy walked over to me.

"You never stop working your miracles!" he told me, beaming.

The half-mask of his helmet distorted his smile, turning it into a predatory grin. Oh wow. If I was scared looking at my own beaming friend, imagine what the enemy would feel staring at his furious scowl.

I shrugged. "I told you I'd think of something, so I have."

"How many of the clan craftsmen received similar gifts from you?"

"All of them," I replied honestly.

It was true. I hadn't forgotten a single one of them, be they cook, a tradesman or a healer.

Having said that... I hadn't been exactly honest, no. There was someone I still had to see.

* * *

"I just don't seem to get warm," Laosh said in a weak voice.

He wasn't in a good way. I found him wrapped in firs sitting in front of a blazing fire. Every now and then he'd offer his trembling hands to its warmth and blissfully close his tired eyes.

Me, I found myself a place as far from the fire as I could, next to a small air vent. The cool draft felt good on my hot face.

Outside, a celebration was in full swing. The sounds of music, songs and laughter hung in the air. Who would have thought that the Calteans would have enjoyed their mini-industrial revolution so much?

I heaved a sigh. I wasn't in the mood to

celebrate. I had too many things to discuss with the shaman.

"You shouldn't have let Amai go so lightly," Laosh grumbled.

I didn't think so. "He's young and inexperienced," I said out loud. "We just might steer his thoughts in the right direction."

"What are you up to?"

I might tell him, why not?

"I'm not making any plans," I said. "The moment isn't exactly right. But if we could forget our problems for just one second, I'd tell you that this place could become a Caltean capital city."

He perked up. "Have you been thinking about it too?"

"Can't see why not. As long as we survive the first few attacks. It might get easier after that."

Laosh' eyes filled with sadness. "You think they *will* attack us?"

"Absolutely."

"In that case, you shouldn't have let Amai go."

"Who told you I let him go? He'll be back. Quite soon, too. He'll be bringing us food and fodder. Lots of it."

"What does he want in return?"

"To begin with, he wants some weapons and tools."

He grew restless. "You're right! Now we really

have something to offer! All thanks to your magic! No Caltean has ever had the kind of weapons and tools we have now! And made by our own craftsmen, too!"

"Exactly. Who did Amai see yesterday? I'll tell you. He saw a bunch of fugitives running away from danger. Now look at your people! The tables have turned. And I'll tell you something else: this is only the beginning."

We fell silent. Laosh watched the flames dance, shuddering despite the stifling heat.

I breathed in the fresh air, listening to the sounds of the party forcing their way in through the tiny air vent.

"You know I have gifts for you too, don't you?" I rose and offered two scrolls to the surprised shaman.

"What's this?" he asked, accepting my presents with shaking hands.

"The merchant who sold me this said that only someone that possesses the right powers can work it out," I bluffed with a poker face.

In fact, those were two spells. I didn't even know which ones. All I'd cared about was that they didn't have class restrictions.

Laosh unraveled the first scroll and began reading. In the meantime, I decided to stretch my legs and get a breath of fresh air.

The camp was awash with the cheerful sounds of drums, flutes, psalters and bagpipes. Everyone was busy partying.

It felt admittedly good. They needed a break. They deserved it.

I lingered there, taking in the festive atmosphere, then walked back in.

Hearing me, Laosh raised his head from the scroll. "Thank you, Olgerd! These are extremely useful spells."

He didn't look it, though. His face was sour as if he'd just eaten a lemon.

"Is something wrong?" I asked.

He waved his hands in protest. "Absolutely not! How can you say that!"

"Then why are your eyes so sad?"

"I'm sad because I wish I'd had one of these spells earlier... and now it's too late."

"What do you mean?"

"Do you remember the magic you used to heal Droy's son?"

"Sure," I nodded as I began to understand.

"Had I had this earlier," Laosh took one of the scrolls, "a lot of people would have survived."

Chapter Ten

I AWOKE IN THE MIDDLE of the night from the soft pinging of a system message. Yawning, I rubbed my eyes. What's all that about?

Congratulations! Your warriors have become much stronger! From this day on, no enemy will dare call them a disorganized crowd of peasants!

Your Reward:
The rank of Commander General
A Shield Wall scroll, 1
An Extended Formation scroll, 1
A V-formation scroll, 1

Now I was fully awake. I hurried to open the clan control panel.

That's right! There wasn't a single Caltean warrior left wearing their old gear. The blacksmiths had made good on their promise, with a day to spare. What a great surprise. They must have received quite a few bonuses too, that's how they'd managed to finish the job in three days instead of four. I might need to look into that later.

I began to shiver. I didn't know which stats to check first. Get a grip, Olgerd. Take a deep breath. Good...

Let's look into my new rank first. I suppressed a smile. Sveta would laugh her head off. A Commander General, me!

Her sweet dear face stood before my eyes. Her dimpled cheeks; her fathomless topaz-colored eyes... the unruly lock of golden hair on her forehead...

I stopped shivering as my body filled with warmth from the memory. My gaze alighted on the Log Out button.

No. I couldn't. I still had lots of things to do.

I shook my head like a dog, freeing myself from the memory. Inhale. Exhale. I massaged my temples and sat up. I had work to do.

Congratulations! You've been promoted to Commander General!

Remember this day! This is your first step on your way to glory and greatness! Keep defeating your enemies and consolidating your army, and you'll be on your way to new successes and promotions!

Important! Now you can appoint commanders! Take your time choosing your assistants: your choice can't be undone!

Reward:

+35 to Morale

+20 to Discipline

Now that was interesting. Let's have a look.

The extra 35 pt. to Morale were very good news because I already knew how that particular stat worked. But Discipline?

Name: Discipline

Description: the prompt and efficient execution of orders issued by higher officers is one of the headstones of military science. The increase in this characteristic will result in the soldiers' improved discipline regarding their commanders.

That was extremely useful. And timely. I used to spend hours explaining the simplest of things to them.

Let me be honest with you: I was still quite

worried about the Calteans' behavior in their battle with the Darks. My men had aggroed the enemy's tanks like brainless mobs when we'd really had to split into two fronts. Had they attacked the Dark players' magic support instead, the outcome of the fight could have been entirely different.

I didn't count on their absolute obedience. Also, I really didn't fancy being surrounded by unquestioning machines a bit like my Scarabs. Even though the Calteans' emotions were only an illusion, it admittedly helped to preserve my sanity. But then again, there was definitely more to these Mirror Souls that met the eye.

Assigning more commanders was an excellent idea, too. Reputation was a great thing but if I wanted my clan to function like a healthy system, I needed something more precise than the fickle Reputation ranking which could soar one moment and plummet the next. And if my choice of commanders couldn't be undone, I was curious how it could affect the respective clan members' reputation. A high rank and low reputation? I dreaded to even think. Having said that, this scenario was commonplace in real life. There, the higher-standing individuals can't really boast popularity with the masses...

Okay. That much was clear. Now the scrolls. They were "gray": nothing particularly special.

I moved closer to the fire and fingered the

corner of one of them. Leather, tied with strips of rough dirty-gray fabric.

I pulled at the end of one of them, untying the scroll. Nothing extraordinary happened.

Very well. I unraveled it.

It was filthy, its ragged edges burned in places. Some of the spots looked suspiciously like caked blood.

I struggled to make out the faded letters. The game designers had definitely overdone it. But the moment I peered at the writing, a message helpfully popped up,

Greetings, Commander! You're holding the ancient Shield Wall Treatise, written by General Conceallo Iron Beard in the Era of Black Rain.

Important! In order to study the treatise, you must be a Commander General!

Would you like to study the treatise:
Yes/No

"Well, what do you think?" I whispered. "What new general would refuse some ancient knowledge?"

Congratulations! You've studied the ancient treatise: Shield Wall! Now your warriors will be able to

---

fall into battle formations!

Attention! Don't forget to convey your new knowledge to your subordinates!

I closed the message and chucked the dirty piece of leather into my bag.

What's that? A new icon appeared in the bottom right corner of my interface, depicting a row of shields.

Shield Wall

Description:

One of the oldest battle formations, first used by the hird of Conceallo Iron Beard in their war on the Sixfoots in the Era of Black Rain.

Effect: +15% to your warriors' protection from physical attacks

+5% to your warriors' protection from magic attacks

+15% to your small arms damage

Minimum requirements:

Shield-bearing heavy footmen, 3

Archers, 2

Maximum requirements:

Shield-bearing heavy footmen, 30
Lancers, 20
Archers or wizards, 30

I opened the *Formation* tab. It was pretty self-explanatory. Three rectangles symbolized the three troop types with their respective icons: three serried shields on the top one, lances on the middle one and a fiery strung bow on the bottom one.

I clicked on the lances. Didn't work. How strange. Why?

I soon found the answer. Apparently, I needed to assign commanders before I could start moving the troops around. Very good. That made it easier for me.

Now, the next scroll.

Greetings, Commander! By studying this ancient treatise, you will learn the secret of Dryx Stoneheart who managed to continuously fend off the army of Desert Dwellers in the Canyon of Two Moons.

Important! In order to study the treatise, you must be a Commander General!

Would you like to study the treatise:
Yes/No

Very well, let's study it.

Congratulations! You've studied the ancient treatise: Extended Formation! Now your warriors will be able to successfully confront the enemy, armed with only the lightest of weapons!

Another icon appeared in the bottom right corner of my interface, depicting a lance and a strung bow.

Extended Formation
Description:
One of the ancient battle formations used by the archers of Dryx Stoneheart during the battle with the Desert Dwellers in the Canyon of Two Moons.

Effect:
+15% to your warriors' speed
+25% to your light weapon damage
+15 to your stabbing weapons damage
+15% to your magic attack damage

Minimum requirements:
Lancers, 3
Archers or wizards, 2

Maximum requirements:
Lancers, 65
Archers or wizards, 45

Excellent.

And finally, the V-Formation!

Oh. It refused to open. It was a cavalry formation — and cavalry was something we didn't have... and might never have, unfortunately.

Still, it was better than nothing. We had to work with what we had.

Which was actually a lot. Before, my Calteans would attack the enemy in a motley disorganized crowd — and I now had the chance to change all that. All I had to do was assign some commanders.

But first I needed some fresh air.

Quietly so as not to wake anyone up I slid out of the tent.

Brrrrr! It was freezing cold! I should have put on the fur coat. My body felt well and truly paralyzed.

Snorting, I rubbed my face with snow, then hurried back into the tent and offered my shaking hands to the fire's gentle warmth. Much better.

"Right, let's take a look," I whispered, opening the clan control panel.

I wouldn't be surprised if the game developers just made up all this stuff as they went along. I'd hate to become their new guinea pig.

Aha. There it was. A new tab appeared, entitled Military Ranks.

As I studied the chart, I couldn't help thinking about all those TV crime series. There, too, police officers pin the picture of a crime boss and his minions to a corkboard in order to study and discuss them.

This was similar. A picture with my avatar topped the chart. *Commander General*, the sign beneath said. Better than a crime boss, I suppose.

The squares underneath were still empty. Each had a sign below, describing the respective commanders' ranks.

The one directly below me was a Colonel. It was gray and inactive, however. Little wonder: according to the prompt, a Colonel was in command of a thousand warriors. We were yet to grow an army that size.

Below the Colonel was a Captain, in command of a hundred warriors. This we could manage.

Below the Captain were empty openings for Sergeants, each in command of ten warriors.

The chart didn't provide a place for regular soldiers. Apparently, I as the chief commander wasn't supposed to bother myself with such trivialities. My job was to assign their commanders who would then proceed to choose their subordinates.

Let's do it, then.

First, the Captain.

Predictably, the system offered me the choice of two candidates: Droy the Fang and Laosh the Shaman. This was a no-brainer.

Congratulations! Your army now has a Captain! Make sure you teach him everything you know so that he becomes your faithful aide on your way to glory!

I grinned with pleasure, studying the new golden symbol shaped as two crossed swords next to Droy's name.

This was fair. He deserved the honor like nobody else. With all due respect to Laosh, I couldn't entrust the post to him. And if the truth were known, he might not even have liked it...

I was about to move to the Sergeants when I heard Droy's sarcastic whisper behind my back,

"Are you doing your magic again instead of sleeping?"

"Yeah," I replied mechanically, then paused, thinking. What had the message said about teaching Droy "everything I knew"?

I reached into my bag and produced the three scrolls. "You see, I bought these from a vendor. They look very old. I don't think he knew how old they really were."

I offered the scrolls to my freshly-minted Captain Droy.

He opened them and began to study the script as if system restrictions didn't even exist.

The system kept mum as he read them. The

change of expressions on my friend's face was the only clue to what was going on. Droy frowned, grunted, kneaded his beard and scratched the back of his head, showing all signs of some serious intellectual activity.

Finally, all three scrolls had been read, studied and even tasted. The moment he handed them back to me, the system finally informed me of its verdict,

Congratulations! You've shared knowledge with your Captain!

Excellent. Now we were cooking!

"So what do you think?" I asked Droy.

He'd changed a lot in the last week. He seemed taller... fitter even. Or was it his new armor? I really couldn't tell.

"Strange writings," he said, looking at the fire. "The first two scrolls we can definitely use. Not sure about the third one, but I know someone who might be interested in it. Do I understand correctly that this is secret knowledge not to be shared with strangers?"

"That's right. This knowledge is the property of our clan."

"Well said," he suppressed a smile. "In the morning, I'll start training the warriors."

"Good," I said as my heart filled with joy.

Actually... "There's one more thing... Captain."

"Tell me."

His new title didn't seem to have flustered him in the slightest. He'd just accepted it as his due.

"You'll need assistants to help you do everything you're planning to do," I said.

He nodded. "I'll appoint a few Sergeants in the morning."

The moment he said it, a new message appeared before my eyes,

Warning! Are you sure you want to delegate the choice of junior officers to the Captain?

Yes/No

You bet! I was a quick learner. Droy knew better indeed. With his skill and knowledge of his people (our earlier conversation about hunting and camp-keeping was proof enough) he certainly knew all the best candidates.

That was it, then. I pressed *Yes*.

The system promptly replied,

Function delegated to the Captain.

And another one in its wake,

Congratulations! You've successfully assigned

---

your army's command! The 10-warrior squads will be formed automatically.

Now your troops can engage in Military Exercises!

What, already? That was quick! Then again, why was I surprised? In order to make decisions, Droy didn't need any charts or interfaces.

I glanced over the list of sergeants' names.

All of our team was there. Which was right. I would have done the same. A few of the candidates were yet unknown to me. I needed to get to know them better. Droy must have had a good reason to promote them.

And what about these Military Exercises?

I hurried to read the description. Aha. This worked similar to a repeatable quest which my troops could complete every other day, receiving 15 pt. of Discipline.

What a strange feeling. Even though I hadn't quite worked it all out yet, I was excited and impatient to see what else the future had in store for us.

Chapter Eleven

*W*ARNING! THE WEST GROTTO *had remained unclaimed for many a century until finally it became home to a colony of Thorn Rats.*

Warning! This location can be too dangerous for players under level 290. Please turn back.

I turned around and cast an appraising look over our ranks. "Let's just hope we're good enough."

Several dozen eyes stared closely at me. They betrayed no fear: if anything, they were focused. Impatient, even.

These were the warriors Droy had picked personally.

When rumors of the upcoming dungeon raid had spread around the camp, we'd had to fight off all the applicants. If the truth were known, I'd very nearly agreed to forming a larger group. Still, having talked it over with Droy, Laosh and the sergeants, we'd decided it would be better to first send in a small recon team, just to work out what we were dealing with. And then we'd see.

We'd carefully weighed all the pros and cons until we arrived at a number of thirty. Thirty of the choicest warriors, the clan's elite, all levels 280+.

As for our formation... the very first Military Exercise had shown us that the gorgeous new gear wasn't enough to call the Calteans an army. Still, they'd managed to complete the first round of the quest — mainly thanks to Droy's unquestionable authority as Captain.

And as for the quest itself... at first I'd thought it might have been something truly special, like a campaign against a lone Noctean group, for instance. Still, it had turned out to be much more mundane. All the Calteans had to do was split into two groups and beat the heck out of each other using the formations they'd studied.

In the end, they did earn their 15 pt. Discipline, but what had it cost them! There wasn't a single warrior who hadn't received some kind of minor injury. We even had a few broken limbs. Still, in the end I didn't see a single shadow of doubt or disgruntlement on their faces.

Funnily enough, Amai and his bodyguards had arrived just in time to watch the last few minutes of our first Military Exercise. They'd delivered the promised supplies in exchange for our "gray" weapons and tools, and stood on a nearby hill watching the new Red Owls in training.

You should have seen their faces. At least Amai and his alter ego Pike tried to keep their expressions in check — but the others didn't even try to conceal their excitement.

I could understand them. I was still under the impression from our Shield Wall training. My guys' last scuffle had been especially impressive. Imagine fifty heavy soldiers marching in lockstep. The earth groaned under their feet. The clangor of steel. The calls of their bugles. The rattling of shields. Their battle axes, glinting predatorily in the blinding sunrays. The clapping of their bowstrings. The hissing of many arrows through the air. All of it happening in synch as if controlled by an invisible hand. Impressive? — You could say that!

Amai's eyes filled with childish admiration — and just a tad of insecurity which lasted but a few moments, replaced by indignation. A proud clan leader couldn't afford even a moment of weakness.

In all modesty, I was more than pleased to

showcase my new Red Owls to the arrogant Northern Wolves leader. His allusion to a "handful of Caltean hunters" still smarted. Watching their faces was well worth it, I tell you!

Now Amai was shaking with excitement. No wonder. Descending to the Forbidden City dungeons was an adventure any warrior could only dream of. This was the stuff of legends and ballads.

I was happy too because it meant we'd have a strong shaman with us. Even though his group wasn't subordinate to us, we could use his help, that's for sure.

Pike had hand-picked their best fighters. One of the Wolves must have spilled the beans about the upcoming raid because the entire Wolves clan competed for the right to escort their leader to the dungeon. Just imagine: fifteen hundred people all eager to join a group of a few dozen simply because they'd hate to stay behind. Did we really expect them to sit it out in the camp with children and females while their leader was busy exploring the ancient dungeons? No way!

In the end they'd added thirty warriors to our raid, not counting Amai and Pike themselves. Judging by the Wolves' sly grins and the greedy glint in their eyes, it wasn't really their leader's safety they were worried about. They just couldn't wait to lay their hands on the fabled treasures of the Forbidden City.

Someone might say it was stupid of me. They'd say I shouldn't have been squandering the legendary riches by sharing them with our contrarious new friends. I beg to disagree. A joint raid was bound to cement our reluctant alliance.

That wasn't the problem. Discipline was. And I'm not talking about the game stat.

It took me ten minutes of watching Amai's men to conclude that they were bound to run into problems.

It wasn't that they didn't obey orders. Oh yes, they did. Pike ran his team with an iron hand. It was their ability to execute his orders that worried me.

Let me explain. What's going to happen if a factory foreman tells a janitor to do a machine tool operator's job? This janitor may even be a well-organized guy, disciplined and hard-working. He'd approach the task in all seriousness and might even learn how to switch the complex machine on. Over time, he might even master it — but definitely not straight away. His first results would probably be pathetic. Without proper knowledge, experience and qualifications, the guy is bound to screw it up big time.

Here it was the same. The Wolves were all highly disciplined and responsible people — and still they had no idea of proper warfare. Only from watching our training had they gleaned anything

---

about proper battle formation.

So basically, I had a bad feeling about Amai's group. Besides, they couldn't boast much in terms of gear, either. Next to my well-equipped warriors they looked especially shabby.

I'd shared my concerns with Droy. His reply was calm and simple. We had to worry about our own warriors, he said, and let their commanders take care of theirs.

You couldn't argue but still... If, God forbid, anything happened to Amai, our alliance with the Wolves would go belly up. I had to do everything to make sure he came out of the dungeon alive and in one piece.

* * *

Based on the formations' bonuses, we decided to use the Shield Wall. That way we'd have protection from both physical and magic attacks as well as an improved small arms damage.

Crym's squad was in the first line. His guys were the hardest to crack. All of them were ex-Black Axes: this gray-bearded giant had gathered around himself all the strength of his old clan. The mere sight of them sent shivers down your spine.

The second line was formed by the squad of Orman the Bear. At first glance, they didn't differ much from Crym's men but still they were marginally lower in levels, their powerful frames slightly less bulky.

We followed in their wake: ten archers headed by Seet the Burly, with Droy as our captain. And last but not least, His Illustrious Highness the Commander General, a.k.a. humble me complete with my little menagerie.

Arrum Red Beard had completely recovered from the arrow wound he'd received by the River Quiet and was impatient to get back into action. Although he'd been given a squad of his own, he was quite eager to join us as a common archer as long as he could go to the dungeons with the rest of his friends.

Horm the Turtle had been promoted to sergeant too, but being more levelheaded, he'd obeyed Droy's personal request to stay behind in the camp.

Calteans! No amount of military ranks and subordination could sever the ties of kinship between them. Obeying orders was all good and well but their relationship with the person who'd issued the order was much more important to them. Also, I'd already noticed that Droy tended to single Horm out among the rest, using every opportunity to leave him in charge. Based on our reputation rankings, I could safely say that we were potentially looking at our next Captain. That's provided our ranks would somehow miraculously swell.

Shorve the Hasty who'd missed his chance to participate in our battle with the werewolves was chomping at the bit, impatient to see some action. He was still angry with us, thinking we'd stripped him of his well-deserved glory. We, on the other hand, were amazed at his own valor: he'd spent several nights trekking through the Icy Woods taking a message to Laosh — and he'd survived!

He had Observational Skills, Stealth, Pathfinding and Hunting all maxed out: a perfect combination for a scout. What could I say? Also, he was the only one who hadn't received a squad to command. It might actually have been for the better. Don't know about Droy but personally, I had some quite far-reaching plans regarding this particular Caltean.

In the meantime, I'd posted him to Seet's squad. Later I'd have to think how to use him for our best advantage.

Droy's voice distracted me from my musings. "It's time."

I turned to him, still pensive, and nodded.

The formation was complete. The raid was ready to set off.

Droy the Fang stood next to me, eyeballing the sergeants. Although he himself was already a captain, he wouldn't have missed this raid for the world. Which made me quite happy.

I looked at the disorderly crowd of Calteans who'd gathered to see the raid on its way. There wasn't a single woman among them.

"Where are your females?" I asked Droy softly. "Don't they want to say goodbye to their husbands and sons?"

Amai who stood to my left replied instead, "This is our custom. Only men should see warriors leave."

"They don't need to see all the tears and stuff," Droy added. "They had plenty of time watching their womenfolk cry last night. But not when they set off. In the morning, it's up to their grandfathers, fathers, brothers and comrades to wish them a good journey and a glorious fight. Now, greeting them back is a woman's job. The warriors' hearts rejoice at seeing their loved ones..."

Oh well. They might actually be right, of course. But as for me... If I could only see the face of my loved one, I'd feel rejoiced already. And knowing Sveta, she wouldn't have minded joining the raid, either.

Whoever had written the history of the Calteans had grossly underestimated human nature. Which was a shame indeed.

For a brief moment, the crowd fell silent. Old Laosh raised his hands to the skies, begging the spirits to bless our raid and deliver us home in one piece.

As he prayed, something clenched my heart. I remembered the last time I'd had to say goodbye to my girls. Sveta crying; Christa's happy eyes... I too had promised to come back in one piece.

What's wrong with me just lately?

Inconspicuously I doubled my hands into fists, taking a surreptitious deep breath. Inhale. Exhale. I seemed to be feeling a bit better.

The moment Laosh had finished praying, I received a system message informing me of a 4-hour protection raid buff. Well done, old man. Today we needed all the help we could get.

It was time to say our goodbyes. The raid members grinned and cracked jokes as if they weren't leaving on a perilous journey. It was easier that way. The remaining Calteans waved their hands, wishing us luck and plenty of loot. The warriors waved back, asking them to take care of their families.

Laosh gave me a bear hug which defied his age. "You're obliged to come back!" he said with a confident smile on his weathered, furrowed face. "And you will!"

He stepped aside. One by one my other clanmates walked over to me, wishing me luck and giving me more bear hugs, asking me to come back safe, once again very nearly driving me to tears. I was only going on an instance raid, for crissakes, not descending into the Inferno!

"Come back safe," Laosh repeated. Was it my imagination or had I just seen a tear glisten in the corner of his intelligent, forever serious eyes?

I smiled back to him. "I'm afraid I'll have to."

Chapter Twelve

"THREE MONSTERS," Shorve reported the results of his brief recon mission.

He'd only been away for a few minutes. That meant that the mobs were real close.

"What can you tell us about them?" Droy asked.

"They're a good head and shoulders lower than myself," Shorve began. "Skinny as hell. But the teeth in those jaws!"

"Are they bipeds?" I asked.

"Yeah... sort of."

"Do they have weapons?"

"No. Just teeth and claws."

"What else?" Droy asked.

Shorve faltered.

"Speak up," I told him.

He cast me a sideways glance. "I'm not sure. You told me not to get too close."

I nodded. He'd done the right thing. I hadn't wanted him to aggro them. We didn't need casualties right at the beginning of the campaign.

"I got the impression they had no eyes," Shorve said.

We exchanged glances.

"That's normal," Crym said. "Most underground monsters are deaf and blind. They'll still know when there's quarry nearby."

"How do they do it?" Amai asked in amazement.

"They can sense the vibrations of the rocks," Crym replied. "I'm pretty sure they know about our arrival already."

I didn't think so. In that case, Shorve would have already brought back a nice little train.

"Prepare for action!" Droy commanded.

The Red Owls interlocked their shields and readied their spears. The archers raised their bows.

The Wolves got moving too. Amai closed his eyelids, whispering something. Pike stepped forward with a scimitar in each hand, covering his master.

Right from the very start, the Wolves had

---

refused to follow in our tanks' wake and walked demonstratively along in a large disorganized crowd, seeing as the tunnel was wide enough to accommodate such an unorthodox formation.

I had a bad feeling about all this. They were going to become a liability, I just knew it.

Droy, however, preserved his habitual cool. During our conversation last night he'd made it perfectly clear that he would neither risk nor sacrifice his own men in case of any problems. If Amai wanted to play the hero, let him do so, as long as we stayed out of it.

I was ready too. Both summoning charms had long been activated. Prankie was running to and fro under the warriors' feet like a ball of mercury, ready to heal whomever I might point to. Boris waited next to the serried ranks. His Triumphant Crow might come in very handy if the enemy did breach our Shield Wall.

Also, just as we'd entered the dungeon, I'd cast three 5-hour buffs on our group. The Red Owls greeted their activation with a victorious roar, earning us quite a few quizzical stares from the Wolves who hadn't gotten any buffs at all.

As for me, I'd bought myself plenty of Life and Energy stones at auction as well as some Life and Speed elixirs. As they say in the Glasshouse, I was "all kitted out". I looked rather like a Christmas tree hung with all the buffs and stuff.

"Advance," Droy commanded softly.

The warriors moved forward.

Had those mobs indeed reacted to the vibrations of the rocks, they would have been upon us a long time ago. Our tanks stomped their heavy boots so hard you could probably hear them above ground. And that's without vibrations.

As we marched, I had some time to take a look around. The tunnel was rather wide — plenty of space for our ranks to regroup. Its walls and ceiling were covered in spots of some shimmering substance which looked like a sort of moss even though the system offered no prompts.

We'd extinguished our torches. Droy, however, told us to keep them at hand. One never knew what might lie ahead.

My gaze habitually searched all the dark nooks and crannies. With my Observation Skills, I had every chance of discovering something useful. Unfortunately, the tunnel was pristine as if it had been swept, mopped and polished just before our arrival. Quite weird, if you consider the place's gory fame. It didn't look as if it had ever been the scene of any fierce battles as the Wiki claimed.

We came across the first mobs less than a hundred feet later. The Thorn Rats must have sensed our arrival somehow and hurried to greet us in their own fashion.

I wouldn't say they were that impressive. I'd seen worse monsters in Mirror World.

They were about the same height as myself, with pale humanoid bodies. Their skinny spines, sharp elbows and knobbly knees were covered in sharp spikes. They had small elongated skulls covered with more spikes instead of hair.

Just as Shorve had said, they had neither eyes nor ears. These defects was more than compensated by their generous jawfuls of sharp teeth.

"Attack!" Droy's voice echoed through the ancient tunnel.

Attention Commander General!
Your group has been attacked by a Sentry Thorn Rat (270)!

Oh. First impressions can be misleading, that's for sure. The Thorn Rats managed to surprise me, after all. I'd never seen such speedy mobs before. They moved in leaps and bounds as if microporting.

Predictably, all of our archers missed. Not to even mention me with my humble slingshot.

The first Rat flashed through the air like lightning, ramming our Shield Wall with his whole body. Still, despite its speed, our tanks didn't budge an inch.

Aha. So that's how it was, then. These mobs

weren't very strong, were they? Their stats seemed to be invested exclusively in speed and agility.

Well, if that was the case, excellent! An agile mob had few chances against a tank. At least that's what they said in the forums. The beasts' only chance was if they attacked us in large numbers.

Before the mob knew what had hit him, his skinny frame was already peppered with arrows and skewered by several spears.

The remaining Rats met the very same fate. The first attacker's death hadn't taught them to change their tactics which boiled down to a lightning attack followed by an equally prompt death.

A system message popped up, informing me of our first victory and the XP received. We'd also earned 3 pt. Discipline — one per Rat, I suppose. That was nice of them.

Everything had happened so fast and felt so *mundane* that my Calteans exchanged puzzled stares. As they curiously studied the ugly little corpses, Crym called us aside.

"Did you see this?" he asked grimly, offering us his shield. Its steel-lined wooden surface was covered in the mobs' shallow claw marks.

As the others studied it gravely, I struggled to suppress a smile. Lia! The tiny artist must have gotten her little hands on our new gear! Both Crym's shield and his entire armor were covered in minute patterns.

I checked the other warriors — the same! She was quick, wasn't she? What could I say? She'd done good!

"They may look like nothing but their claws are something else," Orman commented, studying Crym's shield.

I wouldn't say it had suffered that much. Its Durability was still going strong. The shield was far from reaching its breaking point; but still, provided these attacks were numerous, our tanks risked losing them at some point.

"Fast and aggressive but absolutely defenseless," Seet summed up, kicking the Rat's corpse.

"That's not what worries me," Droy murmured, nodding meaningfully at the Wolves. "If these monsters get to our horse dealers, they'll be in trouble."

Orman shrugged. "That's what they wanted, wasn't it? We did offer them to join our formation."

"They're too good for that," Seet snickered.

I just stood there admiring their poise. Who would have thought that my Calteans — who used to be the same savage "horse dealers" if the truth were known — would have transformed into a fully functional combat unit? Now they were criticizing their allies for what they themselves used to be less than three days ago.

And before I forgot... I walked over to each

corpse and picked up the loot.

Just some teeth and claws, not much. Still, this was only a beginning. Besides, you never knew how much they could fetch back on the continent.

"Stay focused!" Droy's growl made everybody jump. "These were only sentries. Keep going! Keep your eyes peeled!"

We'd barely advanced another fifty feet or so when I heard a weird noise coming from the tunnel.

I looked around me at the warriors. They pricked up their ears.

"Sounds like the rustling of leaves," Shorve said.

Those who'd heard him enthusiastically nodded their agreement.

"Shield wall!" Droy shouted.

"Shield wall! Shield Wall!" the sergeants snapped after him.

The Wolves' commanders began disorderly spitting out orders, too. Amai's men huddled together in a thick mass bristling with swords and spears.

Better than nothing, I suppose.

The weird noise was getting closer and clearer with every moment. I already knew what was making it. And once the first pale monsters appeared out of the dark, I knew I'd been right.

The spooky rustling noise was made by hundreds of Rats' claws scraping the rock floor.

The spine-chilling sounds combined with the sight of the Rats pouring out of the tunnel's dark mouth was enough to make my blood curdle.

"Archers!" Droy barked.

The sound of his voice, the snapping of bowstrings, the singing of arrows and the sergeants' encouraging bawling — all this seemed to shake me out of my stupor. I cast a quick look around. No one seemed to have noticed my momentary lapse of focus. So much for their great general.

The mobs indeed proved to be virtually defenseless. A couple of arrows was well enough to finish them off. System messages reporting their deaths kept flashing before my eyes.

This time they came in two kinds: sentries and guards. They looked identical, apart from their levels. Guard Rats were level 280 — but despite this impressive level gap, they too needed a maximum of three arrows.

Despite the mobs' fierce attack, we'd had no casualties as yet. What a good job I'd upgraded their gear! Had they entered this dungeon in their old "gray" armor, things might have taken a totally different turn.

Until now, the Wolves had been lucky: my warriors had pulled all the aggro to themselves. All the Wolves had left to do was shoot their arrows from a safe distance.

Good. Let it stay that way. I didn't want them to stick their respective necks out.

I didn't take part in the shootout. I was their general, after all. A general's job is to control the entire picture. None of my men was wounded even though Prankie was prepared to offer his medical services whenever needed.

Come to think of it, buffs are really important. They're especially beneficial at low levels — all those blessings and performance enhancers whose effects aren't really that remarkable at top levels. They can turn a regular char into an epic Incredible Hulk-style superhero. Your body bursts with power; in moments like these, you can take on the world.

There was one thing that worried me, however. What was going to happen to me once I climbed out of my VR capsule and reverted to my old human body? I was gradually turning into Olgerd, getting used to his speed, agility and excellent eyesight. His joints didn't ache on rainy days. He didn't need glasses. His blood pressure didn't play up. He didn't have headaches in the mornings.

No wonder people preferred to spend most of their lives in VR modules which gave them freedom from pain and helplessness. Logical. It couldn't be any other way.

As I now stood shielded by my warriors watching them as they made mincemeat out of the

---

attacking mobs, I began to realize that my life had changed irreversibly. I'd changed, too.

My XP bar was filling up. The system kept showering me with messages reporting new levels. My warriors' eyes betrayed their enthusiasm and the sense of their own superiority over the enemy. And it wasn't exactly ungrounded. They had indeed become stronger — tougher.

If the logs were to be believed, the battle had lasted 9 min 23 sec. A victorious roar shattered the tunnel, celebrating the death of the last mob. The Calteans' bearded faces betrayed their disbelief at their lightning victory.

I counted 85 mobs in total. That was the number of Discipline points we'd received. I couldn't quite believe it myself.

Chapter Thirteen

"SO WHAT DO YOU THINK?" Droy asked, peering warily from behind a rock.

I opened the raid tab. The buffs would last another hour and a half.

"We might just make it," I replied.

"We might," Amai agreed, then added, "Can't we just surround them?"

Surround them! I don't think so, Comrade Shaman.

"If we break the formation, we'll die," Droy snapped.

Out of the corner of my eye, I watched Pike's reaction. He gave an inconspicuous nod, as if agreeing with our Captain. He'd had plenty of time to witness the superiority of both our weapons and our formations.

Amai, however, pursed his lips, sulking.

What was wrong with him? I didn't recognize him. What's with all the mood swings? This wasn't the focused level-headed leader he'd been before we'd entered the dungeon.

Didn't he have enough casualties? The Wolves had already lost thirteen warriors. That was almost half of his group! And it's only because at some point their brave leader had thought that sitting it out behind our tanks' backs was losing face!

It had all happened too quickly. During one of the Rats' attacks, the Wolves' archers had suddenly showered them with arrows. Predictably, they'd aggroed the entire pack who'd then lunged on the virtually armorless Wolves.

As a result, they now had thirteen dead and another ten wounded.

Had it not been for his faithful giant of a bodyguard, Amai would have already joined his ancestors in a Caltean afterlife. True, he was a powerful shaman who'd helped us a lot on our way here. But he was such a dumbass sometimes. Worse than some stupid hyperactive teenager.

Or was he just trying to confront some inner problem of his? Hadn't he told me that someone had called him a coward when he'd taken his clan out onto

___

the steppes? It was very possible he was trying to make up for it. But thirteen bodies! And we'd asked them not to shoot without our permission, too! He must have gotten an adrenaline kick when he'd seen that the Rats were an easy kill and decided to show us that his Wolves were every bit as good as the Red Owls.

True, they may have been just as brave but as for the rest, the Wolves were a far cry from my warriors. The moment the Rats had gotten near them, they'd promptly taught them a lesson in humility. The sight of the Wolves' mauled bodies was sickening. I didn't even want to think about it.

Now Pike had managed to surprise me. I hadn't expected that from him at all. I used to think he was a Caltean like any other, only a higher-level one, a perfect match for our Droy, Crym or Orman. But the moment his scimitars had begun to glow as he'd engaged in combat, my jaw dropped. He was much faster than any of the Rats, killing each one with a single well-aimed stroke.

What a shame I didn't have enough Reputation with them to check their stats or the stats of their weapons. Pike was full of surprises. Never mind. I was sure I would get my answer, given some time.

The very last fight had proved to be the hardest. We had to gain access to the grotto's last cave. The creatures were so numerous that several dozen of them had fought their way through our ranks. I thought this was the end of me but my men didn't let me down.

With every fight, their experience kept growing — as did their Discipline. The importance of this little stat was hard to overstate. It affected virtually everything, especially the speed with which they fell in, as well as their synchronization and promptness in following orders. The Calteans fought as one man: a single wall of shields bristling with spears, hammers and poleaxes which barreled through the incoming enemy.

I didn't envy the Rats. They'd lost about fifteen hundred. Unbelievable.

Their claws and teeth were the only loot they'd dropped. Nothing else. Actually, Weigner had told me about these types of dungeons: they mainly rewarded you with XP, allowing you to level up faster.

The thing is, when you've just started playing, the system showers you with new levels. But with every new level gained, your XP bar keeps growing — and once you make level 300, it becomes virtually infinite. High-level players go on evolved military campaigns against the strongest monsters in Mirror World hoping for a pittance of new XP.

So I had a reason to celebrate, really: I'd made level 140 already. But that was mainly due to the percentage I'd received for leading an NPC raid.

Happy? I was overjoyed! The only thing that ruined my good mood was the death of Amai's men. We'd already gotten used to them, you see. They were our comrades in arms. The tunnel had brought us closer together, turning us into a proper team. If only Amai had stopped his nonsense...

I just hoped that Pike might reason with him before they lost all their warriors. We still had the dungeon boss and his army to tackle.

Because it looked like we'd finally arrived.

The main cave was absolutely enormous. A grotto? More like a spaceship hangar lying at our feet. It was at least eight by six hundred yards long and another couple of hundred yards high. You could park fifty Boeings in there, easy.

The shimmering moss allowed us to see everything below. The place was absolutely covered in terrace after terrace of handmade ledges shaped as honeycombs. What on earth might it be?

"That's the biggest farm I've ever seen!" Crym whispered in admiration next to me.

"A farm?" I asked.

Droy nodded. "Of course. We call them mushroom nurseries. You liked the meat stew Orman made, remember?"

How could I ever forget? The stew had been delicious. Orman was an excellent cook, and I'd told him as much.

"Those were cave mushrooms," Orman explained. "It's a good job we stocked up on them before setting off on our journey. Do you remember who we bought them from? Was it the Axes or the Stone Fists?"

"It was us," Crym confirmed with a dreamy smile. "It was an excellent year for them. We had one hell of a crop."

With a wistful sigh, the Calteans nodded their agreement.

Suddenly I felt very sorry for them. They used to live happily raising their children and working their land. They'd had dreams, they'd made friends, they had gotten married; they'd even grown mushrooms. Then before they knew it, an enemy had taken it all away from them.

Not good.

"Did you have farms like this one?" I asked Crym.

He shook his head. "Not this big, no."

"A crop like this could last the entire Caltean race at least three years," Orman said. "I don't think your ancestors used to go hungry, Olgerd."

"Enough of your mushroom talk," Droy grumbled. "First let's do what we've come here for, then we can discuss it. So Olgerd, what do you think? How should we go about this monster?"

Good question. The Rat King lair was right at the very center of the cave. I could see him, sitting of a large rock surrounded by Guards.

Huge bastard. Even from where I was, I could clearly see his big teeth and long claws, with a level to match: 400. This would be a challenge.

And he was only half our problem. There were also his guards to tackle, about a hundred in total. They were much bigger than the Rats we'd smoked by the dozen earlier. All of them were level 350.

I checked the buffs. We still had just over an hour left. We should be able to make it.

"Now," I said. "That one over there is their King."

"You can see he's strong," Orman murmured respectfully.

"He is," I agreed. "He's been around the block a few times. And as you might have noticed, he's not alone."

Crym nodded. "That's his retinue."

"Yeah, sort of. They're very strong too."

"They're better protected as well," Shorve the Hasty said without taking his watchful gray eyes off the creatures scurrying around below. He raised a reluctant hand, pointing at the nearest mob, "Take a look at that one. Can you see the bone warts protecting his chest, back and belly? We need to tell the archers to aim better."

"If they attack us all together, we won't be able to keep the formation in shape," Droy summed up grimly. "And if they surround us..."

"The tunnel's walls give us an advantage," I said. "Which means we need to take up defensive positions here and lure them out."

"You're right," Droy agreed. "The tunnel's walls are our allies. Besides, the Rats would first have to climb up here to get to us. That'll give our archers plenty of opportunity to show what they can do."

I looked up at Amai. His magic skills made him one of our strongest links — but his impatience also made him our weakest.

"Chief," I said as amicably as I could, "I'm afraid we'll need all of your magic skills. You're our trump card in this battle. We all count on you."

He stood up proud with his arms crossed.

Enough flattery. Time to get down to business. "But in order for us to use your magic gift more effectively, I have to ask you to move to the center of our formation. You and your archers."

Amai was about to say something when Pike's large hand lay on his shoulder.

"Nobody's asking you to act like a coward," Pike said once Amai turned to him. "This is only a ruse. You're our weapon, one that's important for us and deadly to the enemy. The City Keeper has a point. You're our trump card. Besides, our warriors might do more good with their arrows than they did with their spears."

"Very well," Amai grumbled, obviously pissed by our decision. He shook Pike's hand off his shoulder, swung round and walked, sulking, to take cover behind our tanks' backs.

What an obstinate dumbass!

Pike cast a calm glance at me. He could probably read my face like an open book. And not only me: my sergeants' faces, too, betrayed their true feelings.

"He won't let you down," Pike said. He didn't sound as if he was trying to defend his student — no, his voice was cold and emotionless. Oh, well. Interesting.

"Good," Droy nodded. "In that case, let's begin. All we need to do is lure them out. And I think I know who's gonna do it," he looked at me with a cunning grin.

* * *

In the end, we didn't have to lure anyone out. The Rats sensed our presence.

"They're a bit sluggish, don't you think?" Orman said, watching the mobs unhurriedly moving toward us.

"They crawl like a tortoise on ice," Crym

agreed.

"Look at the size of them!" Shorve exclaimed in amazement once the wave of monsters was halfway upon us.

"They're at least two heads above any of us," Orman concluded, adding grimly. "We've got our work cut out for us."

The mobs' powerful bodies were covered in bone armor. Their speeds were low. These must have been the enemy's tanks. Judging by the size of their teeth and claws, their damage numbers were nothing to sniff at.

I hurried to check our shields' durability. It was less than half. Oh well. Had it not been for Lia's drawings, we'd have been in real trouble.

They kept closing in, slowly but surely: nearly a hundred creatures level 350.

As they approached, I began to realize that our shield wall wasn't going to hold them. And then... I dreaded to even think. I had to change tactics if I didn't want to lose all of my warriors.

I even wondered if Amai had been right offering us to fight separately. Still, this moment of doubt was gone as soon as it came. We'd gain nothing by splitting up. We would die faster, that's all.

"Lock shields!" Droy thundered. "Don't let these stinkers break our ranks!"

Our eyes met. His gaze betrayed the same

thoughts I'd just been entertaining. But it also glowed with hope: the hope that I just might come up with something.

Very well. Who was I to disappoint him? Time to play *my* trump cards.

"Droy!" I shouted, leaping into the saddle. "I'm going to distract them! You need lots of arrows! Loads! You need to shoot non-stop and very accurately!"

My Captain's eyes cleared. His face dissolved in a predatory smile. "You heard him!" he barked.

In one long leap, Boris sprang over the heads of our tanks.

I turned to the Calteans busy checking their weapons. Heh! Whatever had happened to those reindeer herdsmen clad in animal furs? They were gone. I was facing a wall of warriors armed to the teeth, their eyes burning with enthusiasm and determination.

Suddenly I felt an urge to say something to them before the battle.

"Brothers!" I didn't recognize my own voice brimming with strength and confidence. "You all know why we came here! Which one of you hadn't dreamed of seeing the Forbidden City and its ancient dungeons? Which one of you hadn't heard of their incredible riches? The tales of this place and its miracles were handed down from one generation of Calteans to the next! And now we're here! No one has ever come as far as we just have! You've already covered your names in eternal glory! They will make ballads about our journey! Old men will tell your great-grandchildren stories about their ancestral valor! This dungeon is rightfully ours! All we need to do is smoke out these creatures and their sorry excuse for a king! Are you ready to have fun?"

An ear-shattering war cry echoed through the grotto. A forest of brandished swords, spears and battle axes rose over the crowd. Some warriors banged their shields with their weapons. Someone blew his bugle. Boris felt obliged to add his spine-chilling crow to the mayhem.

At that moment, we were quite capable of taking on the devil himself. Honestly speaking, I hadn't expected this from myself at all.

I gave my army one last once-over, trying to think of something I might have overlooked. Twenty heavy soldiers blocked the cave entrance, with archers waiting behind their backs. Amai was already busy casting some magic. Let's see if he could surprise us.

I'd taken only the best of our warriors on this raid. The clan's elite. I'd done everything possible to protect and further empower them: the chainmail shirts, the helmets, the armor, greaves, swords, long spears and several thousand arrows and crossbow bolts. Our archers had the best bows and crossbows. Every single item was "green".

This was the strongest army the Calteans had ever had — and thanks to our advance through the tunnel, also the highest-level one. I couldn't see a single warrior under level 320.

And I was about to offer this little army to its first real enemy, a.k.a. the Rat King's personal retinue.

"Are you ready?!" I bellowed.

"Yaaaaah!" the warriors roared.

"Don't shoot until I tell you!" I warned them, then turned Boris toward the wave of approaching mobs.

They were running heavily toward us.

Less than two hundred feet away.

I could already hear the unpleasant sound of their claws scraping against the rock.

A hundred and fifty feet. Now I could see the bone warts covering their bodies in every detail.

A hundred feet. Their eyeless heads were tilted upwards, as if they were trying to sniff out their enemy. Drool dribbled down their angular jaws.

Eighty feet. I raised my hand. Behind me, the archers' bows creaked. Arrows left quivers.

My warriors were ready.

My turn.

You've built the simplest mechanical creature: an Armor-Plated Scarab!

Current level: 270

You've built the simplest mechanical creature: an Armor-Plated Scarab!
Current level: 270

You've built the simplest mechanical creature: an Armor-Plated Scarab!
Current level: 270

You've built the simplest mechanical creature: an Armor-Plated Scarab!
Current level: 270

You've built the simplest mechanical creature: an Armor-Plated Scarab!
Current level: 270

Their arrival was met with a unanimous gasp of admiration. I could imagine their faces. I couldn't blame them: I was a bit shaken myself.

This time my little beasties turned out just fine. Each was the size of an armored police truck. Their steely crests glinted. Their shells, head and legs were covered in sharp spikes.

The scarabs froze. My pounding heart was about to jump out of my chest. Every single hair on my virtual body stood on end. Had I really created these monsters? My brain refused to believe what my eyes were seeing.

Fifty feet. Time to do it.

As if by magic, the scarabs stepped forward in synch. Slowly they began to accelerate their lethal approach.

Despite their weight, their fat legs were fast and agile — soft even. The heavy screech of metal was the only sound making you aware of the deadliness of their descent.

They crashed into the Rats' ranks about forty feet away from our formation.

I expected to see anything but that. My scarabs' armored-truck bodies cut into the crowd like hot knives through butter. Their attack was dreadful. They smashed, crushed and rammed all the way through the Rats' ranks, leaving oily crimson trails in their wake.

I'll never be able to forget the sound of it. The snapping of bones and the ripping of flesh. The mobs screamed and howled, choking on their agony.

Then the scarabs about-faced as if on cue and plowed their way back through the helpless crowd. More of the same.

"Shoot!" Droy bellowed behind my back so that I nearly jumped. I'd lowered my hand, hadn't I?

Several dozen bowstrings twanged in unison, launching a cloud of arrows which fell upon the shrieking bloody mass like an angry swarm of bees.

The steel arrowheads easily pierced the Rats'

bone armor, sinking into their pale bodies. Their protection proved not as good as we'd thought before the battle.

Twice more the Scarabs plowed through the crowd. Finally, the last Rat fell. Our arrows had finished what the Scarabs' legs and crests had missed.

Judging by the results of the battle, the Scarabs had lost 30% durability. I'd gained 24 levels.

I glanced at the clock in disbelief. We'd defeated the King's retinue in 10 minutes flat. Time to tackle their master.

Chapter Fourteen

*C*ONGRATULATIONS! *You've won the battle against the Rat King (level 400).*

> *You've received experience!*
> *You've received a new level!*
> *You've received a new level!*
> *You've received a new level!*
> *Current level: 184*

The location boss hadn't played hard to get. Despite his high level and several nasty abilities like Reinforced Blow and Magic Shield, we'd made rather quick work of him.

We'd used the already-tested technique, with

---

the attacking Scarabs pulling aggro to themselves while the others showered the monster with arrows. By the way, Amai hadn't even gotten the chance to cast his magic, so quickly everything had happened. After the scarabs' arrival, Amai kept himself to himself, casting occasional grim glances my way.

His clanmates were suitably impressed, too. But unlike their sulking leader, they stared at me with respectful admiration. Respectful indeed: I'd earned another 200 Reputation with the Northern Wolves.

Pike surprised me again: according to another system message, our relationship had improved from Neutral to Respect.

What was wrong with him? Even my relationship with Droy paled in comparison. I had a gut feeling that surprises wouldn't end here.

Right. What next?

Congratulations! You're the first player in Mirror World to defeat the Rat King!
Your reward has been upgraded!
Reward:
A Bone Chest Plate of the Rat King, 1
The Battle Claws of the Rat King, 1
A Large Magic Chest, 1

My hand shaking, I scratched the back of my head. The first "purple" items I'd won in battle! I mustn't forget to take a screenshot of Rrhorgus' face watching me pour all my latest loot onto his shop counter.

Let's take a closer look. First, the Breast Plate.

Name: A Bone Chest Plate of the Rat King
Item class: Unique
Effect: +350 to Protection
Effect: +255 to Stamina
Effect: +255 to Health

Effect: +345 to Strength
Durability: 1250/1250
Restriction: level 150

Collect the full kit to receive a bonus!

Actually, my current level allowed me to wear it. Should I try it on? Why not?

I pulled the breast plate out of my backpack. Oh. This wasn't my style to say the least. Besides, it looked more like a shield than a piece of armor. This item was meant for a tank.

The Claws proved to be the same. Excellent. Both would fetch me some good money.

What next?

The Magic Chest was "red". Restriction: level 100, excellent. I could open it.

I held my breath and pressed *Open.*

Congratulations! You've opened the Large Magic Chest!
Reward:
Gold coins, 5,000

Dumbfounded, I watched the brief animation as the gold coins moved to the top of the panel, increasing my funds count. I won't lie to you: it felt good. Actually, this was my first monetary loot. Now I could understand why other players were so desperate to be the first to lay their hands on virgin dungeons.

Congratulations! You've received a Legendary Achievement: A Regicide! You're a legend!
Reward: The Order of the Wind's Fury

Not another reward. The message had already been made public in the common chat. I could imagine Tanor's reaction.

And not only his. They weren't happy, that's for sure. Some noob opening new dungeons and amassing all the perks? Something told me they weren't going to celebrate my success.

Never mind. Let's go back to my prizes. One more Legendary Achievement in my collection.

What is it about, actually?

Name: The Order of the Wind's Fury

Description: +45% to the damage dealt with small arms and missiles, applicable to all of your group or raid members.

Excellent. As one of my neighbors used to say, just what the doctor ordered.

My backpack's icon continued to flash. More surprises?

I drew my attention away from the menu in order to check the battlefield. My Calteans seemed to have forgotten their fatigue and had gotten busy investigating the grotto. They walked around it alone or in small groups, studying the ancient structures. Veneration was written all over their faces.

The honeycomb terraces were everywhere you turned. It felt like being inside a giant beehive.

Crym slumped on a rock next to me, groaning with exhaustion, "I've never seen anything like it."

I turned to him. "I thought you said you had things like these?"

"We did! But this... this is-" he swept his hand around the cave by way of describing its majestic glory, then shrugged helplessly, "Well, you know what I mean."

I nodded. I did indeed.

"My father spent his whole life working his farm," Crym sighed. "He wanted me to follow in his steps, heh. He would have loved it here. Shame he didn't live to see it."

"Nocteans killed him?" I asked.

"Oh, no. He died in his bed surrounded by his family. It had been five years before the Horde came."

"I'm sorry," I said.

"So am I," he heaved a sigh. "Never mind. What was I saying? I was still a young boy then. I used to help him a lot in his mushroom nursery."

Well, well, well. It was getting interesting. I pricked up my ears.

"I didn't have to do anything special," he admitted, oblivious of my interest. "Just fetching things and all that. But I still remember a few things. I've had a look around this place. One thing I can tell you is that the irrigation system isn't damaged. Can you see those sluices over there?"

I looked where he pointed. "Do you mean all those mechanisms with levers and things?"

He nodded. "That's right. They appear to be in working condition. All we need to do is clean the cells and the water canals, bring down some fresh soil, plant new mushrooms and start the irrigation machine."

"Are you sure?"

"Absolutely," he said with a confident smile. "If we plant one-quarter of this place, we'll never have to worry about going hungry again!"

I sat up like a bloodhound that had sensed a trail. "What exactly do you need?"

"Heh! You'd be surprised. We have everything already. Every self-respecting Caltean woman has mushroom spores in her pantry. Bringing enough soil down here might be a problem but I'm pretty sure we can manage."

"How many workers do you need to tend the nursery?" I asked with bated breath.

He waved my question away. "That's nothing. Mushrooms are easy to grow. Once we get back, I want you to meet Peet the White Eye. He's the expert."

I remembered a skinny, emaciated man whom other Calteans called White Eye for his pale blue eye color. I'd already met him when I'd brought him some new agricultural tools.

"I actually know him already," I told Crym.

He stared at me, uncomprehending, then slapped his forehead, "Of course! You know everybody now, don't you? Every mangy dog in the camp wags its tail to you! Ha ha!"

I laughed, too.

He was joking, of course. But the really funny thing was that I indeed knew every dog in the camp, whether mangy or not. What would he say to that? And not just every dog but also every cat, pig and chicken. We even had a hedgehog. He was Lia's new pet.

No point telling him that. I could use the occasion to pick his brains about other things. Like our allies.

He shrugged. "We told you everything we knew about them."

"How about Pike?"

"Well..." Crym paused, thinking. "We call him Pike of Many Hands. He wields his sword like you can't imagine. I've never seen another swordsman as good as him."

"I know what you mean."

I meant it: I still couldn't forget Pike's glowing sword tricks. "But as far as I can see, he's not just a great swordsman but also a leader and a wise councilor."

Crym grinned. "You're dead right there. Had it not been for him, Amai would have died in the tunnel like the idiot he is. I swear to you by all the underground gods that it was Pike who must have talked Amai into taking his clan out onto the steppes before the Horde came."

That was a surprise. "You think?"

"Absolutely."

"Anybody else think so?"

"Lots of people."

"But Laosh-" I began but Crym interrupted me.

"Laosh!" he sneered. "He can't see anything

beyond his own nose. Had it not been for you, the Red Owls would have long been dead, all of us."

"Well, the clan owes its survival to lots of people and not just me-"

"Aha! You see? Your modesty is a sign of wisdom!"

"Your words are pleasing to my ear, my friend. But still you're mistaken. Modesty's got nothing to do with it. A clan is like a human body which can't live without its organs. Its heart, liver or kidneys must work in synch like a single mechanism otherwise the body will die. But I agree with what you said about good leadership. A lot of things depend upon it."

"Exactly," Crym said, rising from his place. "Amai would have never plucked up enough courage to take his people onto the steppes."

His last words concerning Pike and Amai were the missing piece of the puzzle I'd so desperately tried to put together for the last few days.

I looked around me, searching for Pike. There he was, standing behind Amai who was sitting on a rock. The old man stood cross-armed, cold and impassive like a block of ice, keeping his eyes peeled for any more blunders from his young leader.

I watched Crym's broad back as he left. Then I returned to the business at hand and pressed the backpack's flashing icon. I probably had some more stat points that required distribution. Or did I have

100% knowledge? I really needed to spend a few moments sorting that out.

When I saw the reason for the icon's impatient blinking, I didn't believe my eyes. I even rubbed them. My heart missed a beat, freezing in my chest like a scared rabbit. My lips stretched in an idiotic smile.

Finally.

The icon of the Twilight Castle map was finally active.

I'd thought it would never happen. I remembered that night in the Footworn Traveler's Inn when I'd first opened Pierrot's app which had scared me out of my mind. Then, all those maps, plans and schemes had felt like something way out of my reach. An impossible dream.

And now I was standing here, right in the middle of a giant mushroom field, a pace away from a new discovery.

I opened the map with bated breath. A bright red mark glowed at its center.

The Armory.

My back erupted in cold sweat. Was it really possible?

Those of the Calteans busy by the opposite wall began shouting. I looked up. Droy was running toward me. I rushed to meet him.

Only when I came closer did I see his happy grinning face.

"We've found another door!" he shouted from a distance. "The underground gods seem to like you, Keeper!"

* * *

The rock walls of the Armory exuded warmth and calm. The room was dry and even felt cozy in the torchlight. Then again, it could be my Ennan nature: I always felt safe and cozy these days whenever I was down a rock hole.

The torches cast their orange light on the Calteans' long faces and dropped jaws. Some of them looked quite funny. Their eyes glowed with the anticipation of more loot. Like impatient youngsters, they waited for me to give them the signal to strip the place bare.

The door into the Armory looked identical to the grotto's front door back on the surface overhead.

I'd already made some calculations. A loaded cart pulled by two buffaloes could easily go through the tunnel. The room itself was big enough for such a cart to turn round. And I was probably seeing only a small part of it within the torchlight's reach.

When we'd just opened the door, the familiar smell of steel, wood and oil had hit my nostrils. The room was lined with shelves stacked high with all sorts of boxes and crates.

I could see large barrels, iron-bound wooden chests and bolts of fabric and leather. A wide table by the door was crowded with all kinds of precious boxes.

"So what do you think, Keeper?" Droy whispered impatiently into my ear. "You need to make up your mind. Everybody's waiting."

I forced my gaze away from the scene and rubbed my eyes again.

Then I smiled to everyone. "Should we share the spoils?"

A shattering "Yaaaaah!" flooded over me.

* * *

Seeing as both the grotto and the Armory were now the Red Owls' rightful property, we decided to leave our loot here.

Now Droy and I watched the Wolves file out of the grotto, ant-like, loaded with Amai's share.

"I still think that a quarter of the loot is too much for them," Droy grumbled.

"That's all right."

"These so-called warriors didn't deserve one-tenth of it. We did all the work."

"They lost thirteen dead, you know."

"That's another thing," he complained. "Why did you have to give anything to the families of the dead? What's it called now... a cop... conp..."

"Compensation," I offered.

"Exactly. That's what I meant, dammit. It's the clan's leader's duty to make provision for them."

I locked his gaze with mine. "You're right, my friend. A clan leader is obliged to take care of his warriors and their families."

Frowning, he gave me a long look. Gradually his face cleared as he began to realize what I'd meant. "Do you mean to say that the Wolves-"

"Why not? I can't see what's stopping it."

My confidence in our future merger had been born the moment I'd received the little green medal certifying my reputation with the Northern Wolves.

Let them help themselves to as much loot as they can carry. Sooner or later they were going to join our ranks, anyway. And as for the loot, most of the items we'd found in the Armory were "blue", anyway. All the materials, all the leather, wood, metals and stones were marked as Rare and came with Craftsmanship restrictions. Neither the Red Owls nor the Wolves could use any of it yet. By the time the Wolves would be able to craft something out of the steel they were now so excitedly carrying toward the grotto exit, we'd have already become a united clan.

In fact, I could have offered Amai to have left their share in the grotto. In our safekeeping, so to say. That would have saved them a lot of time. Still, on second thoughts I'd decided against it. They might have thought we were trying to rob them of their share. Until the last moment, they'd believed we weren't going to give them anything.

Interestingly, once I'd failed to live up to those expectations by sharing the loot with them, my relationship with Pike had grown to Trust. Not bad.

Strangely enough, everybody had ignored all the precious chests and boxes sitting on the table. It was as if NPCs simply couldn't see them. Apparently, this was what the system considered my personal share.

And they were actually quite interesting. A few of the boxes contained all kinds of Reputation stones. Three of the chests were absolutely packed with all sorts of potions and elixirs. Plus five more chests which contained three thousand gold each.

I must have been dreaming.

Let me be completely honest with you. As I watched the Calteans fuss around collecting the loot, all sorts of funny thoughts entered my head. Like, that I could appropriate everything without having to share it with anyone. I'd even made a quick estimation of what it might fetch me at auction. The answer was, *a lot.*

Still, my other self — the one which was normally kind, honest and level-headed — had ultimately gained the upper hand. According to its reasoning, it was nowhere near enough to pay off my loan. So I wouldn't be gaining that much, really.

But I'd be losing quite a lot. I'd lose the Calteans' trust — and without them, I'd never be able to keep the Ennan city.

But that wasn't all. Everything I'd just mentioned, all the materials, Reputation stones and even gold, paled into insignificance compared to what we'd discovered in the far corner of the Armory.

We'd found several dismantled Ennan war machines.

And their blueprints.

Chapter Fifteen

AMAI'S NERVOUSNESS APART, our farewell from the Wolves was cordial. Logical, really, considering they were our comrades in arms. We'd fought side by side. We'd eaten together by the fire. We'd defended each other. We'd shared the loot. We'd become brothers. Which was worth a lot to all of us.

Amai was decidedly ill at ease watching this. He must have sensed the affinity his elite warriors felt to me. His own authority was plummeting. Pike was the one who still kept his clan together.

As I watched the Wolves ride into the sunset, I had a funny feeling they'd become part of us one day, just as I'd predicted.

Still, I had no time to indulge in musings. We

had work to do. Lots of it.

We counted ten long massive crates packed with machine parts. Plus seven glaive throwers and three stone mortars. At least that's what the blueprints located in one of the boxes said. There were quite a few scrolls there, even though I'd only managed to read two of them. The rest were, for now, out of my competence.

The news of the Ennan machines soon spread around the camp. Everybody came running to take a look at the wondrous things: warriors and craftsmen, women and old men, and naturally, the omnipresent kids.

Master Pritus, our expert gunner, was especially excited. Thanks to him, we managed to find enough carts to transport our precious cargo. Admittedly, lots of people had come to take part in the action.

Without even discussing it, we unanimously started by putting a stone mortar together. Why? No idea. Probably because all the numerous parts made it appear much more powerful than a glaive thrower. We must have subconsciously wished for something big and powerful enough to assure us of our security.

According to the blueprints, in order to install the mortars — referred to as *Brocks* — we first needed to build a 30-degree ramp. A group of diggers were already busy shoveling.

While the others opened the crates and laid all the parts on the ground, I read the lengthy blueprint. As it turned out, the Brock's inventor was none other than my very own Master Grilby, my first mentor who'd died in my arms.

What's more, it looked like this invention had been the reason why the Ennan race had been destroyed and all the Black Grisons exterminated.

My heart clenched when I thought of the old man. Of course he was only an NPC, a lifeless piece of program code, but the memories of our meetings were still more than alive.

Pritus stood next to me, staring blankly but reverentially at the blueprint. To him, of course, this was all gobbledygook. Shame. I'd have loved to delegate to him all the dirty work assembling it. No such luck, apparently. I'd have to do it myself.

As my doctor used to say, *a good beginning is half the battle.*

The voice of one of Pritus' assistants distracted us from the blueprints, "It's all done. The ramp is compacted."

I looked at the small clearing littered with all sorts of machine parts: all those levers, pulleys and cog wheels. It was about thirty feet away from the wall. Should be enough for a backswing. If it wasn't, we could always make another ramp.

"Let's do it," I told Pritus, crouching next to

the array of steel junk.

With an impatient nod, he squatted next to me.

"Now," I said, studying the parts gleaming in the winter sun. "I'd like to ask you, Master, to note these symbols which cover each element."

"These are runes, if I'm not mistaken," Pritus replied.

"Exactly," I said. "Have you seen them before?"

He moved undecidedly closer and spent some time peering at the fancy swirling symbols. His eyes opened wider. Beads of perspiration covered his forehead.

I couldn't take my eyes away from the runes, either. They intertwined like the branches on a grape vine, creating a design which was both beautiful and cryptic. The unknown master had wound it all around the steel parts; now the ornamental chain of symbols was silently speaking to us, whispering its secrets to our hearts. Amazing.

With a deep sigh, Pritus forced his gaze away from the array.

"I'm sorry," he said, rubbing his eyes. "I've never seen this language before. The ancient rune makers guarded their secrets closely," he shook his head with regret. "I can't read them."

Never mind. We still had to do it. But first, we had to do one other thing.

"The blueprint says that each piece is numbered," I told Pritus. "Apparently, the numbers denote the assembly order."

He immediately knew what I meant. "In which case, we need to lay them out in numerical order. That might make the assembly much easier.

We spent a few more minutes sorting the pieces out by number. Finally, I could start the assembly process.

I lay my hand on a small block of steel marked with a tiny number 1 in its top right corner.

Warning! You're about to activate Brock Part #1!

Energy required: 1,000 pt.
Accept: Yes/No

How very interesting. Under Pritus' surprised stare, I reached into my pocket for an elixir and activated a "purple" Stamina stone. Now we could do it.

I pressed *Accept*.

For a while, nothing happened. The runes remained gray and lifeless.

Then my right hand sensed a pulsating warmth coming from the runes, as if something was trying to break free from its invisible fetters. The small gray pattern began to fill with a dull blue glow that

---

grew brighter with every moment like a ripening piece of fruit.

It was going nicely. Unhurriedly, the ancient artifact continued to syphon my energy. Devoured by the glowing light, the runic patterns turned an intense blue. I couldn't take my eyes away from the wondrous spectacle.

I cast a sideways glance at Pritus. He too seemed transfixed, admiring the process. The other Calteans crowded around us in silence, taking in the beautiful performance.

Congratulations! You've activated Brock Part #1!

I turned away from our bewitched audience, looking for the next piece. Ever-watchful, Pritus snapped a quick order. His assistants brought us the next part.

I smiled to him. Let's do it!

Warning! You're about to activate Brock Part #2!

Energy required: 1,000 pt.
Accept: Yes/No

Yes, absolutely.

The crowd gasped as the second piece glowed

with blue light.

Congratulations! You've activated Brock Parts ##1 and 2!
You can now assemble Brock Parts ##1 and 2!
Energy required: 200 pt.
Accept: Yes/No

This didn't look so exhausting, after all. *Yes, why not?*

And now Part #3... and #4... and so on and so forth. Levers, pulleys and cog wheels followed one after the other.

Despite all the Stamina stones and elixirs, I soon felt paralyzed with exhaustion. My temples were throbbing; both my neck and the small of my back were in agony. I felt like a hundred-year-old who'd never once taken rest in his lifetime.

But the insatiable runes kept demanding more and more energy.

When you're busy doing some boring monotonous task, your mind starts looking for distractions. Usually, music helps — as does focusing on the end result, providing the energy necessary for one final push. For me, the actual assembly process offered the necessary distraction. It required less energy and allowed me a quick break to catch my breath and take a look at the emerging machine.

Each part had its own unique design contributing to all the others like puzzle pieces contribute to the resulting picture. But even as the runic patterns linked in perfect harmony, with every part added to the emerging device it looked more and more clumsy and misshapen.

Gradually, the curious crowd of onlookers got bored and disappointed. They began cracking jokes and offering sarcastic advice. I couldn't blame them.

Finally, I added the last piece to the runic puzzle, then slumped to the ground feeling completely drained.

Congratulations! You've built a Brock, an Ennan Siege machine!

Reward: +350 to your Craftsmanship.

I wiped my sleeve across my forehead, mopping up the sweat, then checked my life stats. I seemed to be okay. What a job. I still had nine more machines to build. The good news was that glaive throwers had fewer parts.

"Couldn't you make it uglier?"

I turned to the sound and saw Droy's boots standing next to me. "That's the best I could do."

The shapeless steel monstrosity towered on the ramp, its runic nodes pulsating with a sapphire glow.

"How does it work?" Dory's voice rang with doubt.

Grunting like an old man, I scrambled to my feet and stepped toward the weird contraption.

Warning! The Brock is in sleep mode!
Would you like to load it: Yes/No.

Yes, I would.

The machine began to vibrate. The runic script glowed brighter. The Brock actually appeared happy to see me.

For a brief second, nothing happened. Then the shapeless mechanism shuddered to life. All the blocks, cog wheels, steel bars and strips of metal came into motion, vibrating and expanding. The amorphous lump of steel began to grow, gaining shape and purpose with every heartbeat.

We stood open-mouthed, unwilling to move, as this illogical and meaningless collection of unrelated parts transformed into a monstrous creature. The runic script wound around its powerful body. The steel bars had become its six limbs: four spidery legs and two arms which ended in large digging buckets.

"I'm taking my words back," Droy croaked. "He's even uglier than I thought."

I drew my gaze away from this amazing creation of ancient masters and turned to him. Droy stood open-mouthed, gawking at the steel monster. His face betrayed the same emotions that I read in the Calteans' expressions all around me: a mixture of fear and respectful awe.

Droy cleared his throat, breaking the deadly silence. "Impressive. What can it do?"

"One moment," I said, opening the Brock's settings.

Oh wow. Its stats were something else. In brief, what we had here was a miracle of top durability with a range of a thousand feet — more even, dealing enormous blanket damage.

Its rate of fire said nothing to me. Still, I had a feeling that somehow it was going to be much faster than Caltean trebuchets.

Its launching mechanism somehow resembled my good old slingshot. Most likely, all of these stats directly depended upon the weight, size and quality of the missiles used.

I looked up from the stats. "Should we try it?"

"Bring us some rocks!" Droy thundered.

Two warriors promptly dragged a large boulder toward the Brock's right shovel. They swung it several times until they managed to lay it in the machine's open "hand".

As soon as the boulder dropped inside the shovel, the giant effortlessly raised his arm, as if taking a swing. And then... he stopped.

The Brock is loaded!
Type of missile: a rock
Fit for purpose: Yes
Range: +1,000 feet
Rate of Fire: +0.02
Blanket damage: +18,000 ... +26,000

A shiver ran down my spine. If a rock like that landed on my group, we were toast. I'd go directly to my respawn point and my clanmates, to visit whatever Gods they worshipped.

The Brock is ready for action!
Energy required to launch a missile: 250 pt.
Would you like to continue: Yes/No

No, wait. This wasn't good. I didn't mean the energy requirements. I could live with that. The problem was, this machine needed me to activate it. It had even offered me a synchronization option similar to the one I had with my two pets, but I'd refused it point blank. This thing would bleed me dry like an energy vampire.

"Are you ready?" Droy asked.

I nodded. "Yes."

"So what are we waiting for?"

Instead of an answer, I pressed *Yes*.

The Brock's giant arm swung back like a steel

spring, devouring the energy offered to it, and launched the huge boulder into the air.

Rotating slowly, the rock winged its way toward the center of the valley. A few seconds later, a giant snow flower blossomed on impact. From our vantage point, it looked unpresuming, even pretty, but all of us seemed to realize the nature of its destructive beauty.

Then the crowd exploded in catcalls and cheers. What could I say? I too threw my hands in the air, screaming with joy. We'd just received a very hefty argument in any potential confrontation. It towered like an impassive cliff of steel over the tiny sentient animals scattered at its feet, its very shape granting us some hope of survival.

Chapter Sixteen

FOR THE NEXT TWO DAYS, all I did was assemble Ennan machines. I'd used up almost all of my elixirs and energy stones. Still, it was worth it.

We had new sentries guarding our rapidly-growing town wall now: three giant Brocks, seven glaive throwers and the Calteans' trebuchet which looked admittedly ancient next to the Ennan wonders. Earlier this evening, I'd given myself a three-hour break, after which I'd assembled the remaining glaive thrower.

Admittedly, I'd already gotten the hang of it. After the three Brocks, assembling glaive throwers was a breeze. In total, I'd spent about 2,000 pt. Energy on each one.

I couldn't help smiling whenever I remembered my attempts to assemble the first glaive thrower. Just like the Brock, it had resembled a shapeless heap of haphazardly connected parts. But once activated, it had turned out to be a harpoon gun on a tall steel tripod.

Each machine came with a chestful of steel bolts packed into 20-round clips. Their faceted tips were made of some hard black metal which, however, looked chewed, almost as if something had gnawed on it. When I took a closer look, I realized that the tips had been completely covered in complex runic patterns.

The glaive thrower's principle was considerably different from that of the Brock. The latter was easy: you just filled its Herculean shovel full of rocks and pointed it in the right direction. The downside of it was, I was the only person who could control it.

The glaive throwers were different. They didn't need me to issue orders. As soon as they received their share of energy, any of Pritus' assistants could pull the trigger.

However, the Brocks didn't have a power accumulator — something that glaive throwers had, even though their charges were only enough to fire one clip. Which was better than nothing, I suppose.

So all of the Ennan machines required my

assistance in one way or another. Which wasn't a good thing. The moment we had a war on our hands, these contraptions would suck me dry of energy.

My intention had been to assemble all the machines first and then get some practice in. I didn't want to spread myself too thin. So now the entire clan had gathered around me in anticipation of a new spectacle.

Honestly speaking, I'd hoped to get some sleep and test the machines in the morning. But the expectation on all the beaming Caltean faces had made me reconsider. I'd told them to make some targets to test-fire our new weapons.

They fashioned a dozen dummies stuffed with straw and clad them in some old armor. Then they placed a shield in front of each one and jammed helmets on their heads. It wasn't bad at all.

They carried the straw warriors out to a distance of about five hundred feet from the wall. The dummies looked seriously militant from afar.

I set the firing mode to single shot and took aim. Holding my breath, I used both my hands to pull the firing lever at the back.

The recoil was impressive. I physically sensed the machine release the accumulated energy. The bolt hit the exact center of the shield held by one of the dummies.

I hadn't expected to see what happened next.

The dummy disintegrated. Straw flew everywhere.

The crowd gasped.

"Great shot," Droy said an hour later, turning a mangled piece of steel in his hands. That was all that was left of the shield.

"How is it possible?" Orman asked, warily studying the glaive thrower.

"Take a look at the bolt tips," I said. "They're covered in runes. I think they make the tip disintegrate on impact, turning it into shrapnel."

I knew it for sure. After all, I'd read the description.

"And that was just one bolt!" Crym said, his eyes gleaming. "But if you fired several at once... simultaneously..."

Everyone hummed their agreement. Even I was suitably impressed.

A short burst of seven bolts made quick work of our DIY army. Their straw bodies exploded like a ten-ton bomb.

"Can't wait to see what they're gonna do to the Nocteans," Orman hissed predatorily.

I sighed. "I'm afraid, very soon you might get the opportunity to find out."

"The magic sphere is about to expire," Droy added, looking grim.

The long call of the Red Owls' bugle drowned out our voices. What now?

We hurried to climb the wooden scaffolding surrounding the city wall. Our builders hadn't wasted their time. The wall kept growing surprisingly quickly. Very soon it would reach 7 ft.

No wonder: this was a game, after all. Everything that happened here seemed to take place in fast forward. Also, I'd made sure that all of my workers had already made their next level in Craftsmanship.

We'd decided to build the new wall on top of the old ruins. That way at least we saved on the foundations. Also, once we'd cleared the ruins from the snow, we discovered whole surviving sections of the wall that were at least 12 ft. high.

The wall formed a semicircle which linked two impregnable cliff ridges. It looked as if they'd just grown there, gray and grim, obeying the wave of an invisible hand. Their impenetrable embrace protected the upper city which had once been home to the king and his entourage.

We had no shortage of building materials, that's for sure. Ruins were everywhere.

Flooded with the light of hundreds of torches, the building site seethed like a giant anthill where everyone was busy doing his or her task. The air rang with the constant tapping of hammers, the screeching of pulleys and the hacking of axes. Buffaloes bellowed; builders yelled over each others' heads; children laughed and ran around... yes, this was the Calteans making themselves a new home.

And they didn't look too eager to give it up lightly.

The sentries who'd raised the alarm already awaited us on a large platform. I used the chance to inspect it, knowing it was about to become one of our towers pretty soon. We might actually lift one of the glaive throwers up here tomorrow morning. We could install another in the East Tower and place the remaining ones along the wall's perimeter. Not mentioning the Brocks which already lined the wall. We kept growing.

Heh! I honestly hadn't expected such rapid changes. Initially, our situation had been a little less than hopeless — but that was because I used to look at the city ruins from a real world perspective. I should have been thinking as a gamer right from the start. Things would have been dramatically different in real life.

Naturally, we were no match for the players' army, not yet. We still had plenty of weak points. For one, our impregnable fortress could use a gate! A proper one, I mean, not the sorry excuse which currently plugged the only access in the breached wall. Which was basically several carts and wagons reinforced with some planks and crude logs nailed together.

* * *

"What's up?" Droy asked the sentries.

"Over there," a stocky red-bearded Caltean pointed south. "Can you see?"

"What the heck?" Orman uttered. "What's that, a river of fire?"

I peered in the direction they pointed. The sun had long set but the sky was still clear. The large disc of the Moon cast a bright light onto the valley and part of the hills.

A snaking line of twinkling lights was crossing the valley. Orman had a point: it did resemble a river of fire moving toward us.

"Nonsense," Droy replied. "That's not a river. That's torchlight. It looks like Olgerd was right. These are the armies he used to tell us about. They've made it here, after all."

Dammit! That was quick. Just as I thought things were working out.

Orman cussed. Crym who hadn't said a word yet slammed his fist on a stone crenel.

Droy opened his mouth to say something when we heard a powerful bugle call coming from the river of fire.

"No way!" Orman whispered, incredulous.

The Calteans looked at each other, their faces

a complex mix of joy and disbelief. Their eyes were open wide, their nostrils flaring.

Crym guffawed and slapped a sentry's shoulder.

"Mind telling me what's going on?" I demanded.

Droy lay his hand on my shoulder and squinted, "The sound of this bugle means, my friend, that the Calteans can't be killed so easily!"

"Oh, no!" Orman growled. "This is Badwar the Thunder Warrior coming to pay us a visit!"

"And he's not alone," Crym added. "It looks like he's brought all of his Stone Fists with him!"

We greeted the Stone Fists delegation outside, in the same place where we'd met Amai and his warriors only a few days ago. We made a large fire on the city border to serve as a beacon for their clan braving the darkness.

I'd wondered if I should go on a recon flight, just to take a look at our new guests. Still, the others had talked me out of it. According to them, both Badwar and his men were probably at the end of their tethers. They might shoot me down first and ask questions later.

Our little army walked out to meet them in full

combat gear. According to Droy, we had to display our power to them. Badwar was a willful sonovabitch. He only understood the language of steel. We had to put on a good show. Especially as we could afford it.

Rank after rank of armor-clad warriors froze motionless around the fire.

We didn't have to wait long. Several figures emerged from the darkness at once.

"Shield Wall!" Droy bellowed.

With the clatter of wood and clanging of steel, our warriors serried their ranks which now bristled with spears. Then they froze again, awaiting our guests.

They couldn't be very far, judging by the crunching of snow and the shadowy silhouettes gliding through the night.

"If that's not the Red Owls! You've changed a lot, haven't you?" a rude sarcastic voice called out of the dark. "I can't believe it!"

The darkness parted, releasing a stocky figure wearing a round masked helmet. A broad shield peeked from behind the warrior's back. He was holding an enormous axe.

"That's Badwar the Thunder Warrior," Laosh told me under his breath.

Two more warriors appeared next to him: one slightly taller and broader than his commander, the other a mere youngster next to those two. He was probably the armor-bearer of one of them.

"The big one is Gukhur the Black Serpent from the White Lynxes clan," Laosh resumed his running commentary. "And the one next to him is Lavena the Vixen, the right hand of Bevan who is the shaman with the Mountain Hawks."

His voice betrayed his surprise. Our ranks rustled with puzzled whispers. What could have baffled them so much?

I very nearly asked Laosh as much when Droy addressed our visitors. I'd better wait and see what happens next.

"Badwar the Thunder Warrior! Gukhur the Black Serpent! And Lavena the Vixen!" Droy announced. "This is a surprise for me as well! The greatest warriors of our people have decided to honor us with their presence! I'm equally amazed seeing you here standing shoulder to shoulder!"

Admittedly, our guests showed different reactions to his words. Badwar continued to smile while Gukhur stared impassively at the fire as if Droy's words didn't concern him at all. Lavena, however, showed some signs of impatient anger, knotting her eyebrows and white-knuckling the short sword dangling from her belt.

"When we saw your torches from our city walls we thought that a river of fire was flowing toward us," Droy continued. "But when I took another look, I realized that the river would have been much bigger had all the warriors whom your shamans had lured away been with you!"

The steel wall of shields shifted as our warriors hummed their agreement.

"Our shamans are dead," the Black Serpent said. His voice indeed resembled a snake's hissing. "I killed them all!"

Laosh next to me startled. A dead silence hung over the clearing, only disturbed by the crackling of the firewood and the bellowing of nearby buffaloes in the dark.

"Why are you still alive, then?" Laosh shouted vindictively. "Our ancient laws would have had you burned at the stake!"

Lavena stepped forward, inconspicuously shielding him with her shoulder. Had it not been for the gravity of the situation, it would have looked comical: a tiny female outline, lithe and slender, trying to protect this great oaf.

"We didn't burn him simply because he'd saved our lives!" she shouted.

The tone of her voice, her angry face and clenched fists — I was pretty sure she'd have gladly added Laosh to the dead shaman list had she had half the chance.

The face of the Black Serpent was impassive, his wide open eyes watching the play of the flames.

He'd said what he'd had to say and didn't care about the rest.

"We know the laws, old man," Badwar said conciliatorily.

"Then why did you disobey them?" Laosh countered.

"Because your buddies the shamans deserved to die!" Lavena spat out.

Badwar lay his heavy hand on her shoulder. "This is a good question, Shaman," he growled. "But before answering it, I want to ask you something too. All of you! Do you know how to perform the Desolation ritual?"

The Red Owls grumbled their discontent. Someone in front of me cussed. I turned to Laosh. He was dark as a thundercloud.

In the meantime, Badwar continued, peering into the faces of each of our warriors. "Apparently, you do! Now I'm gonna answer your question. It wasn't enough for them to have brought us to the Dark fortress so that our best warriors lost their lives under its walls! Oh, no! They also wanted to perform the Desolation ritual! They wanted to sacrifice our women and children so that they could save their own worthless lives! So yes, they *are* dead! And If I could kill them all over again, I'd have gladly done so!"

* * *

I didn't get much sleep that night. We had a council — Droy, Laosh, the sergeants and myself — deciding what to do with all the refugees.

Personally, I'd come to a decision a long time ago. As soon as I'd heard about Laosh leaving magic marks behind, I knew this was going to happen. So had it been up to me, I would have gone to bed a long time ago. As it was, I had to preside over my clanmates playing the part of the Great Keeper of Twilight Castle, listening to their debating with each other.

As far as the newcomers were concerned, they were the remains of the three strongest clans which at the time had left their home valley and headed in the direction of the Dark Citadel. But if the Black Axes shaman, seeing the complete defeat of their army, had wisely turned back, the shamans of the three other clans had decided to keep going.

Those so-called generals had thought that a powerful magic attack on the Citadel's defenses would allow the warriors to storm the walls and slaughter the defenders. So naïve. Had it indeed worked out as planned, the players would have had a ball.

Naturally, a powerful strike like that demanded a wealth of energy which the shamans simply hadn't had. Still, they did have a solution. They could perform this so-called Desolation ritual. As far as I gathered from Laosh' reluctant explanation, it was nothing more than a mass sacrifice which sucked energy out of living creatures.

Laosh cringed when he spoke about it. I could see he would never have agreed to something like that. He'd much rather have sacrificed his own life to save his clanmates than killed them. I'd already witnessed that during our battle by the river.

"What were they thinking of?" he kept whispering. "Killing women and children! The future of their clans! And what for? They must have lost their minds! I know whose idea it was! It must have been Joddok! The leader of the Stone Fists! The Great Shaman! The strongest amongst us! That must have been his fault. He was toying with forbidden knowledge!"

"And he paid the price!" Orman growled.

The others nodded,

"Yes!"

"Oh yes, he did!"

"They're dead now, anyway," Droy summed up.

He could say that. The game developers seemed to be conspiring to strip my army of any magic support. First it had been the Black Axes' shaman, so cleverly killed by Furius. Now it was Gukhur who'd executed the remaining three. Granted, there was still

Amai roaming around the desert, but I'd had plenty of opportunity to realize that he was more harm than good.

Besides, I wasn't at all sure if I'd ever see the Northern Wolves again. They knew the Noctean horde was coming here. As long as we were battling them, they were unlikely to leave their steppes. I couldn't say I blamed them.

"Which is why we need to take care of the living," Droy summed up. He turned to Shorve the Hasty, "How many did you count?"

"Almost two hundred warriors," Shorve reported. "The rest are old men, women and children."

I made a quick calculation. In total, that was about five hundred new arrivals.

"Many of them are sick or injured," Shorve continued. "They told me they'd been constantly attacked on their way. Lots of monsters and Nocteans around."

Droy turned to me. "Do you think your magic could help them?"

The Red Owls already knew I was in possession of some magic that could heal them and make them stronger. I was pretty sure Laosh had something to do with it. He must have told his clanmates that the City Keeper was basically a healing artifact on two legs.

I nodded. "It might. On one condition. You

know it, don't you?"

"Yeah," Droy kneaded his beard, thinking. "In order to be healed, they need to join the clan."

I shrugged. "Sorry, but that's how it works. Alternatively, you can ask your wise women to help them. They've become much more skillful now, don't you think?"

"Thanks to you," Crym gave me a friendly slap on the shoulder.

He was right. Thanks to all the new recipes and materials, the clan's medicine women could now treat the simplest first and second-degree injuries. Unfortunately, there were no monsters in No-Man's Lands capable of dealing such minor damage. The smallest of the wounds they gave you were type "blue".

"So what do you think they're going to do now?" I asked the question which worried us all the most that night.

Silence fell in the tent. I peered at my clanmates' faces, trying to second-guess what they were thinking.

Seet frowned, biting his lower lip.

Crym sat there impassive, polishing his battle-axe blade with a leather cloth like he had nothing to do with any of it.

Orman was studying his friends' faces just like I was. A skeptical smile lurked on his lips. He must have already made up his mind; now he was waiting to hear what his comrades had to say.

Shorve was busy with a needle, mending a piece of gear. He was never idle, that one. Constantly busy doing something. He didn't seem to give a damn about the newcomers' fate.

Arrum Red Beard was snoring away, his arms crossed on his chest. Ditto for Horm the Turtle.

Droy was silent. I knew what he was thinking, anyway. I was curious about Laosh, though. What did he have to say?

As if reading my thoughts, the old man spoke,

"One can't see the future in every detail. There're too many variables. What we can see, though, is our present. The way we use our present will decide our future."

Everybody nodded.

"So what do we see in our present?" Laosh continued. "We see the remains of three clans which used to be quite powerful. Most of them are women and children, emaciated and sick. Their warriors' morale is low. They don't have single leadership. They're about to starve. Many of them are seriously ill. I'm afraid, we might see the first funeral pyres in their camp already this morning."

Laosh must have noticed me frowning because he added, "Olgerd, I know you wanted us to allow them into the city. Still, we can't afford it. Yes, they are Calteans like ourselves. True, we have a

---

provisional truce in place. Still, they're more numerous. Unlike you, we know their leaders and what they're capable of. We can't risk it."

"He's right," Droy agreed. "We've done a lot for them as it is. We've shared our food supplies with them even though there won't be enough for us now. Our healers are doing what they can. And most importantly, you've let them enter under the protection of the magic sphere. Trust me, that's more than enough."

"To spend a night in a perfectly safe place without having to worry about a surprise attack in the night is worth a lot," Crym added.

"But even despite everything Laosh has just said, I don't think they're going to stay with us," Orman summed up.

"I agree," Shorve nodded without looking up from his sewing. "Badwar is too proud. I don't think he's going to go hat in hand to a Red Owl. Besides, they already know about the Horde's arrival. If they chose not to fight when all of their warriors were still alive, what makes you think they'll do it now?"

That was a killer argument. We had nothing to say to that.

Droy was about to object when his son hurried into the tent. "Father, you're wanted on the wall."

Droy rose. "What now?"

"The boy messenger said that the Northern

Wolves were back."

* * *

The morning seeped a dull sunlight by way of greeting the earth. It might actually snow later. We had to hurry. Despite the early hour, works were already in full swing in the outer moat which encircled the fortress like a giant snake trail.

The open areas outside the wall had been cleared of snow. Fires burned all along the perimeter, warming the ground and thawing out the ancient ruins.

Dozens of Calteans were bustling about in the moat, scooping out the molten slush and hammering in sharp stakes of different sizes. They'd been putting in a united effort, relieving each other day and night. No one was shirking: this was a matter of survival.

The newcomers watched them closely, exchanging comments in low voices and casting glances at the wall and the glaive throwers mounted upon it.

Oh, well. Let them look. That might give their thoughts a push in the right direction. Even in their work clothes, the Red Owls looked dramatically more civilized now. And the wall they were building kept growing in leaps and bounds. The Calteans had never made anything as good as this wall.

Still, at the moment we had more important things to think of than worrying about the newcomers' state of mind. Droy's son had been right: we had the Northern Wolves on our doorstep. Not a small recon group: this time we were looking at their entire clan.

The proud steppe riders trudged in silence, looking pretty worse for wear. There wasn't a single warrior among them. Holy mama mia, how many of them were there?

My warriors lined up along the perimeter of the magic sphere's radius.

What kind of groundhog day was this? We'd been standing here only a few hours ago just like we were now, greeting Badwar and his group.

But in this case, we had no reason to be too strict. We had a treaty with the Wolves, after all. They could come and go as they pleased.

The Red Owls crowded by the wall, greeting the tired Wolves with tears in their eyes. About two hundred armed men rode in the rear. This must have been what was left of Amai's little army.

Actually, I couldn't see him anywhere. Pike appeared to be in command. Exhausted and wounded, his left arm bandaged, he was the last to cross the magic protection border.

His horse snorted as it stopped a few paces away from us. Pike dismounted unhurriedly and with dignity.

"Greetings, O Keeper!" he croaked.

"Greetings, valiant warrior," I replied, studying him closely.

He had an impressive black eye. His clothes were covered in blood — others' as well as his own. Oh. He'd had it rough.

"Brave warrior, I can't see your leader," I said.

Still standing tall, Pike heaved a sigh. "My leader and two hundred of our best warriors have met their end fighting the Nocteans."

The devs had to be kidding! I lost another shaman!

"I remembered our treaty," he continued. "Which is why I brought the survivors here."

"You did the right thing, O Pike of Many Hands," I motioned them to enter. "My Owls and I, we hold our treaty sacred."

Chapter Seventeen

"I THINK I'VE FOUND something," a grinning Pritus slapped the Brock's ample leg.

He had asked to see me as soon as our "round table" with all the clan leaders had finished. Predictably, it had ended in nothing.

You couldn't imagine a more fruitless pastime. It reminded me of a well-known Russian fable telling the story of the Swan, the Pike and the Crab who tried to pull a heavy cartload. Naturally, it didn't work because each of them tried to pull it each in their own direction.

I hadn't taken part in the discussion. What was the point? The Caltean leaders didn't recognize my authority: I didn't have enough reputation with them. Having said that, my personal relationship with Badwar had improved from Suspicious to Neutral. Ditto for the other two: Gukhur and Lavena.

I had a bad feeling about the four of them. First Pike, and now those three. They actually had a lot in common: all four were celebrated warriors whose names commanded respect from every Caltean. I just hoped I wasn't going to get into trouble.

Which wasn't so improbable, knowing me.

A hand lay on my shoulder. "Are you listening?"

"Eh? Sorry?"

Pritus squinted at me. A sarcastic grin played on his lips. "Are you with me?"

"I'm sorry," I said, rubbing my eyes. "All these council meetings are exhausting."

Pritus and I had grown quite close over the last few days. Having to assemble a bunch of Ennan machines does that to you.

"They don't want to become Owls, do they?" he grinned his understanding. The glasses of his pince-nez glinted. "Not the first time."

I remembered the Black Axes. They used to scream and dig their heels in, too. "You could say that."

"Olgerd, you know what? Out of all of us, I was the one who was most against joining the Red Owls."

"So what do you think now?"

"Now I think joining you was the best thing I ever did."

"Really? What made you change your mind?"

"You did. Our other leaders used to send us to a sure death, deceiving us with high goals and made-up prophesies. Their inflated egos and their fear of losing power prevented us from joining together in order to confront the enemy. Their cowardice forced us to leave our homes. When our shaman died, followed by some of the stronger warriors who could have claimed leadership, we felt free for the first time. Can you imagine? Nothing like that had ever happened to us before. For the first time in its history, the council of elders could actually decide something. Before, they only used to go through the motions. And this time, the fates of the clan depended on our decision."

Despite Pritus' praise, I still had my doubts. What if I was just as stupid as their previous leaders? What if it didn't work? What if I *had* brought them to a sure death?

In the meantime, Pritus continued,

"Freedom intoxicated us. We were our own masters! And you know the important thing? Yes, we became Red Owls, but that was our own choice. Can I give you some advice?"

"Good advice is always welcome."

"Give them some space. Let them enjoy their

freedom. Let them experience the full extent of it. Once the euphoria wears off, it'll leave behind the great responsibility for one's clanmates' lives. Then they'll need someone who knows what to do without losing their precious freedom."

"You think I can do it?"

"Well," Pritus smiled, "we're still alive, aren't we? And I don't think our shamans had anything to do with it."

"I don't think so, either!"

We laughed. Finally, Pritus asked,

"So fancy doing a bit of work?"

"Sure," I replied. "What's all this about?"

"I've studied all the machines," Pritus explained readily, "and I noticed a very interesting thing. All the Brocks and glaive throwers have indentations in the same place, same size. What's interesting is that these indentations spread energy canals through the whole length of the machines."

"Strange," I said. "What do you make of it?"

"I had a talk with a few fellow engineers and we think that this indentation is in fact a plug to plug a power block in. Which means that the machines are self-contained. As long as we supply them with power blocks, they can work non-stop! Naturally, we went directly to the warehouse. We looked everywhere but we didn't find anything which even remotely looked like them."

"Show me," I said, curious.

Pritus motioned me to approach, then pointed at a small indentation. "This one."

"You're right," I said. "Did you say all the machines have them?"

"Yes," Pritus replied. The Brocks have them on their second right leg. The glaive throwers, just next to the trigger."

"It's hexagonal," I commented.

Pritus nodded. "That's right. I can bet all you want they're meant for plugging in accumulator crystals."

"Which can't be big. Incredible. Can you imagine that a tiny piece of crystal can power something this huge?"

I was about to touch the indentation to see how deep it was when a new system message appeared before my eyes,

Would you like to plug in the Charm of Arakh: Yes/No

Startled, I jerked my hand away, then reread the message.

The Charm of Arakh... The Charm of Arakh... The name rang a few bells. Where could I have heard about it?

Wait a sec...

I had a head like a sieve, really. By assembling the machines, I'd leveled up my other profession really well. I'd had those old blueprints in my bag ever since I'd built the Replicator, albeit dimmed and inactive. Now that I'd assembled the Brocks, they'd finally become available, so I'd studied them just in case, then happily forgotten all about it. No wonder. Too many things had been happening just lately.

"Can you feel anything?" Pritus' voice asked just above my ear.

Oh. I'd forgotten all about him.

"I think so," I said, theatrically closing my eyelids. "I need to concentrate."

"Got it. I'll be silent as a grave."

Excellent. I hurried to press the Blueprints Studied tab. What did we have here... Yes. The Unworked Charm of Arakh. I could do that. I had seventy of the wretched things in my bag.

And I used to think those were useless trash items!

What other blueprints did I have?

Name: A Blueprint of the Frame of the Charm of Arakh

Requirements:
a Bundle of Steel Wire, 1

"Pritus," I said without opening my eyes, "I

might need some steel wire. A few bundles will do. Ask the blacksmiths, they should have loads there. They use it all the time to make chainmail."

"Got it," Pritus replied.

The sound of his footsteps faded quickly.

Good. What next?

Name: A Blueprint of the Charm of Arakh
Requirements:
A Frame of the Charm of Arakh, 1
An Unworked Charm of Arakh, 1
5,000 pt. Energy

I made a quick estimation. That was enough for twenty rounds from the Brock and five glaive clips.

My heart pounded like mad. That meant that I wouldn't be tied to the machines anymore!

When I opened my eyes, Pritus was scurrying toward me with Zachary in tow.

"Here! Take your pick!" he offered me several bundles of steel wire in different sizes.

I began trying them — but the system rejected each and every one of them.

I very nearly cussed. There I was, one step away from an energy breakthrough had it not been for a miserable piece of wire!

Damn those blueprints! I might need to leave the city and go back to the continent.

"This is all chainmail wire," Zachary said who until now had been watching my manipulations in silence. "Try this one. It's thinner but just as strong. It's jewelry wire I use to make chains with."

I took it from him.

Yes! It worked! The system was happy with our offering!

Congratulations! You've just built a Frame of the Charm of Arakh!

I reached into my backpack for the fragment of Blue Ice.

Would you like to build a Charm of Arakh?
Warning! Building a Charm of Arakh will deprive you of 5,000 pt. pure Energy!
Would you like to continue?
Accept/Decline

The moment I pressed *Accept*, my hands began living a life of their own. This time I wasn't even scared. The experience was familiar.

My right hand picked up the Frame, my left one, the Unworked Charm. In one smooth motion, I joined the two parts. A flash followed, depleting me of 5,000 pt. Energy. Out of the corner of my eye, I watched Pritus' and Zachary's open-mouthed faces.

Congratulations! You've built a Charm of Arakh!

All done!

"Is this what I think it is?" Pritus managed.

"I think so, my learned friend," I replied, walking over to the Brock. "All we have to do now is test   it.

Would you like to connect the Charm of Arakh to the Brock: Yes/No

The moment of truth. I pressed *Yes*, then plugged my creation in. It fit the indentation like a glove.

Congratulations! The Brock's power charge has grown 5,000 pt.!

Warning! The depletion of the power charge will destroy the Charm.

A small handle appeared next to the plug. Now Pritus and his assistants could control the Brock without me. Excellent.

The only problem was, the Charms had turned out to be disposable. And I only had sixty-nine fragments of Blue Ice left. No idea where I could get any more.

Suddenly an idea struck me. And what if...

"If you refuse to work now, I'll scrap you, I promise I will!" I murmured, producing the Replicator.

"You sure you're an engineer?" Pritus laughed, watching me.

I smiled to him. "Good question."

The moment I placed the Charm into the Replicator's tray, the system generously offered a new message,

Would you like to start the replication process?

Finally this weird contraption which resembled a school microscope was good for something! It had been worth lugging it around the No-Man's Lands, after all.

Yes, I would! I would very much like to start this wretched process!

Upon receiving my consent, the strange device came to life. Its tiny cog wheels, springs and little coils started moving.

The charm lying in the tray dematerialized.

What was that now? What if everything went wrong? What if I'd misunderstood the meaning of replication? What if the game developers had their own ideas of what it was supposed to signify?

Twenty seconds seemed like twenty hours. Still, the little machine hadn't let me down.

Congratulations! The replication process successfully completed!

Replication results:

The Charm of Arach, 3

Time until next replication: 23:59:59

Chapter Eighteen

THE PREVIOUS NIGHT, I'd warned Droy I was going to go on a recon flight. I'd already assembled all the Ennan machines. Camp life was more or less under control. I could safely entrust the whole caboodle to him. We had too many enemies: the Noctean horde as well as the players of both Dark and Light, and we needed to know where they were exactly. I was the only one up to the task. Without the intel we were blind.

There was another reason, though, and I wasn't in a hurry to divulge it to anyone. And that was the question I'd asked myself a thousand times before: if I failed to discover the Twilight Obelisk, then what? What was to happen then?

And the more I tried to analyze the situation, the grimmer it seemed to me.

This Ennan City was in fact a trap. A choice morsel whose job it was to attract all the vultures in the area.

Naturally, I still hoped that this wretched Obelisk would one day declare itself, but in the meantime, our magic protection was dwindling — and nothing was happening.

Honestly, I felt worried: on the brink of panic, even. In such cases, I always need a backup option. Two would be even better. In other words, I was desperate for Plan B.

So while the sphere was still active, I decided to spend some time working on it.

I decided to start with the Silver Mountain Valley which was in the south, about two weeks' hike from Ennan City and a month' away from the players' territories.

That was the Calteans' original home which they'd been forced to surrender to the Horde. According to them, it used to be a great place to live. Lots of fields and lakes, mountains and meadows. It only snowed there in winter time.

So naturally, I had a question: if the Noctean horde was already on its way here, what was going on at Silver Mountain?

So I decided to check it out.

* * *

The thick viscous fog covered the ground like an enormous, endless quilt. I couldn't see anything below in the white haze which promised an approaching snowstorm. I had to land.

A rocky ridge nearby looked just the thing. Obeying my mental command, Boris began to descend.

The rocks were unbelievable. I stared, transfixed, at their bizarre shapes carved by Mother Nature, thwarted by the realization of my own insignificance in the face of these behemoths. At moments like these, I didn't want to remember that they were only stage props created by programmers and game designers.

Their powerful tops seemed to be piercing the sky. The thick snow clouds got caught on their massive primeval bodies. Finding a natural wonder like this here had come as a complete surprise.

I looked around me. The barren surface was covered in dry tufts of some scrub sprouting out of every crack and fissure. I couldn't see a single creature sheltering within their entwined branches: not a bird's nest nor a single rodent. The place looked dead.

We were still too high. The fog prevented me from seeing anything below.

A touch of frosty breeze brushed my face, growing stronger with every minute. It swept the fog away, replacing it with a fresh crisp transparency. Soon I was looking at a truly fascinating picture.

A boundless valley lay below, studded with clusters of cliffs. The wind had dispersed the last of the fog, revealing the panorama in all its majestic serenity.

But that wasn't what had made my heart miss a beat. A countless herd of some animals was grazing below at what looked like a deceitfully close distance.

Wait a sec. Aren't they buffaloes? So many? I almost choked with the discovery.

I leapt into the saddle and told Boris to descend.

A large herd like that was bound to attract unwanted attention. I was almost sure some large predators were already lurking nearby.

The ground below was a filthy mess of slush mixed with animal excrement trampled in by thousands of hooves.

Was it my imagination or the further into No-Man's Lands I advanced, the more lifelike everything had become around me?

Those were buffaloes all right. They were slightly bigger than those bred by the Calteans, tall with long powerful legs and broad hooves. Their long hair was gray spotted with black. They had small ears and long horns that pointed forward, crowning their large heads.

Without straying too far from their enormous herd, buffaloes grazed calmly, scooping the mud with their hooves in order to get to the blue moss covering the frozen ground. The air hung heavy with the smell of dung.

The herd had ignored our arrival entirely. Either the wind was blowing toward us or they were too short-sighted. Or most likely, they simply didn't consider my flying beast to be a threat.

The boundless valley stretched to the horizon. There was enough blue moss here to feed dozens of herds like this one. The buffaloes flowed across the valley unhurriedly like a gray river, feeding, bellowing, defecating, leaving the ground in their wake plowed as if by a thousand tractors.

We continued our flight along a rocky ridge that stretched the entire length of the valley. I noticed several streams babbling happily amid the cliffs. A few minutes later, I came across a family of wild pigs.

I decided to stop for a while to watch them from above. We landed on a cliff ledge. Immediately Boris stretched out on the rocks, lounging happily.

I too was enjoying the peaceful break watching a totally cute family of wild pigs. Their daddy the boar was enormous, the size of an adult rhino. His powerful yellow tusks protruded far from under his lower lip, making him look a bit like a forklift. He used them to peruse through the frozen ground with ease, leaving deep furrows in his wake. He was a mountain of muscle propped on fat stubby legs.

A few smaller males were feeding nearby, snorting contentedly as they dug through the earth. The tuskless females followed closely behind with their snouts pressed to the ground, vacuuming up any remaining food. Baby pigs frolicked around, squeaking happily and adding an extra note of cuteness to their family idyll.

I leaned against Boris' soft belly, admiring the scene. I'd always loved animals and enjoyed watching them. And now, with every hour that I spent in this dangerous and formidable land, I realized I was becoming one with its forest, growing into these cliffs and this valley.

I definitely liked it here, and not just because of the breathtaking views. I was yet to see a mob below level 50. The daddy boar was level 600+! A huge territory densely populated with high-level mobs was an excellent addition to my Plan B.

The forest beyond the cliff ridge looked perfectly normal. I even noticed some conifers, their evergreen needles standing out bright amid the bare trees still awakening from their hibernation.

Spring was in the air. After the lifeless and silent snow dunes, the valley felt like some kind of wildlife metropolis.

A flock of birds arrived and began dashing around on their own errands, chirruping and trilling in a multitude of calls.

We resumed our flight and banked to the right, following the buffalo herd. We seemed to be heading in the same direction. Such a huge mass of potential prey was bound to attract predators.

Speak of the devil.

I could clearly see a large pack of some black animals exit the forest. Big cats, by the looks of it. Their young, restless and quarrelsome, followed the pride.

A group of a dozen adult felines led the pride. They slid across the valley like unstoppable black torpedoes, stealing up on the unsuspecting herd in a predatory semicircle. The sight was breathtaking.

The cats' giant leader broke into a run, leaping toward the buffaloes who seemed to be already aware of the danger. The cat's blood-curdling growl sent shivers down my spine.

The buffaloes nearest to it seemed to have frozen in panic. Admittedly, I couldn't move, either.

Finally, the herd heaved and flowed away, trying to escape their pursuers. Still, they'd wasted too much time. The leading cat, as fast as an arrow, rammed the edge of the herd and clawed its way into the very thick of the terrified animals. Drunk on blood and their fear, it towered over their gray bodies.

The other cats followed, trampling the poor buffaloes and ripping them apart. Seeing the adults feasting on their prey, the cubs darted for a long-overdue meal too, rolling into the mutilated herd like a ball of yelping, fighting fluff.

"I think we've seen enough," I grumbled to Boris. "Let's go."

Midday enveloped the valley and the cliffs in its warm sunny veil. Unable to resist the all-pervasive sunrays, the snow had melted into hundreds of little streams trickling away from their home to new unknown horizons.

The winter-tired cliffs offered their frozen flanks to the sun. Spring was traveling across the valley, her every fleeting green step reviving the frigid, unyielding soil from its anabiosis.

The more I saw, the more I liked this location. At least it was much warmer here. The further we flew, the nicer the temperature got.

We'd parted ways with the giant buffalo herd which continued its flow deep into the valley while we were still skirting it, following the mountain ridge.

The cliffs seemed to be changing too. Overgrown with low shrubs and new grass, they now resembled fluffy green giants. Bird flocks clamored amid the greenery, busy with their own agendas.

We landed on a mountain top. I jumped down from the saddle and stretched my legs, then reached into my backpack for my fur coat. With my back to the valley, I unfolded it while casting an absent-minded eye over the forest to the other side of the ridge.

I froze in disbelief. A thin streak of smoke rose swirling to the sky from the thick of the forest quite close to where we now stood.

I blinked and rubbed my eyes, then looked again. The weak gray trail hadn't disappeared anywhere. It reached bolt upright to the sky and dissipated high overhead.

What was that now? Players? Other Calteans? Or other NPCs?

I checked my clothes and weapons and leapt back into saddle.

Boris made off toward the smoke.

As we flew, I gave it some thought. It probably wouldn't be a good idea to expose ourselves to any Tom, Dick or Harry. The fact that they didn't even try to conceal the smoke could only mean one of two things: they were either clueless beginners or they had no one to hide from. You had to be really careful in this world of hungry, toothy, angry mobs who considered you to be their rightful meal. What kind of creature could it be that could control fire but wasn't afraid of prowling cats or Noctean hordes?

How sure was I they would be happy to see

me?

Lots of questions, and the only way to answer them was by going on a recon mission. Right, Sir Olgerd, off you go!

* * *

The smoke trail brought me to a small farm surrounded by a flimsy low stockade. Parts of it had collapsed, revealing the still-smoldering skeleton of what must have once been a log hut.

The stockade appeared very old. The logs it was built from were dark and dried with age, crudely sharpened and spotted with patches of green moss. This looked like an illustration to a Grimms' tale: the stockade baring its rickety teeth against a backdrop of gnarly gray wood.

Having made a few circles over the farm and found no signs of life, I decided to drop down.

Having landed by the forest edge, I looked around me, listening out for any sounds. Then I noticed some weird paw prints on the ground, leading toward the stockade.

At first they were large with sharp claws. After a few feet, they seemed to have transformed, becoming smaller and smaller, until they reached the stockade where they turned into the prints of a small human.

I got the impression that something huge and

very carnivorous, judging by the size of its claws, had walked out of the woods very recently and headed for the farm grounds — and this something had turned into a human in the process, the size of a ten-year-old child.

Then again, I could be wrong. I'm not a boy scout, am I?

I followed the footprints until they brought me to a hole in the stockade.

Here, the thick black logs clumsily driven into the loose ground had listed as if having been hit by something very big and very heavy.

Whoever had lived on the farm had paid a high price for their recklessness. They should have fixed the stockade when they'd had the chance. Apparently, whoever had left the weird footprints in the snow didn't forgive this kind of oversight.

I peeked through the gap.

The entire farm was about an acre. All of its outbuildings were burnt. Everything was covered in brown spots of caked blood.

The trampled snow sported all kinds of footprints, including the clawed ones. Oh. I must have been right, then.

This looked like one of the remote Caltean settlements. Maybe a family which had split away from their clan.

Judging by the miserable quality of the fence

and the buildings, they'd been in a bad way. Or had they relaxed without the threat of an external enemy?

God knows. In any case, this farm was dead.

Time for us to go.

Chapter Nineteen

LESS THAN TWO HOURS LATER, Boris brought us to an endless expanse of water. It was marked on the map as the White Sea. Between the heavy swell, the freezing wind and the dark clouds, I wouldn't call its shores particularly welcoming.

Despite the obnoxious weather, Boris soared effortlessly under the clouds on his powerful wings. He even looked pleased, enjoying this bit of extreme flying.

I was about to tell him to head back inland when I noticed a few dark oblong spots on the shore. From afar, they resembled the dead bodies of either beached seals or very large birds.

That wouldn't be so bad if it wasn't for the way

they were positioned. The bodies were lined up neatly, as if by a sentient hand.

When I approached, I realized I was only half-right. The dark oblong bodies turned out to be upended boats lying on the shore. They looked very old, too, their blackened sides cracked, rotten and gaping with holes.

What did this imply? The first thing that came to mind was that there must have been a settlement of sentient creatures nearby. They must have dumped their old boats on the shore to rot. The game offered no prompts when I focused on the boats which meant they were simply part of the scenery.

Wait a sec. Now this was getting interesting.

A skeleton lay on the sand next to the last boat. Even with its skull smashed beyond recognition, I couldn't mistake a Noctean for any other race under the sun. And the stone axe which was still lying under the boat was a sure giveaway.

Plus, all the footprints around were old and barely discernible. These weren't Nocteans.

How very interesting.

"Let's follow them, kiddo," I told Boris, leaping back into the saddle.

We didn't have far to go. I discovered the next skeleton lying about five hundred feet further on.

This Noctean had large boulders piled up on him. His head was a mess. Apparently, he'd tried to climb out from under the rocks: I could see that by the deep claw marks left on the boulders' surface.

Now why did this look familiar?

"I think I was right," I whispered, casting watchful glances around.

"Let's land over there," I pointed at a wide cliff ledge overhanging the rocky trail.

The ledge was easy to access and offered plenty of space to lie in hiding for whoever had used it to surprise their unwanted guests.

There! The entrance to a cave, just as I'd thought. It was cleverly concealed by some bushes which — I was pretty sure — hadn't grown there on their own accord.

I set Prankie free for a bit of a run-around and let him check the place out.

His lithe predatory shadow disappeared within the dark passage. A few minutes later, he was already back. All clear.

I patted his hackles and stepped into the darkness.

The rock corridor wasn't that long. Soon I was already through to the other side.

I took cover behind a large boulder and blinked the sunlight out of my eyes. The cave hadn't been that dark, especially not for Ennan eyesight, but still the harsh sunrays had momentarily blinded me. I waited for my eyesight to restore and continued on my way.

An abandoned settlement, dead and silent, appeared unexpectedly amid the cliffs.

At first sight, it looked dramatically different to the farm I'd encountered earlier. This stockade was well built and fortified with rocks piled up to half its height, discouraging any unwanted visitors.

Cliffs protected the settlement from both sides. A sturdy gate towered at the center, bristling with sharpened staves. This was a well-conceived and well-kept compound. Skulls of unknown animals topped some of the stakes. Judging by their impressive fangs, they were definitely predators.

Two wooden watchtowers flanked the gate. I didn't notice any sentries or archers on them. The little fortified settlement appeared perfectly dead.

A few Noctean skeletons lay under the wall, apparently killed by arrows and other missiles. The weapons themselves, however, seemed to be missing. Someone must have collected them after the battle.

That was good news. It meant someone might still be alive.

I couldn't help admiring the formidable little structure. Everywhere I looked, I saw evidence of a mercilessly bloody battle. The walls and the gate were covered in dark spots which seemed to have permeated the wood and caked on the rock, telling me that the settlement's defenders met their foe honorably, spilling a lot of enemy blood in the process.

A growl came from below. I couldn't confuse that sound with anything.

Gingerly I stepped toward the edge of the cliff ledge.

Nocteans. Just as I thought. Five of them.

They staggered along, dragging their feet with exhaustion and growling at each other. Their front limbs hung listlessly at their sides. All of them seemed to have been wounded.

Ah-ha. And there were the defenders coming! A few creatures appeared in the stockade: two on the walls and one on each of the watchtowers.

They were definitely Caltean. Having said that, they were sort of small... puny... their armor was definitely too big for them.

I was an idiot! Those were kids! Young boys!

Judging by the Nocteans' happy growling, they'd noticed them too. They scurried toward the settlement as fast as they could.

The first arrows flew from the walls. Too early!

What were they doing on the walls, anyway? Where were all the adults? Why had they allowed children to defend the place?

Never mind. I'd find that out some other time. Hold on, kids. We're coming...

On my command, Boris soared high in the sky, then darted downwards.

"Your entry, Steely Guts!" I shouted, releasing a Scorpion.

* * *

"So when did that happen?" I asked.

"A fortnight ago, maybe more. We didn't count the days," a teenage Caltean boy replied. His name was Unai.

"No one came here after that?"

It had been two hours since we'd finished off the Nocteans who'd been quite the worse for wear to begin with. I'd been lucky: their energy had been depleted, their Life bars hovering at 20%. The latter must have tipped the scales in our favor, I suppose.

The children had met me warily at first. Still, through some inexplicable insight of their own, they'd recognized me as a Red Owl. From then on, their mistrust had disappeared.

Sitting on the wall's broad ramparts, I was now talking to the young defenders.

"No, no one's been since then," Unai shook his head.

I looked at them in disbelief. It was incredible how much they'd suffered in these two short weeks.

The clan of the Sea Tigers had been attacked by a large Noctean tribe who'd slaughtered all the adults in a one-sided battle. Only a few children had survived: four boys and two girls. Having said that, now that you looked at Unai and the squat little Torm, you wouldn't call them children anymore.

Once all the adults had been killed, they became responsible for the settlement's survival.

"Which one of you dropped the boulder onto the Noctcan whose bones I found by the boats?" I asked.

Torm and Unai exchanged surprised glances.

"I did throw a rock at him, yes," Torm replied.

"Did you finish off the other one too?"

He nodded, then added vaguely, "I used the same rock."

"The same boulder, you mean?"

"Yeah. It was the best I could find. Hard and sharp. I spent some time picking the right one."

I chuckled. "I see."

'A rock'! The kid was strong, that's for sure. That's probably what Crym or Orman used to be like when they were young.

Torm was a real giant for his age. He had large hands, broad shoulders and big feet. He was almost the same height as myself. But that wasn't what worried me. It was the weird look in his eyes... hard and cruel.

Then again, what did I know? The kid had just lost his entire family killed before his very eyes. What kind of look was he supposed to have?

So all in all, the young Sea Tigers had left a most favorable impression on me. Especially Unai, the eldest, who now was their leader.

I couldn't help comparing myself to the boy. Would I have been able to preserve my own courage and integrity in his place?

He, too, had had his entire family killed before his eyes by hungry Noctean cannibals. He had no one but a handful of scared boys like himself to turn to. Still, it hadn't prevented him from getting his act together and saving the few survivors.

"How did you know?" Torm asked.

"How did I know what?"

"That we threw a rock at him," Unai explained, curious.

"I followed Torm's footprints."

"His footprints?"

"Yes. Actually, I only saw three of them. Two were by the old boat and one more in the passage between the rocks. At first I thought they belonged to a small man because I couldn't imagine such a big boy could exist," I nodded at Torm who puffed his chest out with pride.

Unai gave me an understanding smile.

"It's been days! How did you see them?" Torm demanded.

"Just by being observant, that's all. Your footprints were the deepest because you carried

---

something heavy — the boulder, apparently. Did you know that that was the only way you could break a Noctean skull, throwing something heavy from a great height? You don't have to be very observant to notice the cliffs overhanging the shore exactly where it happened."

"But surely the rain and wind would have destroyed our prints after so many days?" Unai pointed out.

"Absolutely. That's exactly what happened. Which is why I only found three footprints. Two of them had survived because they were left next to the upended boat which protected them from the wind. The third one on the rocky trail was even easier. Torm must have stepped accidentally into the Noctean's blood and left a footprint on the pebbles next to the body. That's basically it."

They fell silent. Unai sat mouthing something, as if trying to memorize what I'd just said. Torm was contemplating his own feet as if he was seeing them for the first time.

"Where did you come from?" Unai asked, changing the subject.

"From the Forbidden City," I said.

Their eyes opened wide.

"I'm the Keeper of the Forbidden City," I explained. "In actual fact, I've offered refuge to the surviving Caltean clans, whatever's left of them."

"*Surviving* clans?" Unai asked in disbelief.

"Of course," I replied. "Silver Mountain Valley was invaded by a Noctean horde. Didn't you know?"

They exchanged glances, then shook their heads in unison.

Oh. I didn't expect that.

"But what are the clans doing in the Forbidden City?" Unai asked. "It's in the North, isn't it?"

"Lots of reasons. The shamans couldn't come to an agreement so the clans split to go each their own way."

As I spoke, they kept exchanging bewildered stares. Heh! If Laosh could only see the boys' reaction to the "clever" decisions of his supposedly wise colleagues!

So I had to tell them everything from the start: about the Calteans' each going their own way; about the Red Owls and the Black Axes; about the Nocteans and how we'd fought them. About the arrival of the other clans — or rather, what was left of them.

On hearing the names of Badwar, Gukhur and Lavena — and especially when I'd told them that they'd killed their shamans and why — the boys' fists clenched. Torm even cussed almost like a trooper.

I could understand them. Their familiar world was falling apart in front of their very eyes. First the death of their families and now the news about the horde coming. For them it must have been nothing short of an Apocalypse.

We spoke about the future of their settlement. I offered to have them moved to the city. Surprisingly, they declined my invitation. As it turned out, they had the place up and running. They had plenty of food and materials. They even had a few buffaloes. They were actually rich by local standards. They even had a big boat and a dozen smaller ones.

Despite their age, the boys were all levels 200+. The two girls were slightly less — but both of them already had some very useful abilities and skills, especially the young one who promised to become a very strong medicine woman one day.

I didn't invite them to join the Red Owls. I simply didn't have enough Reputation with their juvenile clan yet. The little gray medal I'd already earned definitely wasn't enough to influence these kinds of decisions. But we did strike up an alliance, to our mutual pleasure.

Then they offered me a meal. I had to tell them all about the Forbidden City and its dungeons. Everyone loved Boris and Prankie so much they didn't want to let me go because of them.

Still, I had to go back. What a shame I couldn't do anything for these kids — not at the moment, anyway. One thing I did do, I left them the Scorpion I'd just used fighting the wounded Nocteans.

It still had about 60% durability. Let it stand by the gate guarding them. Now that we were allies, Steely Guts identified the Sea Tigers as friends.

To say they were happy to receive it was an understatement. Once I got back to the city, I'd have to get the others to think of ways to help these brave kids.

Boris banked into a farewell circle over the settlement before spiriting me back to Silver Mountain.

The river was incredible in its serenity: an expanse of gray glass spilt into the valley. Rough and raging only the day before, it now half-heartedly licked the rocky shore. Mist drifted low over its surface, promising a sunny day later.

I was sitting on a half-submerged rock by the shore watching and listening, taking in my surroundings. The river resembled a giant beast lying in ambush before springing at you, the splashing of its waves lulling its victims into a false sense of security.

With bated breath, I admired the momentary quiet. The lapping of the wavelets helped my thinking.

I'd just seen everything I needed to see.

We were in it well and deep.

An eleven thousand-strong Noctean horde was

moving directly toward us. And that was not all. The Dark players were rapidly approaching us, moving at the double. They'd already crossed the Black Stream. I'd taken an inconspicuous peek at their numbers: four thousand at least. That's not counting their supply train.

And that wasn't all, either. Over there beyond the mountain ridge, the allied army of the clans of Light was about to enter the Icy Woods.

We were being surrounded. Having said that, the Nocteans were bound to arrive first.

This was how the cookie crumbled. There was still a remote chance that all these countless armies could go for each other's throats under our walls. But that would be too good to hope for.

A soft rustling behind my back distracted me from my sad musings. Reluctantly I turned around, already knowing whom I was going to see.

A slim female figure froze on a rock nearby. She was clad in pitch-black armor which must have cost her a fortune, judging by its "purple" glint. Two scimitars peeked from behind her back. A small crossbow hung by her side.

A couple of weeks ago, the sight of her would have made me realize my own helplessness. Not anymore, though. I was different now. I'd changed.

"Hi Sir Olgerd," the Alven girl said. "I didn't recognize you. I'm so happy to see you."

"Hi Liz," I smiled back. "Nice to see you too."

"You're crazy, flying over the clan army. What if they'd noticed you?"

I chuckled. "They wouldn't have. I fly above the clouds, don't I?"

"How did you see me, then?" she asked.

"My friend list began flashing," I explained. "I opened it and saw you were in the local chat. So I left you a message. Was it hard to find the watchtower?"

She shrugged. "So that's what it was, then. You okay here?"

"I'm becoming savage gradually," I said with a crooked smile. "How are things going on the continent?"

She laughed. "Same old. Uncle Vanya told me you'd started a Godawful mess here."

I heaved a sigh. "He's right. I had no choice. How is he? I didn't see him over there."

She waved my question away. "The caravanners have their own rules. They'll wait till this area is completely civilized, then they'll arrive. Uncle Vanya disapproves of pioneering new routes. It isn't going to bring them any extra profits, so what's the point in ruining good carts and animals?

"Logical," I said. "At least you're here."

She nodded. "Sure. And not just me. Everyone who's managed to raise some money for good gear, they're all here."

"Are you marching against me?"

She waved at the mountains in the direction of the arriving army. "Them, yeah. But not my group. We can't fight against you. That's what all the caravanners say, too. Lots of people say that, in fact."

I smiled. "Thanks. That's nice to hear. You might want to know that in a couple of days you risk coming across a Dark army of a similar size. Please be careful."

She shook her head. "They won't fight us."

That was a surprise. "Why not?"

"The leaders of the Dark and Light clans have an agreement. We have a temporary truce."

I scratched my head. "Oh. That's not good news. Why would they do that?"

She laughed. "Good question! Everybody keeps asking themselves the same thing. Our leaders are up to something."

"How weird."

"I must be off now," she said. "I don't want them to notice I've been gone. You take care of yourself, okay?"

"Bye, Liz," I said. "Say hello to everyone!"

Her jaw dropped when she saw Boris arriving. We circled the shore a few times to allow her an eyeful of our tandem. Then, with a farewell wave of my hand, the two of us took off for the watchtower.

It was even more gorgeous up close. It was

built with well-cut slabs of stone gray with time. It in fact resembled a tall donjon ready to receive a small group of warriors.

The tower may have appeared old but it wasn't fragile. You could see it was abandoned. No one had taken care of this beautiful fortification in centuries. Grass grew out of the cracks, its roots forcing the stonework apart. One of the clans was bound to claim it pretty soon.

It towered on top of a rocky plateau, the highest in the area. In order to get to it, you had to climb a rather steep path for five minutes at least.

I flew up closer. Now I could make out the neat rows of arrowslits. This was in fact a small fortress which a small group of archers could hold until the arrival of main forces, provided they had enough food and supplies.

The tower offered an excellent field of fire. An enemy wouldn't bother to waste either time or resources on such a trivial target. This place was perfect for a small group wishing to sit it out. They had an excellent visibility and the bonus of being able to signal at will.

"Good! I think we've seen enough! Time to go home."

Chapter Twenty

WARNING! The Magic Sphere will expire in:
05:00 min...
04:59...
04:58...
04:57...

The last few days of the magic protection had flown by like a flock of sparrows assaulting a freshly-filled garbage bin in the backyard.

Biting my lips, I stood on the castle wall watching the timer mete out the remaining seconds. The devs were real bastards. They could have easily given me a month's protection if they'd really wanted to.

You'd think I was a fully grown man but I felt jittery as if I was about to sit a school exam. It was as if I'd forgotten something very important despite all the nights I'd spent poring over textbooks cramming page after lengthy page, realizing I couldn't possibly remember it all.

Normally, this would plunge you into a state of panic and anger with yourself — which strangely enough, nudges you into action. You look back at the last few days you'd spent studying, admonishing yourself for wasting a whole evening at the movies the other day when you could have been studying instead. Or the trip to the river a week ago! What was the point of lugging textbooks along if all you did was lounge around with friends playing cards? That's another day wasted. At night, it makes you feel like a dieter blaming herself for a slice of pie she'd wolfed down earlier.

Unfortunately, we can't control time. It slips through our fingers like water: you can cup your hand as tight as you want but water will always find a tiny crack to escape through.

The previous night had been quiet and remarkably warm. It looked like springtime had finally arrived in No-Man's Lands, gradually reclaiming them from the recent snowstorms. Snow was melting all around the city and the valley, revealing the ugly remains of the once-majestic Ennan civilization.

Springtime. My wife Sveta loved it a lot. She found joy in birds' chattering: this was a signal for her to get us out on bonfire picnics in the woods. She was the main driving force in our family, inventing all sorts of outdoor entertainment. She also loved to dance. I often barged in on her singing into her hairbrush. Oh yes, she loved springtime... a proper one, not the kind we had here.

Also, my Calteans weren't exactly a cheerful bunch at the moment. We hadn't been in the mood for dancing just lately.

I'd managed to convince my commanders to let the newcomers into the city. Also, Badwar had announced that they were going to stay with us even after the protection expired. Wise decision. They wouldn't be able to escape the Nocteans, anyway. And even if they could, they had nowhere to escape to. Even in its deplorable current state, Twilight Castle still offered some sort of protection.

Pike and his Northern Wolves had stayed too, for more or less the same reason.

Unfortunately, none of them had expressed any intention of joining our clan. The Calteans were too proud to betray their own colors. In the real world, that would be highly commendable — but here, reputation was key and my reputation with the other clans left a lot to be desired.

We'd fortified the wall as best we could. The

blacksmiths hadn't stopped for two weeks, the ringing of their hammers echoing across the valley. I didn't even notice the sound anymore.

Others were busy hunting and fishing, amassing food supplies. The siege might last a long time. All the men were armed: as we already knew, the Nocteans took no prisoners.

Calteans were terribly headstrong. Okay, I'd more or less expected that from the fugitives but definitely not from my own Red Owls who'd refused to share their "green" weapons and armor point blank. There was nothing I could do, despite the fact that I'd been the one who, in true fire-bringing Prometheus style, had shared the revolutionary tools with the Red Owls to begin with.

"We've given them food and shelter," Droy had told me last night. "That's more than enough. Don't forget that we know Badwar better than you do."

No amount of me telling him that we were all in the same boat facing the Noctean invasion could smash the brick wall of his reasoning. Just another proof that you couldn't ride the game system. No matter how stupid Droy's arguments might have sounded against the rational logic of my own, I had no chance of ever convincing the machine. The AI which controlled my Captain would never override the existing script.

"Look!" a young voice exclaimed.

I looked up. The boy who'd been helping the builders on the wall stood up straight, pointing his hand.

Nocteans. Just to please. The moment the protection expired, they were here right on cue.

The familiar call of our bugle came from the East Tower.

"Here we go," I whispered, peering into the distance.

The Nocteans were legion. Like a powerful river, the horde flooded the valley, pouring down the hills toward the city. Their howling and roaring had drowned out all other noises. My back erupted in a cold sweat.

"Arrows! Quick! Whatcha starin' at? Have you messed your pants already? To your positions!"

Those were my sergeants barking orders from the north wall: the last bastion standing between the Calteans and their death.

The city had now turned into an angry disturbed beehive ready to assault the intruding bear.

I watched as the defenders, fast but efficient, took their places on the walls. Pritus and his assistants fussed around the Brocks and the glaive throwers. He'd recruited local boys and girls into his special artillery squads. They looked suitably nervous and excited.

I watched them, suppressing the desire to

interfere. Pritus seemed to be doing just fine. He'd already gained some experience in commanding them, and his tuition had proved its worth to everyone during the recent mock drills. Dressed in light "green" armor, they were now trying to do everything they'd been told, bringing the glaive clips and rolling the already-prepared boulders toward the Brocks.

Pritus was walking among them, tapping his hand on his small bag where he kept the charged Charms of Arakh. On top of the seventy I'd had before, I'd managed to replicate another twenty-two. That was all I'd had time for, as the Replicator had turned out to have a twelve-hour cooldown. Still, it was better than nothing.

The Caltean warriors awaited their hour by the gate below. Judging by their expressions, some of them couldn't wait for the enemy to approach, impatient to see what the Ennan machines could do: they certainly inspired confidence.

A slight panic arose in one of Pritus' teams fussing around a Brock. The man himself was on the wall checking glaive throwers. I nodded to him and hurried down to check on his group.

Right, what did we have here? Aha. One of the boys couldn't find the firing lever because they hadn't inserted the Charm of Arakh properly.

I quickly rectified their mistake. The boy looked at me, his beardless face crimson with embarrassment. Wait a sec... that's a girl!

"You've done good," I gave her an encouraging smile. "A bit nervous, that's all. It's gonna work fine now."

I summoned Boris and leapt into the saddle. In one smooth wingbeat, we were already soaring over the camp.

The Nocteans appeared even more numerous from above. The entire valley had already filled with their gray bodies and growling jaws. A true avalanche of death about to crush our tiny camp.

Growling and baring their teeth, the Nocteans rolled toward the wall which had become the only barrier separating us from certain death.

Predictably, the ruins of the lower city had slowed down their advance. It wasn't as easy as the table-flat valley, was it? They had to thread their way among the ruins, climbing and scrambling over them.

The first screams of pain came as Nocteans began stumbling into our traps. We'd expected them to advance through the lower city which was why we'd set up plenty of nasty surprises for them over there.

The snow had turned crimson where they'd walked right onto the sharpened stakes and pikes of our traps. The first system messages started coming in, dutifully reporting our enemy's casualties and the XP received.

When they were about five hundred feet away

from the wall, I signaled Pritus to begin.

His orders resounded below. The Brocks were the first to kick into action. We'd already filled their barrels with large rocks the size of a dog's head. Now they showered the advancing monsters like a flock of deadly birds.

A blast of screaming and wailing assaulted our ears as the rocks reached their targets.

From the wall, it looked as if someone had spilled red paint onto the white canvas of the valley. Spots of crimson kept blossoming everywhere, bringing more agonizing deaths to the demoralized Noctean crowd.

Now the second volley.

That was it. We'd choked their advance. The Noctean leaders bellowed their orders in vain: their hairy soldiers were fleeing the battlefield shrieking with horror.

The sky turned dark with the barrage of arrows and even more rocks which fell upon the fleeing cannibals like swarms of angry wild bees. Caltean cheers added to the cacophony of wailing and screaming.

Done it. The Nocteans were retreating. One nil.

I signaled to Droy to let him know I was going on a quick recon. Once he nodded, I told Boris to take off.

---

* * *

I'd spent until midday checking the area. In the end, I was completely exhausted — but at least I knew what to expect from the enemy.

The leaders of all five clans met me by the gate grim-faced, awaiting the news.

"How many are they?" Laosh asked as soon as I landed by the wall.

"Fewer than I expected," I said. "Two thousand max."

"That means the horde is still on its way here," Lavena said confidently.

"I agree," I said.

"Those bastards breed like rabbits," Badwar spat.

Gukhur turned to Pike, "I think we were followed by their avant-garde."

Pike nodded, frowning. He still blamed himself for Amai's death.

"If that's true, then those were the young ones," Crym offered.

"Which is good," Droy spoke. "They're impulsive and undisciplined. Good for us."

"Did they attack while I was away?" I asked.

"Three more times," Orman said. "We have no casualties. They lost at least a hundred and fifty soldiers."

"You assembled your machines just in time, Keeper!" Badwar growled. "Without them, we'd have been right in it."

All the others voiced their agreement. Crym gave me a hearty slap on the back as was his habit.

My relationship with Pike and the other clan leaders instantly changed to Friendly.

Much better.

"I've checked the whole area," I continued my report. "They're nowhere to be seen outside this valley. Currently they're busy devouring their dead and wounded."

"Did you see their leader?" Lavena asked.

Was it my imagination or did her voice quiver ever so slightly when she said this?

"I think so," I replied reluctantly.

"Why, what's the problem?"

I rubbed my forehead. "He's sort of puny. I expected to see my old friend, Shaggy. He was huge. But he wasn't there."

"And this, what did you call him, the puny one? He wasn't white by any chance, was he?" Badwar asked.

The others tensed up.

He was right, come to think of it. The Noctean leader's white markings had indeed stood out from the gray crowd.

I nodded. "He was. You're right."

"Dammit!" Badwar growled.

"He's a *Kerook*," Gukhur hissed. "He brought them here!"

I looked at Laosh, expecting an explanation.

"As you must have noticed, there're two types of Nocteans," the shaman began. "The normal ones and the shapeshifters. Normally, the strongest shapeshifter becomes the leader of the whole pack. But there's also a third type. These are called *Kerooks*. They can control the packs' leaders. The stronger the Kerook, the more Noctean packs he can submit to his will."

"Two thousand soldiers, not bad," I murmured. "Whatever he is, he's not weak."

The Nocteans kept attacking us non-stop throughout the night. They only stopped early in the morning in order to drag away their dead and feast upon them. I even got the impression that their leaders had sent their men toward our arrows and stakes on purpose.

They would roll onto the wall like sea surf onto cliffs, dying in their dozens but also claiming the defenders' lives. Several times they'd managed to scale the walls and push us back temporarily, but every time our warriors had enough fearless courage to throw them off the walls onto the sharpened stakes of the moat.

Our allies had lost fifty warriors in the last

twenty-four hours. The Red Owls had no casualties so far.

Noctean losses were immeasurably bigger. Still, fifty dead was too many for our small and badly organized army.

And this was only the first day of the siege! If it went on like this, there'd be no defenders left standing after a month of such round-the-clock attacks.

That wouldn't be so bad but what drove me crazy was the Calteans' reluctance to unite. Each clan had its own camp, seeing as we had plenty of space for everyone, including all the refugees and their numerous livestock.

Thanks to my lessons that Droy had communicated to the rest of the Red Owls, their camp was nothing short of perfect even if I say so myself. The newcomers, however, had turned their campsites into pigsties. That especially applied to the Northern Wolves with all their sheep and horses.

That in itself wouldn't have been so bad — but the last twenty-four hours had made me realize that I'd grossly underestimated the sheer scope of the looming catastrophe. What had I been hoping for, thinking that the Red Owls could defend the city on their own? Between the Noctean horde and the players' clans they honestly stood not a chance in hell. Even with our recent addition in the face of the

---

Northern Wolves and highland clans we were unlikely to last until the end of the week.

That's what happened when you entrusted an army to someone who didn't know jack about the art of war.

How I wished I could send it all to hell and press the Logout button. I'd have loved nothing more than to see my girls, Sveta and Christa. I could use a shower and a meal out. I just needed some sleep, come to think of it.

"Keeper! Sir Keeper!" a child's thin voice awoke me from my musings.

"Eh?" I looked around me. "Sorry, what is it?"

A girl of about seven years of age stood below the wall waving her hand to me. "Keeper! My father asks if you will see him!"

"What's his name?" I asked.

"It's Keaven!"

Keaven. I remembered him. He was one of the masons clearing the stone debris. I should be grateful to them for the prompt restoration of the walls.

I came down to her. "Okay, show me."

The girl — her name was Ula — ran in front of me toward the Red Owls' camp. Soon we stopped by an impressive-looking pile of rocks.

Her father greeted me, then invited me to come closer for a look.

"We just cleared this pile as normal," he spoke

in a rapid patter. "We were just about to move on when Povel hit a piece of metal with his pick. We cleared the earth away and then we saw this," he gestured at the ground at his feet.

I peered in the direction he was pointing at. My back erupted in goosebumps.

I stepped toward their discovery. My Map icon began to flash. A new mark appeared on the map of Twilight Castle.

It looked like my masons had just discovered the entrance to the city's Throne Room.

Could that be *it*? Were we safe now?!

Master Satis had been almost right about the notes of Arwein. The Throne Room was indeed located in the very heart of the Castle. The only difference was that it was under the ground, not above it.

The door discovered by Keaven opened with ease. Not really a door but rather a hatch. The game engine habitually highlighted the right key in the bunch given to me by the city's old Keepers.

The door opened, revealing a deep tunnel below. I dove into it under the stares of the crowd which had already gathered around me.

Having received no warnings about any high-level monsters lurking inside, I decided to proceed.

The tunnel was rather well-lit by the green moss which the Ennans had used instead of lamps and torchlights.

I descended the last few stairs and stepped into the wide doorway.

The system helpfully kicked in,

Welcome to Brutville Halls!

Oh. Did that mean that the Throne Room was the same as Brutville Halls?

What, was that it? This was my final destination set by the Reflex Bank?

The mind boggles. Me, with my meager gaming experience and even less confidence?

I began shaking uncontrollably. My whole life in Mirror World flashed before my eyes.

My first full immersion. Myself, lying in a capsule helpless and dumbfounded, barely able to move while the virtual world blossomed around me in full sound and color, a true miracle of our century.

The Spider Grotto. The Steel Spider Queen.

The Citadel wizard's tower. Boris' first flight which had scared the hell out of me.

My first virtual death back at the Nameless Isles. Defeating the Lich. Meeting Droy. The battle with the Darks and the Calteans' acceptance of me.

And finally, the Ennans' Forbidden City.

I struggled to focus. Awesome as it was, I still had to do one last thing. I had to activate the fabled Twilight Obelisk which so far was nowhere to be seen.

The Brutville Halls met me with desolation and spooky silence. I had to agree with Arwein who'd left a brief message about this place. Unlike this famous traveler of old, I hadn't been to any of the places he'd praised — like the Emerald Palace of the Alven Prince, the Brown Deserts of the Narches or the boundless moors of the Dwandes. Still, I'd been in some other places in my lifetime just as majestic as these. And I had to agree: here, the game designers' imagination had indeed added a new meaning to *grandiose*.

I turned my head this way and that, studying the incredible décor. The ceiling was in fact much higher than it had appeared from the outside, its vaults supported by a multitude of columns bearing unusual patterns of intertwined letters, symbols and images.

Lamps hung from the ceiling every several feet, glowing with the same omnipresent green moss which clung to them, enveloping their fancy shapes.

I walked across the hall, casting curious glances at the columns. Each had its own unique design telling a complex story. The unknown craftsmen had done an amazing job retelling fragments of somebody else's life: the person's birth...

---

two armies about to lock in combat... Two small figures on the farthest column held their hands, surrounded by a cheering crowd... on the next column, the same two figures were sitting on thrones, reaching their hands out to the onlookers. This must have been a royal wedding, followed by the newlyweds' happy reign.

When I'd crossed the entire length of the hall, I indeed came to two thrones mounted on a small pedestal. They differed in size but were covered with the same fancy carvings. These must have been the thrones I'd just seen in the picture, once occupied by the royal newlyweds.

Right in front of the thrones, an enormous dirty-gray crystal protruded from the ground. Rather tall and slim, a bit like a spearhead, it appeared to be piercing its way out to a long-awaited freedom.

I looked around me. I got the impression that the whole of Brutville Halls were in fact built around this ancient crystal which had been here long before the castle builders had arrived.

Forgetting everything around me, I admired its primeval beauty.

"So how do you like the Twilight Obelisk, my dear grandchild?"

Chapter Twenty-One

I SWUNG to the sound.

An Ennan man stood just a few paces away from me, cross-armed, his right shoulder leaning on the obelisk.

His crude padded leather vest was covered in oil spots and burn marks. He wore sleeve protectors with plenty of little pockets for all kinds of tools. His face was surprisingly clean-shaven — which was more than compensated by his disheveled head of hair.

A cunning smile hovered over his narrow face.

I looked up at the tag above his head. "Master Brolgerd?" I was so dumbfounded I'd even forgotten to say hello.

"Yeah, whatever's left of him," the Ennan

replied with a sarcastic grin.

I took a better look. Of course. I was talking to a ghost. His translucent shape was proof enough.

He nodded at the obelisk, "You didn't answer. How do you like it?"

I glanced at the murky gray crystal and replied in all honesty, "I've no idea what to think."

"Don't you have an opinion? This is one of the oldest artifacts around. The stuff of legends and ballads. Didn't your parents tell any of them to you?"

I shrugged. "I don't think so. All I know is that this object has something to do with the Gods."

Brolgerd gave me a studying look. "You've come here to activate it, haven't you? Not to steal it or chip off a fragment? Just to activate?"

"Of course. You don't need to worry," I raised my hands in a reconciliatory gesture. "I don't think you'll find somebody more interested in activating this crystal than me. Master Adkhur clearly told me-"

"Adkhur?" the man's furrowed face cleared. "Is he alive?"

"Yes, I suppose so. I hope so."

"No! You don't understand," the man pointed at his own translucent body. "Is he alive *for real?*"

"Oh, I see. Yes, he's alive all right. Gained some weight even."

"Cheeky bastard!" his face dissolved in a smile. "So he managed to avoid the massacre, then."

I looked around me. "Is this where you died?"

The ghost heaved a sigh. "It is. Someone had to defend the Obelisk."

"What do you mean?" I asked, uncomprehending. "I thought it was Master Grilby and his machines that became the Der Swyors' undoing?"

The ghost curved his lips in a smirk. "You could say that, I suppose."

What kind of Machiavellian intrigue was that?

"I can see you don't understand," Brolgerd said. "I find it strange Adkhur didn't tell you. He must have had his reasons. Oh well. No point in me trying to keep the truth from you. Do you know what 'Der Swyor' means?"

"No idea."

"It's the ancient language of the underground dwellers. Literally, it means 'the Rock's Keepers'. Later it became our clan's official name. Ever since the War of Gods, we've been the guardians of the Twilight Obelisk. For centuries other Ennan clans used to respect our mission. But over time, they forgot their fear of the bloodthirsty Gods of old. Craving their magical powers, more and more Ennans longed for the return of their patron God who used to protect the underground folk. Luckily, the Rock's Keepers knew of the god's scheming and of his cruel nature and so managed to prevent a new catastrophe. Still, in their greed and ignorance, other Ennans decided to challenge the ancient laws. As is often the way."

"Does that mean that all this hoo-ha with the 'ancient knowledge' and Master Grilby's legacy was only a cover up?"

"I didn't say that," the ghost said with a sly look. "The creation of the first Brock was what prompted it. I gather, you already got the chance to witness its efficiency."

"Did I ever."

"In which case, you're probably familiar with my little inventions too."

"I am. I can't tell you how grateful I am to you-
"

He waved my words away. "That's nothing. Especially as you've only just studied the first pages of my notebook, haven't you?"

"I do what I can. To tell you the truth, even this small fraction of your knowledge is mind-boggling."

The ghost chuckled. "I'd love to see you when you make it toward the middle of the book."

And so would I.

"But talking about my mentor's machines," Brolgerd looked me in the eye and added, "Or should I say, *our* mentor. As I told you already, our possession of such a powerful weapon promised nothing good to the advocates of the so-called 'Divine Comeback'. And what's more, had we not procrastinated with building them, the future of the Der Swyors might have been entirely different. Unfortunately, procrastinators are every society's curse and undoing. We were no exception. To cut a long story short, we didn't make it. The Divine Comeback supporters — which included several dozen Ennan clans — jumped at their chance. They raised a powerful army and invaded Twilight Castle. The rest you know."

"The Keepers were killed."

"And not only them," Brolgerd said with a predatory smile.

"Pardon me?"

"You don't mean it? Adkhur didn't tell you?"

"He told me about the Black Grisons, if that's what you mean."

"Heh! That's Adkhur for you! Our animal lover! He was always away with the fairies."

"What did happen, then?"

"Well... When the last defender of Brutville Halls finally fell, the invaders seized the opportunity to deactivate the Obelisk."

"Why?"

Master Brolgerd heaved a sigh. "Part of it was my fault, I suppose. At the time, I'd made a divining charm for ore seekers. It was supposed to serve peaceful purposes, like all of my inventions. The charm sought new ore deposits. All you had to do was place a tiny fragment of freshly farmed ore into it and it would give you the vein's exact location."

"What's that got to do with the obelisk?"

"Simple. The Obelisk is also a fragment. It's a fragment of the Divine Portal."

"The Mirror of the First God," I whispered, remembering my conversation with Tronus.

"Aha! You're not as hopeless as I thought!"

I chuckled. "What happened next?"

"Next they tried to chip off a tiny fragment of the Obelisk. Admittedly, that was quite smart. Unfortunately, it also showed their utter ignorance. Their attempt to damage a fully loaded Obelisk caused the instant death of everyone who happened to be in the room. All the clan leaders, the freshly-baked priests, the warlords and their best warriors... not to mention everyone else in Twilight Castle. You saw the state of the city, didn't you?"

"I did."

"Having destroyed the elite of Ennan society in one clean sweep, the Obelisk's magic prevented the Keepers' souls from leaving the city. For centuries, Master Satis, Master Axe and myself used to guard this place, awaiting the arrival of our worthy descendant."

"That's right," I said. "They gave me the keys to the city and the magic sphere which almost discharged. Then they just left without really explaining anything to me."

"That's right," he said in dead seriousness. "It was a test, one of the many you need to take along your way. Only a Keeper who is a valiant defender of the city could find his way to Brutville Halls. Which means you're worthy of the title. Even when the magic sphere expired, you still continued to defend the city."

"We had no choice, did we?"

He pursed his lips. "By 'us', do you mean the descendants of our sworn enemies? Don't look at me like that. The Calteans are the sorry remains of those who attempted to control the obelisk and its magic. Having lost their elite, their society fell into decay, slowly retrogressing until they returned to the stone age. Hah! Had it not been for your help, they might have soon reverted to stone axes and bone arrowheads."

"I don't think so," I murmured. "Their shamans were about to take them south."

"Shamans!" he spat. "That's what's left of their priests! They probably have no idea who they used to be. Did they really think they'd be welcome in the South? Idiots."

"They didn't do it because they wanted to," I tried to defend my friends. "They were forced out of their homes."

"You don't mean it! What could have possibly made them leave Silver Mountain Valley?"

"The Noctean horde," I said. "Which is

incidentally besieging this city even as we speak. No idea how long we can hold Twilight Castle."

I won't lie to you. I really hoped I could save the Calteans by activating that damned Obelisk.

"They can't have fled a bunch of wild animals, surely?" his voice rang with disbelief. "I'd love to have seen the face of the Silver Mountain King when someone showed him the despicable future of his people!"

Now I was getting angry. "Please don't say that."

The ghost's face lengthened in amazement. "Are you defending our enemies, boy?"

Was he getting familiar with me?

"No, I'm not," I said pointedly. "They're not my enemies."

I paused, trying to calm down. "Think for yourself. They've no idea what their ancestors used to be like. They're not responsible for their fathers' sins. And what's more, they're my friends. We fought shoulder to shoulder. We shared food and shelter. No one's going to debase them in my presence. I don't care whether it's you or anyone else."

The ghost cracked a sarcastic smile. "That's an answer worthy of the City Keeper! Sorry, but you can't save them anyway."

I tensed up. My nails dug into my palms. "What are you going to do?" I barked. "If you hurt them, I'm gonna smash this wretched Throne Room and your precious Obelisk to kingdom come!"

Brolgerd threw his head back and guffawed. "What makes you think I can do that?" he wiped away the tears of laughter. "I'm a ghost, for pete's sake. The Obelisk's magic preserved part of my identity and left it here so that I could teach a worthy contender how to use the artifact. I can see you know what I mean. Oh yes, my funny descendant, I can only serve as your guide. It's up to you to do the work."

"Yes, but-"

"Come and touch the Obelisk," he interrupted me again. "Then you'll stop asking useless questions."

Seeing my hesitation, he added,

"Come on, go ahead. It won't bite you."

Reluctantly I took a step forward and reached out.

The moment my right hand touched the obelisk's hard surface, a new system message appeared before my eyes,

Congratulations!

You've found the Twilight Obelisk!

Warning! Activating the Obelisk will deprive you of 10,000,000 pt. pure energy!

Would you like to activate the Obelisk: Yes/No

How much?!

I snatched my hand away. Ten million points pure energy?

That was the end of it. All my hopes had been crushed.

Impossible. It was a mistake, surely? I was probably seeing double. How many zeroes was it again?

Trembling with shock, I brought my hand up to the Obelisk.

Same message.

That's right. *Ten million points pure energy.*

Dammit!

My brain habitually kicked into its stress calculating mode. I could scrape together 20,000 pt. energy every 24 hours just to feed this bottomless pit. That's not counting the emergency reserves I always had to have at hand to feed my Brocks and glaive throwers.

Now. What did we have? Nothing.

This was an utter fiasco. This way it would take me a year and a half just to charge the wretched thing.

"Aha. Do you see now what you got yourself into?" Brolgerd's sarcastic voice came from behind me.

How I wished I could wipe that smirk off his face!

I slumped to the floor. "Come on, spit it out."

His face grew serious. "That's better. Now

listen. It's very important you activate the Obelisk."

It was my turn to be sarcastic. "Is it really?"

"Of course. By doing so, you'll activate the City's extended protection. It works similar to the sphere Satis gave you but it's much more powerful and lasts much longer."

He knew how to get my attention, the bastard. I didn't say anything, inviting him to continue.

Ignoring my reaction, the ghost went on, "And not just that. The Keeper — you, to be precise — will have access to all of the city's secret rooms and passages. You'll have all the maps and schemes offering you full knowledge of the place. When the news of Twilight Castle's revival spreads all over the world, the descendants of our clan will come to you. You'll need weapons to give them. And by weapons I don't mean the miserable pittance you've found in the Armory."

What, did they have more weapons? I'd love to know where they kept them.

Brolgerd chuckled. "I can see you're interested. Forget it. No activation, no weapons. Otherwise the risk is too great that they might fall into the enemy's hands. It's all or nothing. Got it?"

"Yeah."

He fell silent, piercing me with his dark unblinking stare.

"What's wrong?" I finally asked.

"Just thinking."

"About what?"

"I'm wondering if I should share my secret with you, my pro-Caltean City Keeper."

"Why, do you have a choice?"

"Well, I might just as well stay here for another thousand years."

"Yeah, right. Pull the other one."

His translucent face cleared. "It actually might be a good thing you brought them here. The presence of our enemy's descendants might simplify our task quite a bit."

I climbed back to my feet. "Don't even think about it."

Brolgerd ignored my threatening tone. "How many times do I need to tell you, I'm long dead. I can't do anything even if I wanted to. But I might help you."

"How?"

The ghost tilted his head to one side and gave me a studying look. "What do you know about the Desolation ritual?"

* * *

"You're a stupid fool!" he shouted after me. "You'll have to come back here, anyway! You have no choice!"

"You can stuff it," I grumbled, heading for the exit. "The guy has some sick ideas!"

Mirror World Book Four ~

To cut a long story short, that monster had suggested I sacrifice most of the Calteans to the Obelisk. According to him, the released energy — their life energy — would be well enough to activate the wretched thing.

"Think of those who are waiting for you!" the ghost's voice echoed behind. "It's time to fulfil your promise!"

Did you hear that? The devs openly suggested I smoke all of my friends. That was definitely a way out, I agree. For someone else, maybe, not for me. Not at that price.

My inner voice joined the struggle, as if asking, *What's the problem, dude? Just activate it! Then you can go back home to your family. These are NPCs, for crissakes! They're virtual! They're just senseless bits of binary code!*

Well, whatever. They were real enough for me. They'd saved my backside enough times. They'd given me warmth and joy. We'd worked and fought side by side. And how about their children that had been born in the city? We'd celebrated their births together.

It didn't matter what they were. What did matter was my own integrity. Provided I was still a human being and not a heartless player who only cared about his own gains like loot and leveling.

And as for my loved ones... I was pretty sure Sveta and Crista would understand.

~ 328 ~

Killing over a thousand sentient beings albeit NPCs? Oh, no. That wasn't in the agreement. There had to be some other way.

In which case I was going to find it.

As I left Brutville Halls, I could still hear Brolgerd's muffled voice calling after me. He just couldn't leave it alone.

I hurried back through the tunnel and flew up the stairs toward the hatch. For the first time I found it very unpleasant being underground.

I climbed out and squeezed my eyes shut, blinded by the light. Blinking and rubbing my eyes, I looked around.

All of the Calteans stood around me. I saw Droy the Fang and his son. Laosh, surrounded by his disciples. Badwar, Gukhur and Lavena.

Pritus gave me a squinting look from behind his cracked pince-nez. Lia stood in the crowd with her grandfather Crunch behind her, his hands on her shoulders, his gaze focused on me. And all the others with whom I'd traveled many miles across No-Man's Lands.

What was going on?

Seeing my confusion, Laosh spoke,

"When you jumped into the tunnel, many of us followed: Droy and Lavena, Badwar and Pike... When the bewitched ghost of the old Keeper arrived, they decided not to reveal themselves to him and hid behind the columns."

"We heard it all, my friend," Droy said.

"We thank you for keeping your oath and saving our children's lives," Badwar boomed. "As well as our own. You confronted your own to save us! Allow us to follow you!"

I looked around me, uncomprehending. When I finally opened my mouth to speak, my voice was drowned out by the roar of a thousand throats,

"The Keeper! The Keeper!"

A new system message appeared before my eyes, informing me of a thousand-strong addition to the Red Owls clan.

Chapter Twenty-Two

IN TOTAL, the Caltean's miraculous reunion had brought our ranks up to just under seven hundred warriors. I was now a proper medieval seigneur with my own footmen, cavalry and artillery.

I even had my own champions: Pike of Many Hands, Badwar the Thunder Warrior, Gukhur the Black Serpent and Lavena the Vixen. All those weird system messages reporting my Relationship changes with them had now found their explanation. The words *High Esteem* now glowed red and proud in my interface.

In other words, these guys were unlikely to leave my side any time soon.

I'd also worked out the mystery of Pike's

glowing scimitars. Apparently, some NPCs could have the so-called *super blows*. It was their analog of skills, basically, when the last move in a particular combo could activate a super blow. Pike's was called The Fury of a Wolf.

Oh, and one other thing about my champions. All of them were literally hung with "purple" items. You wouldn't have thought so looking at them, would you? I too had tended to believe their gear was all "gray". And once players found that out, my new clan members would be fair game for all those willing to get themselves a pair of "Pike's Scimitars" or "the Hammer of the Thunder Warrior".

Having said that, you had to defeat an NPC like that first. Their levels were 350+ with stats to match — not to even mention their super blows. Besides, I wasn't going to sit back watching them being smoked, either.

We finally had a Colonel: Droy the Fang. Who else? He'd personally appointed the seven captains. Strangely enough, our champions weren't interested in taking up command posts. All four of them constantly stayed by my side as my own personal retinue.

All these appointments and rearrangements had had to be ad libbed during the short breaks between Noctean attacks. But now that the entire Caltean race had been affected by my legendaries, fighting the enemy had become much easier.

Our rearmament race was in full swing. Zachary and Prochorus spent all their time forging new weapons and armor. At the time of the clans' merger, they'd already clad and rearmed more than half of all newcomers.

The results of our local "industrial revolution" were especially encouraging. We now had almost two thousand civilians boasting almost a hundred professions. I'd been thinking about going on a trip to get them more recipes and blueprints but they didn't need it: the entire camp seemed to be busy exchanging "green" knowledge. Blacksmiths trained more blacksmiths. Healers shared their newly-acquired know-how with their apprentices. And so on and so forth.

The stats and charts in my clan interface seemed to have taken on a life of their own. Their numbers blinked, flashed and grew quicker than I could take note.

The renewed clan was seething with life. The camp was gradually taking on a more civilized shape.

I was rubbing my hands with glee watching it all.

* * *

The animal roar of a thousand Noctean throats thundered behind the city wall, mingled with our defenders' war cries.

"Load!" Pritus barked in the heat of the battle.

Fire! And again!

Screams of agony came from behind the wall. Our warriors on the towers shook their weapons, celebrating their triumph.

The Nocteans must have reached the walls, judging by the archers' fast regrouping.

"Fire!"

Bowstrings began snapping.

The growling monsters kept springing up trying to reach the top of the wall — only to drop dead studded with arrows like porcupines. The moat had claimed a generous harvest of bodies, its sharp stakes sticking out like the teeth of a giant monster.

The screams. The hollering. The agony.

I couldn't force my gaze away from the bloodied stakes with guts hanging from their rough spiny shafts.

This wasn't right. This wasn't normal. This was supposed to be a game.

The world had filled with the thick, viscous presence of death. I seemed to be sensing it in every bone of my virtual body.

"You all right?" Droy asked softly. His voice reached me over the screams of agony and the thunderous Caltean cheers.

I managed a nod. My entire body was immobilized by this scene of slaughter.

"Glaives!" Pritus barked.

"Rocks!" his young Caltean assistant echoed, tending to the Brocks.

The Brocks' barrels were refilled, the glaive throwers loaded.

"Fire!"

A shower of glaives shot over the wall, followed by a cascade of rocks.

A new torrent of agonizing screams assaulted my eardrums. Wincing, I closed my eyes. That felt a bit better. I just wished I could block my ears with something. Unfortunately, my commanding rank didn't allow for such luxury.

The Nocteans' last attack was by far the most desperate — and scary. Fear gripped my heart in its insistent sleazy tentacles.

A loud cracking sound came from a distance.

Droy next to me jumped as if electrocuted. "The gates! All available warriors to the gates!"

His captains started running around, issuing orders.

"To the gates, quick!" Droy bellowed.

"The gates!" the captains echoed his order.

Still, the Caltean warriors on the walls already knew something must have changed on the other side. A few of them dropped from the wall like ragdolls and never came back. One of them had a stone axe buried in his back.

"Shield Wall!" the commanders shouted. "Serry the ranks!"

Two giant captains, Crym and Orman, towered over their soldiers like cliffs, repeating Droy's commands. Their two companies locked their shields and raised their spears, making a formation about a hundred feet from the gates.

Behind their backs, the companies of Horm the Turtle and Seet the Burly hurried to fall in, readying their arrows and loading their crossbows. Whoever would attempt to break into our camp wouldn't enjoy it, that's for sure.

The Brocks continued to launch their deadly missiles over the wall. The glaive throwers fired non-stop.

If it went on like this, our artillery wasn't going to last long. Pritus still had about forty charms left; I had another twenty.

We absolutely needed to get rid of the Noctean avant-garde before they exhausted us with their constant assaults. We needed at least a three-day break before the main horde arrived. We were too low on energy. We needed to do something pretty soon.

"Get ready!" Droy continued to spit orders.

"Hold the line!" his captains' commands reached far over the orderly ranks.

The soldiers' faces betrayed a calm determination to die.

"They'll break the gates down in a moment!" someone shouted from the wall.

The miserable makeshift structure we so optimistically called "the gates" was gradually crumbling under the blows of hundreds of stone axes.

Finally, it gave way with a thunderous creaking. I could already see the Nocteans' bared teeth through the splintered gaps in the wood. Froth drooled from their jaws. Their animal eyes glowed with madness.

One last blow.

The jury-rigged arrangement of wooden planks, rocks and pieces of metal listed forward, forming a gap for the Nocteans to pour in. They looked a sight, I tell you. They'd suffered a lot in this last battle.

Ignoring their terrible wounds, they lunged forward blindly like puppets controlled by an invisible puppeteer. The gateway soon filled with a mass of gray bodies which continued to pour forward like a river bursting a dam.

"Fire!" Droy barked.

Hundreds of arrows showered the gateway,

followed by rocks from a Brock which Pritus had promptly had moved over.

Finally I could see the Ennans' killing machine in action. The torrent of rock shrapnel blocked the gateway with the Nocteans' still stirring bodies ground to a pulp.

The system kept showering me with messages. I was already level 230.

"Glaives wait!" Droy commanded. "Another Brock ready!"

"More rocks!"

The Brock assistants didn't have to be told twice. They were already filling its barrels with new boulders, working efficiently and in synch.

Healers threaded their way through the crowd, helping the wounded. Young boys and girls flew up and down the walls delivering armfuls of arrows.

Droy watched as the army executed his orders. "Wait for the second wave!" he thundered.

The Nocteans weren't long in coming. Once again the breached gateway filled with their growling mass. These were considerably stronger, their levels higher. Many were holding clubs and stone axes.

"Aha," Badwar chuckled bloodthirstily. "The Kerook is sending his elite."

"He must be real close," Lavena added.

A double volley from the Brock made quick work of their so-called elite.

Suddenly it dawned on me.

Eureka!

I turned to Droy and my champions. "We need to kill their leader, otherwise we'll still be fighting them until the main horde arrives. And then we won't have any energy left to face them."

Judging by the grins on their faces, they loved the idea.

"You understand, don't you," Droy began, "that you're the only person capable of stealing up on him."

"Oh yes," I agreed. "The problem is, he's clever. I've tried to do it quite a few times already but he keeps a low profile. If we kill him, it has to be done quickly. I alone can't do it. I don't have the right weapons."

"How about your scarabs?"

"They're not right for this kind of job. The Kerook's bodyguards will engage them, allowing their master to disappear. We need to kill him in one clean sweep."

"What a shame," Badwar said. "If only you had Lavena's skill!"

I turned to double-check on her. Lavena the Vixen had the body of a gymnast, small but strong and agile. A powerful composite bow peeked from behind her back.

I opened her stats and looked for her super

---

blow. Aha. The Mountain Hawk, activated by every fifth arrow she launched.

Badwar had been right. This looked like just the thing we needed, with excellent damage and bonuses to Accuracy. And if you added my legendaries to this...

Droy guffawed. "Look at his crafty face! I bet he's already come up with something!"

"Come on, tell us," Badwar demanded, playing with his poleaxe.

"I have an idea," I said. "I wonder if I can pass my skills on to her?"

I looked over their puzzled faces until my gaze alighted on Lavena. "Are you okay with flying?"

My plan was simple. Lavena and I would leave the city hidden in the middle of serried ranks of warriors to make sure the Kerook didn't sniff us out. He was a cunning little bastard, elusive like you can't imagine. I already knew this from experience.

But the moment our tanks drew aggro to themselves, he'd be obliged to take command of the Noctean attack. That's where we would come into play.

Boris' new skill allowed him to carry two riders. And once our tanks had tied the Nocteans down in battle, Lavena and I would do our little double act.

"You must be bored, kiddo," I whispered into Boris' ear, stroking his back. "Time to stretch your wings."

Lavena was stroking his neck in silent awe. He accepted our affection with calm graciousness.

"You need to trust him," I told the girl who was visibly on edge. "Flying is great. You're gonna love it. Now remember. You need to get to him as close as you can and shoot him at point blank."

She kept nodding as she admired Boris' silvery ashen feathers.

"Advance!" Droy growled. "Let's kick some butt!"

The air was shattered with the roaring of hundreds of warriors brandishing their swords, poleaxes and spears.

Our giant mass of steel stirred and headed for the gates. Lavena and I walked behind the tanks' backs. I'd unsummoned Boris, unwilling to expose him too soon.

The earth groaned with the lockstep of our armored boots. The sergeants' commands hung over the ranks clanging and rattling with steel and wood.

An eerie feeling dawned over me. I felt one with these hundreds of warriors, my brothers in arms, who would unhesitantly give their lives for me. Did the devs really think so low of me, believing me capable of betraying them? So which one of us was playing this game, then?

We reached the gateway. There wasn't a single Noctean still alive there. A game, yeah right.

We walked out of the gates — or whatever was left of them — and stopped, taking in the scene of carnage behind the walls. Some Nocteans still stirred, their plaintive groans floating over the battlefield.

The Noctean elite stood in a single line about five hundred feet away from the gates. They looked remarkably calm, with only an occasional growl or show of teeth-baring.

The Caltean warriors lined up to defend the entrance.

"Why aren't they attacking?" I whispered.

"The Kerook is waiting for more food to come out," Lavena replied, also in a whisper.

"In that case, he has to be somewhere around," I said. "He must be very strong to control so many monsters at once. We're obliged to rid them of him."

"He's not going anywhere," Lavena promised. "Today is his last day."

"Once the melee begins, we need to get closer. I'm counting on you to seek him out."

"I'll keep my eyes peeled," she bared her teeth in a predatory grin.

I opened my profile and began activating all

my legendaries. The Calteans met my "Keeper's magic" with wholehearted cheers.

I downed a potion and turned to Lavena. "Let's do it."

* * *

Reluctant to witness a new massacre, the sun took shelter in its celestial halls behind the leaden thunderclouds, leaving the handful of valiant fools to the mercy of cannibalistic hordes.

The two armies froze at a mere five hundred feet from each other. The Calteans' locked shields resembled a wall of steel barring the entrance to the upper city. Their eyes glowed with fury from under their helmets, their strong hands clenching their spears.

Archers were lined up on the wall, ready to do battle. I glimpsed Pritus' black robes rushing to and fro amid the glaive throwers. He was probably busy loading them with the remaining charms. I'd given him mine before I'd left, keeping just one for replication purposes.

The warriors on the walls cheered, encouraging us. Badwar raised his poleaxe, triggering another wave of battle cries.

"Fire!" Droy thundered.

More arrows rustled out of their quivers.

Bowstrings groaned.

The fletched messengers of death escaped the confines of the city wall, enjoying their free flight and celebrating their freedom. Then Mother Earth pulled them back down. In answer to her call, hundreds of arrows began their descent.

From the safety of my position behind our tanks, I couldn't see the arrows pierce Noctean bodies. I was too focused on one single spot at the very heart of the enemy formation. I thought I'd glimpsed something there.

"He's over there," I whispered, pointing at a Noctean group that had caught my eye.

Lavena nodded. "I think so too. I can sense his power. It's like the cobweb of a big black spider. How strong he is! Incredibly powerful. It's our duty to kill him before he becomes even stronger. Whatever it costs! Even if we die, it's worth it."

An icy fear ran down my spine. A primeval panic tugged at my heart. What on earth was wrong with me?

I stood behind the soldiers' backs, tense as a coiled spring, ready to summon Boris and soar up to the skies. My Fix Box was full to the brim, ready to shower the enemy crowds with every bit of metal I had.

The invisible puppeteer gave his troops the order to proceed. I sensed his command with every fiber of my overwrought psyche. Or could it be my imagination playing up?

In any case, the mass of mobs shifted into action. Howling and roaring, they lunged at our ranks.

"Hold the line!" Droy's voice sounded as if from afar.

The barrage of arrows kept coming from the walls, piercing more Noctean bodies.

The Calteans tensed up. Their bristling spears prepared to receive warm flesh.

The first Noctean line was almost upon us, enormous clubs in their clawed paws, their tiny eyes glowing with fury and savage hunger, their fangs grinning.

Fifty feet.

"Hold the line!"

Twenty.

Ten.

"Hold the-"

Droy's order was drowned out by the clatter of steel and screams of agony.

The first strike was horrendous.

The Nocteans barged headlong into us without sparing their lives. Like mindless zombies, they threw themselves on our spears trying to break the first line of our defense, slaying our warriors with heavy blows from their clubs and claws.

The first two Caltean lines had died almost

instantly. Still, their death wasn't in vain as the Noctean attack had become bogged down, their advance hindered. More arrows kept showering the mobs from the walls, sowing death in their collective wake.

Death reigned on the battlefield. The small area in front of the city gates was filled with mortal cries and the agonizing screams of the wounded. All the shouting, the growling and the groaning added to the mayhem.

And there was only one creature lurking somewhere here which enjoyed this gruesome symphony.

Finally, I saw him.

So that was the Kerook, then. Tiny and cute he was, like a cuddly toy. Which had in fact given him away.

His fluffy snow-white coat stood out amid the Noctean leaders' gray bodies. The bastard watched the massacre, pulling the invisible strings like a spider watching a fly struggle in his web.

"I can see him!" I shouted to Droy. "He's very close!"

Droy nodded his understanding and began dishing out orders. A new formation took shape at the center of our ranks, resembling a turtle bristling with poleaxes and spears, the warriors' shields forming its shell.

A few crossbowmen stood at the heart of this new structure shoulder to shoulder, prepared to give us covering fire with a barrage of bolts.

Trying not to betray our presence, Lavena and I ducked under the shields. I glanced at the girl. She was ready.

"Forward!" Droy commanded from behind us.

"Rrrragh!" the warriors grunted in unison, stepping forward. They pushed the last remaining line of Nocteans back, assaulting their armorless bodies with spears, hammers and poleaxes.

The warriors' broad "green" shields absorbed Noctean attacks. Our soldiers winced and frowned with the effort but kept the beasts at bay.

"Forward!"

"Rrrragh!"

"Forward!"

"Rrrragh!"

Bristling with spears, our tiny turtle kept advancing through the raging sea of Nocteans step by strenuous step.

"Forward!"

"Rrrragh!"

The Kerook was very close now. I skulked behind a warrior's broad back for fear of alerting the monster to my presence.

Lavena must have sensed it too. She clenched her bow tight, readying herself.

Finally the Kerook drew his attention away from his army and deigned to notice us. I could clearly see several giant Nocteans forming a gray cocoon around him to shield him. The barrage of arrows kept piercing the gray bodies of his bodyguards who silently fell to the ground only to be immediately replaced by new ones.

Nasty little douche. Sitting there all nice and pretty.

We were already within twenty feet from him when he finally relented and began to retreat.

His hissing sliced through my brain like a shard of broken glass. The Calteans stopped. They couldn't move any further, completely bogged down in the banks of mangled Noctean bodies.

Droy was covered in blood from head to foot. "Forward!"

"Rrrragh!"

Straining every sinew in their bodies, the warriors took the last and probably the hardest step in their lives. The first line of tanks crouched, leaning on their spears.

I readied myself. Lavena the Vixen tensed up next to me.

The warriors' powerful broad backs strained. Their shields moved in unison in a sweeping upwards motion, throwing back the Nocteans pressing against them.

The creatures fell against the ranks of their peers standing behind them, forming a pandemonium of hairy gray bodies.

I used the commotion to activate the summoning charm, then released all of my scarabs.

Sorry, guys. It'll get less crowded in a moment.

The rest happened as if in slow motion: the angry, uncomprehending Nocteans, the retreating Calteans and five steel tanks sinking their sharp mandibles into the screaming mass of mobs.

Boris soared up with an effortless ease. To him, two riders made no difference whatsoever.

Lavena sat with her back pressed against mine. She drew her composite bow.

I told Boris to circle the scene.

"I can see him!" Lavena shouted.

Her bowstring sang. She rapidly loosed off a flight of four arrows, following it with an unhurried fifth one. She must have taken her time for better accuracy.

The arrows avoided the bodyguards' bodies. They had only one target in mind.

As if sensing the danger, the Kerook dodged left, then right, then ducked under a large column fragment.

All five arrows missed. Lavena cussed in a most unladylike way.

"Circle him!" she barked.

Boris flapped his large wings and flew low over the chunk of debris where the Kerook was cowering. The little bastard actually peeked from behind it.

Seeing us, he darted off, apparently intending to take cover in the ruins of a house — like a petrified prairie dog trying to escape a predatory eagle in the safety of its burrow.

Boris was giving it his all. Finally, his swift shadow covered the Kerook. Behind my back, Lavena strained, drawing her powerful bow.

The Kerook screamed, realizing he wasn't going to make it.

This time we wouldn't miss him.

"Boris, chant!" I shouted.

His Triumphant Crow assaulted our fleeing quarry. The Kerook froze, turning into a fluffy pillar of salt.

Five arrows pierced his body almost simultaneously. The fifth one glowed with a pale blue flame.

It hit the little bastard right in the back of his head, shattering his skull.

Dead.

The system dutifully reported his death and the XP points received.

Then something weird started happening below.

The Nocteans seemed to be awakening from a

hypnotic trance. They stopped, looking fearfully around. Some swung round and hurried to flee the battlefield; others assaulted their own.

The well-knit Noctean pack had ceased to exist, turning into a disorganized rabble.

"Retreat!" Droy kept shouting. "Quick! Behind the wall!"

Now that the Nocteans had stopped attacking us, our warriors retreated in a single unbroken formation.

Boris flew us over the wall. The next moment we stood surrounded by friends.

The warriors cheered our arrival, slapping our backs and shaking our shoulders. I received their praise, smiling like an idiot.

Lavena and I exchanged a hearty handshake.

"it was a good idea telling your bird to sing," she croaked. "For a moment, I thought he'd get away."

"What, from your arrows?" I laughed. "Are you kidding me? He had no chance!"

Our celebration didn't last.

A single blood-curdling howl came from the direction of the hills.

Another one echoed it. And another. And a few more.

Not this again! What was going on?

A sentry's warning resounded over the city

walls,

"Werewolves! Werewolves!"

* * *

That was Shaggy again. Cheeky bastard. He'd waited till we went for each other's throats before attacking us. Basically, he repeated what I'd done to him earlier.

Just when I thought we'd won this round.

I remembered the werewolves' tactics well. I dreaded to even think what they would do to our craftsmen, women and children if they broke into the city.

The two remaining scarabs had frozen in the werewolves' path, preparing to ram them. They didn't have much durability left — but they should buy us a little time.

As I tried to arrange them into a defense line, Droy got busy dishing out orders.

"Retreat! What are you looking at? Fall back behind the walls! Move it! Those on the walls, get ready for action!"

The sergeants and captains joined in, nudging the flabbergasted warriors into an organized retreat. The mixture of blood, slush and mud underfoot hindered their progress.

Encouraging his army non-stop, Droy approached me.

"Don't summon any more scarabs," he said in a peremptory tone. "The gates are broken, whatever's left of them. We can't keep the werewolves out. But we can trap them. We'll need a Brock to do that. You must go back. The youngsters won't manage without you. I want you to keep an eye on them."

I nodded, not quite yet understanding his intentions. As I hurried toward the Brocks, I heard his voice again,

"Wait for my command to fire!"

The nearest of the Brocks was facing the gates. The runic inscriptions covering its body glowed softly, enveloping the machine in their shimmer.

I began issuing orders. We didn't have the time to turn the other two machines toward the gates. I just hoped one would be enough.

The system reported the Brock's readiness.

My heart fluttered in my chest. I was too nervous and too afraid for the others' lives.

As if sensing my state, the Brock vibrated softly.

"Rocks! Get more rocks!" Pritus was shouting at a distance.

"The werewolves are coming! There they are!" archers shouted from the walls.

The first Caltean warriors appeared in the gateway, retreating in organized rank and file. Lancers were running toward them, readying their weapons.

Some were pushing empty carts toward the gateway hoping to barricade it for a while.

"They're led by Shaggy!" the archers shouted from the walls.

"How many of them?" warriors asked from below.

"At least three dozen!"

"What about the others?"

"They're fleeing!"

So Shaggy must have decided to attack us in small numbers, anyway. He was apparently putting his hope in the werewolves' strength and speed, hoping to finish us off in one fell swoop.

"Olgerd, are you ready? Wait for my signal," Droy shouted, then immediately addressed the others, "Shield Wall!"

"Line up!" Badwar roared, brandishing his enormous poleaxe.

"Rrrragh!" hundreds of throats grunted in unison.

The warriors locked their shields. Their ranks bristled with spears. They were defending their houses, their wives and children, their parents, their brothers and sisters. They weren't going to give one inch of their freedom to the enemy.

"They're at the gates!"

The sentry's voice was drowned out by the cacophony of blood-curdling animal cries.

The warriors on the walls showered the enemy with arrows, darts and crossbow bolts. The first Noctean screams of pain were met with a celebration of gleaming weapons as our warriors spat curses on the enemy's heads.

The Brock's giant arms swung back, preparing to launch their deadly missiles.

Shaggy barged in first.

He was enormous. His savage primeval rage drew everyone's eyes to him. His body was massive but lithe. His hair was a very deep brown, almost black, with a few graying patches on his head.

And his eyes! They glowed with triumphant fury.

I paused momentarily, admiring this handsome beast. He stopped in the gateway for a few heartbeats, staring at his victims in proud confidence.

Then werewolves began pouring out upon us. Not quite as big, they were just as hungry and desperate.

Roaring, they barged toward our shield wall, disregarding the bristling spears. Studded with lances and arrows and awash with their own scarlet-red blood, they ignored their mortal wounds, throwing themselves into the battle.

In one lightning-fast leap, Shaggy overtook his avant-garde, taking the lead. They were about to crash into our shield wall.

Droy's voice reached me through the thick fog of congealed time,

"Olgerd! Now!"

The Brock's long arms jerked into motion.

Bang!

With every fiber of my body, I sensed the lethal flight of the death-bearing rocks.

Bang! The other arm went off.

Droy's calculations had been right on target. By the time the Brock fired, virtually all of the pack had already crowded inside the gateway.

Two split seconds later — the time the Brock had needed to fire its missiles — the werewolves had ceased to exist. The barrage of stones had literally ground them into a pulp. Their still-twitching bodies were immediately studded with arrows.

This was a clear victory.

I was close to insanity as I watched the gory nightmare. Now more then ever I wished I could press the Logout button long and hard.

I shook my head. I needed to get a grip.

Rubbing my eyes, I tried to concentrate on the work at hand. God knew I had plenty of things to do.

Puffing with pride, Droy supervised the gates' restoration. We exchanged glances, then nodded simultaneously to each other.

Life was moving on. If only we could build a wall like the one around the citadel! Complete with steel gates at least fifteen feet wide.

Yeah, right. Dream on. It was time for me to get down to earth and get working.

Still, I could use a brief break. Nothing wrong with catching a few Zs. My mental state would thank me for it.

As I walked toward Droy's tent, I had to go past a dilapidated shed. I was too busy contemplating my warm bed to notice something which was definitely out of place there. I had to double-check — and once I had, I stopped dead in my tracks.

The shed had a door. But not just any old door, either. It was white and made of plastic. Nothing unusual about it.

Just a standard office door.

Chapter Twenty-Three

I STARED AT THIS real-world object, amazed at my own hesitation. I must have really settled into my role if the sight of a humble piece of plastic could give me a culture shock.

Normal, if you think about it. Anyone would freak out seeing a nice clean office door amid a bloodied medieval battlefield.

My Caltean friends, however, didn't seem to notice it at all as they walked right past it.

Olgerd, Olgerd. Why would they? Come on, put your brain in gear already! This door is for you. Just pull the flippin' handle. The Mirror World bosses must have something to tell you.

I walked over to it.

Aha. The number on the door looked familiar.

That's right. The same old number 1 glistened on the dark-blue sign.

I gave the door a light push, already knowing what I was going to see inside.

The room hadn't changed. The same dark gray filing cabinets. The boxfuls of papers. The printer. The black computer screen. Vinyl windows.

I stepped toward the window, curious to see what was behind it.

This time it was a seaside resort. The golden beach was packed with sunbathing holidaymakers. Colored beach umbrellas cast patches of shadow onto the sand.

Water bikes sliced through the azure waves. Further on, boats large and small rocked on the waves.

The waters by the shore seethed with people swimming, diving, splashing and enjoying the sun.

I gulped. I'd have loved to join them!

The door opened behind me. I forced my eyes from the window and turned around.

A man stood before me. His closely cropped hair was snow white even though he wasn't at all old. Clean shaven, with a firm chin and intelligent eyes. About forty-five, maybe. He was at least six foot tall, with broad shoulders and an air of military bearing about him.

His sharp gaze studied me. "Sir Olgerd, it's nice to see you here, Sir," he finally said. "You can call me Sergei Sergeevich. It's a nice day, isn't it?"

"It is, for some," I nodded at the window. "Not for me, I'm afraid."

He ignored my words. "Please take a seat," he nodded at a black office chair, then sat down himself.

Rattling my armor, I followed suit.

"Sir Olgerd, I'd like to move straight to the point. First of all, I need to tell you that our team is absolutely thrilled with your progress. For somebody with no physical training or prepping skills required by these kinds of survival games, you've done admirably, much to everybody's surprise."

"Thank you," I said. "Honestly, I didn't expect this kind of praise. I thought you were going to tell me off."

He stared at me, uncomprehending.

But now my inner dam had burst. I couldn't hold anything inside for much longer. "What I mean is this weird situation around this obelisk. I know we had an agreement. I would find the city and activate the crystal, and you would fund my daughter's surgery. In actual fact, I kept my word in almost everything. I've found both: the city and the obelisk. Now I'm busting my guts trying to defend it. But if this is about my refusal to perform a mass sacrifice, sorry, I can't do that. I'm not that kind of person. This wasn't in the agreement. I know they're computer characters, but I'm not! I can't just kill two thousand women, children and old people! For me, they're real. They're my friends. They trust me. And in any case, it's not as if I'm late with my loan repayments. Also, I'm giving you some good publicity. The clans' armies are already on their way. You can't complain, really. What with the war and everything..." I minced the last words.

The man listened to me impassively without attempting to interrupt me. Once I'd finished, he leaned back in his chair and locked his fingers.

"So you don't know anything yet, do you?" he asked.

My heart missed a beat. "Pardon me?"

"The thing is, the people you had an agreement with don't work here anymore."

"What do you mean they don't work here anymore? I thought that girl... that lady, Vicky, I thought she worked for you?"

"She most surely did. She doesn't anymore. Nor do her superiors. If I can be completely honest with you, the entire Mirror World administration as you know it has ceased to exist."

"Wait a sec... and the bank..."

"Oh, no, no, no, you misunderstood me. Reflex Bank is still active and in perfectly good shape. It's changed hands, that's all."

I emitted a nervous chuckle. "But what

about...”

“Don’t worry about your loan. Your agreement is still in force. You made it with Reflex Bank, didn’t you? Is that correct?”

Thank God. “Perfectly correct,” I said. “But if you don’t mind me asking... who’s controlling the company now?”

“You don’t need to know that. I can only say that the old administration’s attempt to cash in by activating a new game plan was the reason for the urgent transferal of the controlling block of shares to us. I can tell you more: it was entirely thanks to you that their little scheme failed to succeed.”

“Can you explain?”

“Sure. Their analysts had badly misinterpreted your psychological profile. They made sure you had enough NPCS in order to perform the ritual. One thing they didn’t anticipate was that you might refuse to do it. That created a minor delay which proved critical for us. You bought us the time we needed. We really appreciate that.”

He stood up and proffered his hand. “It’s been nice meeting you. Don’t worry about the loan. Just keep paying it off. I hope it’s not for much longer. Your body is perfectly safe in the module center. Also, as a sign of our appreciation, we’ve arranged for a very decent discount for you on all our services for the duration of one year. Your brother is still working for us, by the way. He might get promoted soon. I don't think I'll see you again, unfortunately. Have a nice day."

He opened the door, about to leave.

"Wait a sec," I finally got my wits together. "What am I supposed to do now?"

He turned back to me. "You're a free man now. Apart from your loan, you have no obligations to Reflex Bank whatsoever. Enjoy the game."

I stood by the window admiring the sea view and replaying our conversation in my mind.

You're a free man now...

You're a free man now...

That was it. Mission accomplished. I was free. I could press the Logout button whenever I wanted to. I could go back to my family.

The sheer thought warmed me inside. But...

I couldn't abandon the Red Owls. That would be just as sick as sacrificing them, only in a different manner.

I shouldn't make any illusions about players, either. To them, every Caltean scalp had a price tag attached. Some of them were quite capable of slaughtering Caltean children wholesale.

"Very well, Sir Olgerd," I muttered. "Is it Plan B, then?"

* * *

The moment I walked out of the virtual office, I noticed that the camp was strangely quiet. Almost deserted, in fact. The sentries were still on the walls, but not a commander in sight. No sergeants, no captains... actually, no adults at all. Where was Droy? Pritus? What on earth was going on?

With a weak cry, a young archer on the wall came tumbling down a ladder, counting all the rungs with his spine in the process. He scrambled up off the ground and darted toward me, his eyes wide open with horror.

He ran blindly, repeatedly stumbling and falling, before he reached me. Gasping for air, he kept opening his mouth like a grounded fish, struggling to speak.

"Keeper! They... you know... over there... it's-"

"Calm down, boy," I said, trying to sound composed. I was about to explode myself. "Take a deep breath... like this... good. Now report."

He obeyed my instructions, then began to explain,

"All the adults are gone. They told me to say good-bye to you for them."

My back erupted in a cold sweat. "Gone where?"

"Over there," he pointed at the quiet camp.

"They went to see the dead Keeper."

I left him and dashed for the door to Brutville Halls.

I just prayed I wasn't too late.

What the hell were they up to?

Women and children crowded around the open hatch. Some were crying. Others stood silent, as if frozen.

Some of them saw me. Hope filled their eyes.

What on earth was going on here?!

I dove into the hatch and flew through the tunnel. I popped out of it like a champagne cork and galloped down the hall praying they hadn't done anything stupid. Faster.... faster...

The Caltean warriors stood with their backs to me. They hadn't noticed me yet. This looked like the entire Caltean army: adult warriors, young men and quite a few women too.

All of my commanders stood motionless next to the Obelisk. Laosh froze with his head bowed low, listening to the Keeper's ghost.

"Am I interrupting something?" I yelled sarcastically.

All heads turned to me.

I looked into their faces. My friends, my brothers in arms. They preserved a grim silence. Some averted their stares; others glared defiantly back.

Whispers ran riot.

"Ah, here's your Keeper!" Brolgerd faked a welcoming smile.

"Shut up!" I snapped, striding through the parting crowd toward Droy. "What's going on here?"

"Can't you see?" Droy replied calmly. "He told us that our lives would be enough to charge the crystal."

I crossed my arms. "Ah-ha."

"Olgerd, you need to understand," Laosh cut in. "This is the only solution. The horde is almost upon us. The united armies of Dark and Light will be here any day. We can't defeat them. What we can do is offer a voluntary sacrifice. If we feed the Obelisk, it'll protect the others. Our children will live. Otherwise we have no future. The old Keeper promised us-"

I looked around me. "Let's listen to what others have to say."

"Please don't stop us," Pike said calmly. "We must do this."

"The enemy's too strong and too numerous," Badwar growled. "There's no way we can defeat them. Had it only been the horde, no one would have contemplated this. But each human warrior, either Dark or Light, is worth ten Calteans. Neither the Brocks nor the city walls can stop them. I'd much rather die in battle but that's too easy. Too irresponsible toward my children."

"If we die in battle, we won't be saving

anyone," Lavena added. "But if we die here, we'll provide the others with the protection they need. We'll give them life."

The ghost was beaming like a Cheshire cat. What a lunatic.

"Is this what you all think?" I strained my voice, looking over the crowd.

"We do."

"Yes."

"Sure."

"And me in turn, I give you my word — the word of the City Keeper — that your families will live!" the dead Master Brolgerd shrieked, his eyes glowing.

"The word of the City Keeper?" I snapped. "I've already believed a few. One wanted me to come here running — but as it turned out, he was a bit economical with the truth! Two more abandoned us in the deserted city, leaving us to fend for ourselves amid all the ruins and desolation! And now you — and what did you offer me the moment you saw me? You wanted me to sacrifice my friends!"

I was adlibbing my head off. I could only imagine the admins scratching their heads in front of their computers.

"My friends!" I shouted, adding a note of remorse to my voice. "This is all my fault! I led you into a trap! No wonder your ancestors nicknamed this place the Forbidden City! All I can say is that I trusted those so-called City Keepers! I thought I could revive the Obelisk on my own! Had I managed to do so, we'd have all been safe now!"

"Don't blame yourself, my friend," Droy thundered. "Had it not been for you, many of us would have been rotting in the ground a long time ago! You were the only one who offered us the chance to survive!"

The throne room echoed with cheers.

"But knowing you," Droy added with a cunning squint, "you've probably already come up with something, haven't you?"

Chuckles ran through the crowd. Smiles of hope lit up some of the faces: the hope that they just might avoid the slaughter.

"You could say so," I replied.

"Speak up!"

"Tell us!"

Their voices rang with newfound optimism.

This felt like a déjà vu. This was how they'd cheered me by the fire when I'd first suggested we went to the Ennan City.

With one difference. Today I wasn't obeying anyone's instructions. No one was offering me prompts telling me where to go. Today, I was choosing my own path.

"Okay, okay!" I raised my hands in the air to quieten them down. "I have a suggestion to make. I'm telling you straight off it's not gonna be easy!"

"Is it better that being slaughtered here like cattle?" Orman shouted.

"Oh, absolutely!"

"Then tell us!"

"Speak up!"

"As you all know, I went on a bit of a recon. I needed to find out how close our enemies were. I saw the horde and the united armies! But that wasn't all!"

"What else did you see?" Laosh said in a fallen voice.

I looked at him. "Shaman, we've both been wrong, you and I. This place will never become a new Caltean home. If anything, it'll become our grave. But I know of a place where there're no Nocteans! The warriors of neither Light nor Dark can reach it! And what's even better, there're no loony Keeper ghosts there!"

"Yes, please!" someone shouted. "Where is it?"

The crowd's thunderous laughter shattered Brutville Halls.

I peered at their severe faces. They were all ready to follow me to hell and back if needs be.

"I suggest we go and reclaim your old home! We're going back to Silver Mountain Valley!"

Chapter Twenty-Four

I STILL SMILE REMEMBERING the commotion that went up in the crowd when I'd said that.

The cheers! As you might have guessed, the Calteans had promptly forgotten all about mass sacrifices. Or psychopathic ghosts. Both the "Keeper" and even the very entrance to the Brutville Halls had immediately been consigned to oblivion.

The camp dissolved into a flurry of packing up.

We'd cleared the Armory and loaded all its contents onto sledges. The Brocks, the glaive throwers and the trebuchet would have to be taken apart and packed into crates. We'd have to do that last thing before leaving.

The death of the Noctean "puppeteer" had bought us some downtime. According to my calculations, we had less than forty-eight hours until the horde arrived. Still, it gave us plenty of headstart.

We didn't even consider the smaller Noctean groups. They were no danger to us. They'd previously engaged us in battle a couple of times but that was nothing compared to what we'd already suffered. It was such a good job we'd managed to kill both Shaggy and his Kerook. Had the Nocteans had a half-decent leader now, we wouldn't have had it so easy.

Droy had appointed a cavalry commander: Bevan the Raven, a sinewy black-bearded guy, one of those who'd descended with us to the West Grotto to fight the king of Thorn Rats. Apparently, Bevan was one of the Wolves' best. Droy must have set his sights on him there and then, so now he'd entrusted him with the command of two hundred riders.

Finally, my third scroll had come in handy. The V-Formation, remember, the one I'd received with my Commander General's rank? It allowed you to organize heavy riders in a, well, V-formation. They would attack the enemy followed by light riders — mainly archers — who would finish off those who'd survived the first wave. Also, the formation had bonuses to damage, strength and speed.

(Later, we'd have a chance to see the V-Formation in action when a small Noctean group attacked our returning caravan. You can't forget that sight in a hurry, I tell you. Even the Calteans themselves couldn't believe their eyes.)

Now as they were busy packing, I checked all the remaining nooks and crannies in the city in the hope of finding something worth my while. No such luck. The admins had run out of freebies.

Still, I wasn't too upset. We had plenty of stuff as it was. The siege machines were a treasure in themselves. Now we had enough protection wherever we went.

We left the city early in the morning. We broke camp properly and walked unhurriedly under the heavy escort of our riders and footmen. I'd activated all of my buffs, too. Just in case, you know.

I had mixed feelings about leaving Twilight Castle. On one hand, it was a shame I hadn't completed the quest. Activating the Obelisk might have given us loads of various bonuses. And whenever I looked back at the long path we'd traveled to get here, I almost kicked myself.

But on the other hand, whenever I looked at the unfinished wall and the clumsy lump of tree trunks and bits of steel we'd proudly called the city gates, and at the black ruins sticking out of the snow like rotten teeth, I felt a huge relief. I was tired of being a pawn in somebody else's game.

At least now I was my own master.

I took the caravan along the northern side of the mountain range that led all the way to Silver Mountain Valley. I called this route the Northern Way. True, it meant we had to make a dog's leg — but it was worth it. The Noctean horde was moving toward us along the range's southern side. None of us was really looking forward to meeting them.

On the second day of our journey, I received a pompous system message telling me that the Nocteans had taken Twilight Castle, therefore I'd failed my mission and had been stripped of my proud title of City Keeper. Immediately, the bunch of the keys to the city and the page of Arwein's notes disappeared from my bag.

That was it. All the tails had been docked.

Strangely enough, I kept all the trade route maps and city plans. Apparently, they weren't part of the quest.

On the tenth day of our journey, I decided to take Boris and go have a quick look at the city.

What I saw there left me speechless. The entire valley had been scorched. There were no Nocteans left there anymore. Apparently, the clans of Light and Dark had already made quick work of them and were now busy slaughtering each other. I couldn't have made a better decision.

Nobody had activated the Twilight Obelisk. It looked like this place was going to attract greedy stares for a long time still.

Good. I just hoped it stayed that way.

* * *

The morning sun enveloped the valley and the surrounding cliffs in its warm sparkling veil. Its touch melted the snow which ran away in hundreds of little rivulets, hurrying away from home to see new uncharted lands.

The cliffs, fed up with the winter chill, offered their flanks to the warm sunrays. The spring walked across the valley, her soft green footsteps awakening the frozen earth from its hibernation.

"Silver Mountain Valley starts behind that forest over there," I told Droy who was standing next to me. "We're almost there."

"Oh yes," Droy replied, peering at the dark depths of the forest. "The Rock Wood. I've never seen it so close before. But I've heard so many legends and ballads about it..."

I chuckled. "You and your ballads! If I listened to you, the Red Owls would sing them all day long."

He grinned, then continued in a much more serious tone. "I suggest we set up camp here. Everybody's tired; they need a break. Three days of rest might do it. You could take Boris for a quick spin, just to check out the area."

I nodded. "Good idea."

It had been twenty days since we'd left Ennan City. I wouldn't say it had been a walk in the park — quite the opposite, in fact. Still, our little exodus had proven very productive.

Every now and again, our caravan had aggroed some very impressive mobs, all of them levels 400+. I was curious to see what kind of creatures inhabited the North of No-Man's Lands. As soon as we arrived and began settling down in Silver Mountain Valley, I might take Boris on a recon mission to those parts of the world.

Apart from fighting off mobs, we'd managed to loot five mini-instances. I'd made level 300 in the last one — a nice round number.

I'd long overgrown my current gear. My bag was packed to the brim with loot. I also had new pages available in my Book of Blueprints. Now I could make a 30-strong colony of ants and a spider which could spin cobweb traps. But to do all that, I needed more materials.

The Owls weren't too far behind. They were long ready to advance to the next development level. So I could use a break, really. It was high time I saw my old friend Rrhorgus. He was probably wondering what the hell had happened to me.

* * *

"To tell you the truth, I'm so happy it worked out the way it did," Rrhorgus said pensively after I'd finished telling him my story. "I was very worried about your relationship with the players' clans. Both of the Light and the Dark. And now it looks like they have more important things to worry about."

"You could say that. I sent you the footage. You'll see what they've turned the valley into. It's like a nuclear bomb site."

"Talking about which," he perked up. "You know that your videos are trending, don't you? That girl's channel has made it to the Top 100."

"I've just sent her more of them. Lots of interesting stuff there. You're gonna love them."

"I'm sure I will. She must be very happy."

I shrugged. "I don't know who'll be happier, her or myself."

Rrhorgus' green Dwandish mug grew long with amazement. "Why?"

"When I came back and checked my inbox, I saw a few letters from her as well as some money transfer reports. Apparently, she kept sending me my cut for the viewings."

Rrhorgus scratched the back of his head. "I must be getting old. Do they get paid for posting stuff?"

"Apparently. Talking about which, I have something to send you too," I forwarded him his share of the gold I'd farmed in both the grotto and the city treasury.

He stared at me open-mouthed. "Where did you get this from?"

"Just looted the city a bit. Was I a Keeper or just a pretty face?"

"That's the way to do it!" he rubbed his hands, then added, raising a meaningful finger, "Loot is an important factor in our emotional security!"

"Don't give me that shrink stuff," I said.

"Come on, don't drag it out! Where is it?"

"It's right here, man!"

As I produced last month's pickings out of the bag, I thought he might need emergency resuscitation. All the bones, fangs, animal pelts, weapons, armor, crystals, materials, stones and elixirs... I had no idea my bag could fit so much!

"And finally, this," I said triumphantly, producing a small pile of steel pieces.

They clattered onto the table with a dull glint.

"Is this what I think it is?" Rrhorgus wheezed, near unconscious.

I really should have been more careful. I only had one best friend. "It is," I nodded. "Field Altar fragments. Four 'red' ones and five 'purple' ones. One 'purple' one is ready to be assembled."

In actual fact, it was the Kerook that had dropped one of the "red" fragments. All the rest we'd farmed in the mini-instances on our way back to Silver Mountain Valley.

"You have any idea how much it costs?" Rrhorgus whispered, his shaking hands fumbling with the pieces.

"And this is only the beginning," I told him.

"So while the players are busy at each other's throats trying to claim Ennan city, you moved on. And? What are you planning to do there?"

"Oh, whatever. A new settlement. A city. A country, maybe?"

Chapter Twenty-Five

SPRING WAS on a roll. The sun shared its heat generously with even the darkest corners of Rock Wood. The birds exchanged the latest news in cascades of happy twittering. The first buds covered tree branches, promising to soon unfold into gentle green leaves.

Whoever had named this location must have been out of his mind. I'd never seen so much vegetation anywhere in Mirror World.

We'd been crossing Rock Wood for four days already. Unlike the Icy Woods with their dead trees, this one was perfectly normal albeit wild and untrodden, overgrown with chaotic clusters of conifers and deciduous species. It differed so much from the organized cultivated forests of the real world with their disciplined ranks of carefully chosen trees.

Our advance was slow but not because we were tired. The Calteans had rested really well during our three-day stop. They'd slept a lot, eaten their fill and were in great shape. The reason for our slow advance was Shorve and his men's constant forays out to investigate the way. Thanks to them, we'd already successfully avoided an encounter with a small but very predatory group of giant level-500 pangolins. We'd been forced to go off route for a while just to make sure we didn't run into their buddies. The fat treetops had rendered me completely useless as a scout which was why Shorve's men's skills were greatly appreciated.

Naturally, we could handle these kinds of mobs these days — but not without casualties.

Every time we stopped, we started by making lots of fires and posting sentries next to them. Caltean strength and stamina never ceased to amaze me. No one complained; there was no bellyaching or protesting no matter how hard the going had gotten.

The Calteans obeyed their commanders' orders indiscriminately without arguing over them. They remained calm even though the trek through the woods wasn't the easiest. Most likely, they managed to grab a bit of rest during the recon stops. That and also my buffs which I kept activating non-stop.

Our champions were especially courageous and disciplined. Their very presence seemed to improve the others' morale. They tried to be everywhere at once, supporting their clanmates.

I too tried to follow their example. Which was why I'd offered to stand the night watch.

I'd spent half the night sitting by the fire waiting for Badwar and Lavena to relieve me. Still shivering from their sleep, they moved closer to the flames.

Even though this place was much further south of Ennan City, this wasn't the real south. No palm trees and sunkissed beaches here.

I stayed by the fire for a while just to make sure the other two had woken up properly, then made myself a bed nearby. I closed my eyes and began thinking about all the recent changes in my life. About my wife and my daughter and everything that had happened lately.

Gradually, sleep enveloped my mind, adding a touch of fantasy to my thoughts. Over the last few weeks, I'd learned to balance between sleep and wakefulness without succumbing fully to my slumber. This is probably how wild beasts rest, ever-watchful.

Also, a weird uneasy sensation didn't let me sleep properly. This was what my grandfather used to describe as a "gut feeling".

Still, gradually the night had taken its rightful

---

toll, suppressing the weak impulse of anxiety. I just needed some peace and quiet...

I sat up and rubbed my eyes. "Who are you?"

I didn't expect to see this at all. A small Alven girl sat by the fire, her blonde hair and light clothing a stark contrast to Badwar and Lavena's heavy gear. They were only at arm's length away and still they completely ignored her. The two exchanged short phrases, keeping a watchful eye on the night forest.

The system refused to identify her. The girl didn't seem to have a name or a level.

She sat by the fire sideways hugging her knees, her slanted blue eyes watching the flames. The fire cast an uneven light on her ponytail and freckled face.

The impossibility of it threw me. How did she get here? Why did no one seem to see her?

"I'm surprised you've noticed me, mortal."

I jumped at the sound of her soft calm voice. She didn't take her eyes away from the flames. She didn't move; she hadn't even turned her head.

Badwar and Lavena continued to exchange whispers. They couldn't hear her, dammit!

She paused, waiting for me to say something, then went on, "I haven't seen sentient beings in this forest for centuries. And now you — so many!"

For a brief moment, her smile seemed predatory — then the calm, impassive expression returned to her pale face. "Do you like our forest?"

I just nodded.

Our? Did that mean she wasn't alone here? Then again, why should she be?

"Please stay. We'll be happy to have you."

The same predatory smile again.

I dared not breathe, too scared to attract her attention. And she just sat there hugging her knees and staring at the fire.

"We have so much space here. You'll like it."

Strange she didn't move. Normally, people are obliged to change their position from time to time. They can't just sit motionless like that. Only her lips seemed to be moving.

I heard a fresh branch crackling in the fire. Pine treetops rustled overhead.

I desperately wanted to wake up but it didn't look as if I was sleeping. This seemed to be for real. The fire, the night, the strange visitor, the unsuspecting Calteans apparently unable to see her...

Talking about which, the sentries would have to be relieved soon.

As if sensing my thoughts, she finally looked up at me. Her slanted pale blue eyes focused, unblinking, as if reaching into the very depths of my soul.

I tried to avert my own gaze but couldn't. Was she trying to hypnotize me of something? What were the admins playing at?

Her voice had changed imperceptibly. Now it sounded hard and insistent,

"I've changed my mind, you know. No, you're not gonna like it here."

Her mouth curved in an unnatural bloodthirsty grin. The rest of her face remained frozen, devoid of any emotion.

Still unable to move, I noticed four small fangs showing behind her pale bloodless lips.

Something was going very wrong here. Spine-chillingly so.

"You know what I think?" she continued. "You might die very soon. Still, you have a choice. Leave these mortals. Fly away. They're a nuisance."

I was completely paralyzed, unable to move a limb. My breathing slowed right down. Every breath became a struggle. I was suffocating. My mouth went dry. I was thirsty as hell.

Panic gripped my mind, immobilizing my arms, legs, my shoulders. My chest heaved. My oxygen-deprived lungs were on fire.

What was going on here? What kinds of special effects were these? The further into No-Man's Lands, the more hardcore it became.

Now my every heartbeat added anger to the chilling panic. A hot, furious rage — and the more I fumed, the weaker my invisible fetters grew. Was the effect wearing off? Was it some kind of warning from the admins?

My suffocation began to ease up. The creature's stone face shifted into a mask of surprise. Her right eyebrow rose slightly; her mouth curved in disdain, baring two of the fangs.

"You seem to be stronger than I thought you were, human."

This voice was different. The apparition began to fade. I'd been right, then: this had only been a temporary visual effect.

What a relief. I'd very nearly freaked out. My blood was still boiling with adrenaline.

A weird little creature was now sitting where the Alven girl had just been. The size of a ten-year-old child, it had weak emaciated limbs covered in hard gray skin. It sat in an ungainly pose with its knock-kneed hind legs tucked under it.

The creature's head was small and wrinkled all over like a shrunken potato. Its teeth were small and sharp with pronounced fangs. Patches of short mousy hair covered some parts of its body.

The firelight reflected in the creature's enormous pitch-black eyes which stared at me unblinkingly like two saucers.

I was feeling slightly better now. Still, the moment I tried to move and take a deep breath, the invisible weight pressed me down again, binding my body with the same spine-chilling stupor.

Bastard admins! Them and their experiments!

After a few more unsuccessful attempts to wrestle myself free, I tried to relax and calm down.

"That's better," the creature croaked. It sounded as if it coughed out every word. "I know you can understand what I'm saying. I've been keeping an eye on you for quite a while, human. Hehe."

"What do you want?"

The fact that my idle immobility was nothing good was pretty self-explanatory. On the plus side, the numbness seemed to subside. I needed to bide for time. This was probably the best tactic for this sick scenario.

The creature didn't seem to have heard my question. Its wrinkled body stretched out, as if awaking from a slumber. Dark webbed wings opened up behind its back, ending in sharp bone spikes. The wings were three times wider than its body, making it look a bit like an oversized bat.

The first flying NPC, LOL. New competition for my Boris.

"Do you remember the farm behind the stockade? I can see you do. I saw you tame that Hugger. Well done, heh. When I told my sisters about you, they didn't believe me. They laughed at me."

Mechanically I looked around, expecting to see more adversaries. I dreaded to even think what the "sisters" of this abomination could be capable of.

I still remembered the dead farm. The caked blood. The ashes. And now the camp full of sleeping Calteans.

So it had been her, then.

The creature croaked, laughing. "Don't worry, human. My sisters didn't believe me. Which is a shame. Now I'll have all of your strength. I'm so hungry. I'm so happy I've arrived here first... before my sisters..."

"How about a deal?" I offered, bidding for time. I could move freely now but I continued to fake numbness, wheezing and gasping as if from lack of air.

There was one thing I couldn't understand. There I was shooting the breeze with a monster from hell — and my Calteans were dead to the world!

"You're stupid. All humans are. Can a spider make a deal with a fly?"

Well, that's a matter of opinion.

My summoning amulets were ready. The Fix Box was fully charged. Thanks to my new "purple" gear that Rrhorgus had procured for me, I wasn't so nice and cuddly anymore. He'd actually promised to arrange a closed auction for me for the set I'd won back in the Isles. According to him, players were fighting over items like those.

I was ready to attack. Still, I needed Calteans

---

to back me up. Even though I'd received no system messages, I'd have been stupid not to see that this was one hell of a powerful mob.

"I'm tired of you... You've made me hungry."

That was the signal for me to attack.

I lunged at the creature like greased lightning. I'd never moved so fast in my life. I gave it my all.

My little fleas also leapt onto her like silver darts, aiming for her shriveled chest.

Her agonizing squeal made the blood freeze in my veins. Twenty high-level fleas can do this to you!

Screeching and wheezing, the creature spread her enormous wings and darted up into the air, trying to brush the fleas off with her scrawny little paws. In her agony, she'd forgotten about her surroundings and revealed herself to everyone in the camp.

You need to give my friends their due. They quickly put two and two together and jumped to their feet, ready to fight. Lavena rolled away from the fire and was already loosing off arrows into the sky.

Badwar rushed toward me, trying to cover me with his shield. The remaining three Caltean scouts hurried to string their bows, about to join Lavena.

Now we were going to show her!

In the meantime, something had happened to the creature. Her body began to grow. Just a moment ago, her shriveled chest had been trembling, pierced by several arrows — and now it was expanding, growing strong before our very eyes.

The weak knots of muscles covering her puny limbs expanded, turning into herculean steel cables. Her clawed fingers extended; her little fangs had grown big and strong.

Her powerful wingbeats raised dust into the air. A mixture of dry leaves, twigs and still-burning embers enveloped us.

The monster wasn't squealing any longer. The night woods shuddered with her powerful roar. The thing's huge black eyes searched for her attackers in the midst of the humans fussing about below.

My fleas died one after the other, leaving scary-looking venomous wounds in the monster's body.

The first one of Lavena's glowing arrows pierced the creature's shoulder, extracting another ear-shattering roar from its throat. More arrows assaulted it as if on cue, piercing its legs and ribs and puncturing its wings. In a desperate wingbeat, the beast managed to dodge the last arrow.

I did my best to keep up with the archers. My slingshot kept firing non-stop. Not that it was much good but still. Rrhorgus had promised me to talk to some craftsman who apparently could improve my fabled "Minor Pocket Weapon". The guy was a Master Blacksmith who did a bit of DIY on the side, making sure it didn't come to his clan's attention. I'd have to wait for that. Same applied to my "red" belt buckle: I needed a Master Leatherworker to make an actual belt for it, and that wasn't going to be easy.

Finally, the monster killed the last flea. There was no point making more because the creature was too high in the air, anyway.

It moved fast amid the trees. Unless it got out into the open, my Boris was no match for it. No point summoning him or Prankie, either. Both were almost the same level as myself now. The last time I'd gone to the continent, I'd paid another visit to Master Rotim who'd leveled their old skills up a bit and opened a couple of new ones. He wasn't getting any cheaper! Still, now Boris boasted a Furious Peck while Prankie could cast a speed buff on me.

Wailing like a banshee, the monster took to the sky until it reached a certain height. It closed its wings and began dropping down, spreading its talons in front of it like a hawk going for its prey.

Oh bummer. It was aiming for me! I must have pulled all the aggro to myself.

Still, that also meant it was going to land.

I stopped and raised my head to the skies. Come to Daddy, little birdie. I have a surprise for you.

"Get ready! It's coming down!" I shouted to the warriors.

My temples were splitting with the strain. Still, it wasn't the right moment to worry about myself. I stood motionless with my legs spread wide, clenching the little mirror in my right hand. Come on now!

It kept dropping toward me like a giant rock, apparently savoring the moment of sweet revenge.

Badwar the Thunder Warrior roared something to his men. Now that I'd seen his battle axe in action, I knew why he was called so!

Lavena was snapping commands to the archers. Now the fun would begin.

Finally, the monster's giant black shadow covered me.

I leapt aside.

You've activated the Magic Mirror of Ishood!

My exact copy was now standing where I'd just stood. I didn't have the time to enjoy the likeness: the beast went right through it, hitting the ground nice and hard.

Warning! Your reflection has been destroyed!
You can use the Mirror again in 01:59...

The monster's attack had been crushing — literally. Had I stood there, I'd have been back at my respawn point already.

The creature raised clouds of wet top soil as it searched blindly around, digging through the heaps of pine needles and rotting leaves looking for me. Its disappointed wail echoed over the camp.

Just what we needed.

"Boris — chant! Scorpy, your turn!"

Boris appeared out of nowhere with an ear-shattering scream.

Oh wow. He was good, wasn't he?

The monster froze in place like a pillar of salt, staring meaninglessly into space. The Scorpion sank his pincers into the creature's webbed wings, pulling aggro to himself and immobilizing it even more. His long steel tail began punching the mob's gray skin with its sharp venomous tip.

"Fire!" I shouted to the archers, releasing another swarm of fleas.

With a furious growl, Badwar lunged at the monster and brought his battle axe down onto its head, again and again, until we heard his weapon's signature sound which resembled a thunderclap.

The creature finally awoke from its stupor and snapped at the Scorpion's steel pincers. Its claws sliced through the shiny armor on his back.

Some damage that was!

Hold on, Steely Guts, I'm coming!

Badwar was getting tired. He'd barely dodged a blow from the creature's powerful spiky wing. One of the monster's claws brushed against his back. Had it not been for his armor, he'd have now been lying on the ground with a broken spine.

The fleas clung on to the creature's body, busy sucking its blood. The Scorpion replied to its every blow with several lightning-fast stings.

Arrows showered the monster non-stop. The battle axe wounds on its body looked awful. The flea and Scorpion toxins slowly corroded the creature from the inside.

It was growing weak. Its body resembled a lump of bloodied meat.

We were nearly there. Victory was close at hand.

What's with the absence of system messages? Why couldn't I see the mob's stats? Not a single damage report! Was it some error? A glitch? A bug?

One of Lavena's "blue" arrows put an end to the battle, sinking deep into the creature's head. The monster choked on its own roaring, emitting a shrill ear-shattering scream. It began to shrink before our very eyes. Its scream of agony stopped mid-note.

It collapsed to the ground.

Silence hung over the camp.

* * *

Congratulations! You've killed a Vapree (level 500), one of the five Icy Dhuries!

Reward: The Icy Heart of Vapree, 1

Kill all 5 Dhuries and collect 5 hearts to receive a Dhurie skill of your choice!

Congratulations! You've received a Legendary Achievement: Epic Monster Slayer. You're a legend!
Reward: the Order of Victorious Gaze

For your information: as the holder of the legendary Order of Victorious Gaze, you bring +30% to Observation Skills of all group members.

We were sitting around a freshly-started fire. The camp looked like military training grounds after a good shootout. Clumps of wet soil covered everything around: a rotting mixture of old moss, pine needles, blackened leaves and dank twigs.

I looked around me, taking in our camp's state.

The sun had long risen but wasn't in a hurry to show from behind the gloomy gray clouds. The air was damp and fresh.

We'd already packed our stuff. The Calteans seemed to have finally recovered from the horror of the previous night's battle. Or at least they'd stopped ambling pointlessly around the camp looking lost.

My pets had long forgotten their ordeal and were now playing chase with abandon. Looking at them, I couldn't help feeling as if this was but a

---

leisurely walk in the park.

Badwar had removed his armor and sat by the fire, his torso bandaged with wide strips of fabric. The monster had grazed him, after all, giving him a "purple" back injury. I could see his life dwindle, then promptly restore again thanks to my Order.

Badwar's pained breathing didn't prevent him from wolfing down the thick stew sitting in front of him.

Lavena and the archers got away unscathed. I was shaken but unhurt. My temples tingled a bit, that was all. As soon as I got out of the capsule, I'd have to discuss all these weird special effects with the staff. Were they trying to experiment on the players or something?

I'd managed to grab a bit of sleep after the battle, but not much: two hours at most. Now I just sat there, taking in the results of last night's party.

Lavena was sitting next to me cool as a cucumber, wrapped in animal skins. This was one tough lady. She'd fought with the best of them and basically decided the outcome of the battle.

I turned to the Calteans. "Thanks a lot, guys. You've saved my life. Had it not been for you..."

"Get away with you!" grinning, Lavena offered me a steaming bowlful of stew made with smoked meat, roots and herbs. "Shut up and eat."

I nodded my gratitude, accepting the delicious

offer. "Do you know what it was?" I asked her.

"Vapree," she said curtly.

Aha. Did that mean they were familiar with that little beastie?

"Vapree?" I asked, faking incomprehension.

"Yes, Vapree, one of the five Ice Dhuries. She's the horror of this land. The true Lady of Rock Wood. Legends say, it was her who gave life to the first Black Groves. I never thought I might see her in the flesh one day."

"Didn't she say something about her sisters?"

"You shouldn't believe everything she says," Lavena said absent-mindedly. She kept turning around, peering into the impenetrable woods.

"Our old shaman used to say his scrolls only mentioned three of them," Badwar mumbled through a mouthful of his stew. "The other two have never showed themselves to us. I always thought those were just fairytales for the kids. And now this..."

"Vapree means *Power over Dreams* in some ancient tongue," Lavena added. "Our shaman used to tell us stories about her too."

"So only three of them have been described, then," I murmured, thinking.

"Exactly," Lavena said. "The other two are Nerkee and Aise, or so the scrolls say.

"*Power over Woods* and *Mighty Mountain*," Badwar translated.

"They say that Nerkee prowls the world in the shape of a giant she-wolf," Lavena added.

"And Aise, what does she look like?" I asked.

"We know little about her. Some say she lives in the Damp Cliffs. Her skin and heart are made of stone and her eyes are blocks of ice. That's all we know. I used to think they were children's stories. Yeah right! So many things have changed over these last few days."

"Did you say she'd been sitting right next to us and we didn't see her? What was she doing?" Badwar asked.

"Who, that monster? I really don't know," I said. "At first she looked like an Alven woman, only she was very small. She spoke to me, inviting me to stay and abandon you. And then my breathing stopped. I couldn't move. I thought I was dying."

"You were lucky," Lavena said softly. "Normally, Vapree assumes the shape of a loved one. A lost son, a dead husband or an old mother who's long joined her ancestors in their celestial halls. The Lady of Dreams has many faces. We know her better than the others because she just won't leave the Caltean people alone."

"She's committed many a black deed," Badwar clenched his fists. "Old legends said that she could appear to a group of warriors resting by the campfire at night, pretending to be their dead leader, casting her charms over them and luring them into the woods. There were stories about deserted villages where everything remained untouched: the livestock still in their barns and people's possessions still in their homes. Only a whole bunch of footprints leading toward Rock Wood. But today, the dreadful legend has ceased to exist!" Badwar's face glowed with triumph.

I chuckled. "You could say that. I bet the whole forest heard her screaming. We might get other nasty visitors in a moment. The sooner we move on, the better."

"I don't think so," Badwar said. "I could bet my poleaxe that no beast will dare come anywhere near this place for a while. They all know what happens to those who stands in Vapree's way when she hunts."

Lavena smiled. "How are they supposed to know she became prey this time? Nothing will happen if we stay here for a while. We need a break, after all."

Badwar paused, thinking, then nodded. "Very well. Let's stay and wait for the main group."

Then he cast her a begging glance. "Is there any more of that stew left? I'd never eaten anything like it, I swear!"

Chapter Twenty-Six

WE ADVANCED much faster now. The forest was changing, becoming clearer and less dense. We didn't have to fight our way through the brambles and undergrowth anymore. Everything pointed at us approaching the sea.

Short squat trees which looked more like oversized shrubs were scattered amid the many glades and clearings. The dark, rich, heavy soil had been replaced by layers of yellow sand.

Sand was everywhere here. It spread in the rippling waves compacted by the incessant sea winds. The trees had all but disappeared, replaced by gnarly low plants which crept over the sand. Sun-bleached and eroded by the briny breeze, they were determined to survive.

As we walked through this sparse sandy forest, I couldn't help thinking about nature's variety. You can spend hours watching all the changes. This very area might once have been the sea bed once inhabited with fish and other marine creatures.

Then again, what was I talking about? This was only a game.

The sand was just as pregnant with history as the dark soil of the forest. I scooped up handfuls of it and brought them up to my eyes, letting it slip through my fingers as I studied the tiny white, pink and purple fragments of seashells where clams had once lived; withered bits of seaweed and tiny fragments of rocks. Kudos to the game designers: they'd done an incredible job.

I shook the remaining sand off my hands and wiped them on my pants, sensing a thin residue still clinging to my palms.

I brought my hand to my face and licked the tip of a finger. It tasted salty. The sea wasn't very far away.

Droy — and not only him — found my actions amusing. Actually, the Calteans had cheered up a lot. The excitement of the journey's end was palpable in the air.

Orman who knew this area well had told us that if we continued in this direction, we might soon reach the old lighthouse — probably some time during the coming night. According to him, there was a small settlement there, five or six houses where we could ask for lodgings for the night.

Then he became crestfallen. He must have remembered I'd already been here.

I'm so sorry, my friend. There's nobody here anymore. Only Unai and his Sea Tigers. The last survivors.

I'd love to know how they were doing, actually. I had lots of presents waiting for them.

It had been three days after the night battle with Vapree. The shock of meeting her had gradually worn off over those three days, dissolving into the air over our numerous stops and campsites. We hadn't seen any evidence of large mobs here anymore. Their packs tended to move further to the left from the route I'd chosen.

Shorve's men had stopped going on extended recons. It was my job now. Open spaces were my forte.

As we traveled, my Calteans did quite a bit of herb gathering. Rock Wood was a true treasure trove of all sorts of plants. The clan's herbalists and medicine women had the time of their lives, scooping up everything under their feet like combine harvesters: all the healing herbs, roots and tree buds which they then used to prepare all sorts of potions and bandages.

The news of Vapree the Lady of Dreams being slain had spread like wildfire. The locals greeted us as heroes, cheering Lavena the Vixen and her archery skill.

* * *

The day was on the decline. The sun was about to retire to its celestial halls. It hurried to share its last golden rays with the tired travelers, saying goodbye to earth and preparing to relinquish its duties to its younger sister Moon.

Our caravan of about three thousand Calteans was making its way through the sparse wood, trying to stay in the shade of the low trees. From above, our column resembled a giant speckled ribbon which snaked warily along the unknown path.

Many of the Calteans had recognized these places. This gave them the extra bit of strength they needed. Some of them even ventured into the woods — although they never strayed too far and only accompanied by warriors.

The commanders turned a blind eye to these forays. The men deserved a bit of fun. They'd been great throughout this perilous journey. Also, I was keeping an eye on them from above, anyway.

Soon the path took us to a large field surrounded by a dilapidated picket fence. After the multi-day trek through the woods, the panorama of the open space held the promise of freedom.

We stopped by the field's edge. Reclaimed from the woods, it was now overgrown with grayish waist-high weeds. The wind ruffled the sturdy plants which had survived the tough winter.

The rippling dirty-yellow sea of grass seemed to glow against the leaden backdrop of the darkening sky. The combination was quite spine-chilling.

The fence was made of rows of crooked horizontal planks nailed to low stakes, gray and rotting. It must have served to protect the crops from some of the larger mobs. The gaps between the planks were wide enough to let in smaller animals — but not a herd of reindeer, for instance. It was also entwined with some thorny creepers.

Longhorn animal skulls were mounted on some of the stakes. The fence had sagged and collapsed in places.

When I approached it, I heard a strange humming sound coming from the field. Focusing, I realized that it was coming from skulls which served as makeshift guardians, scaring away birds and animals.

This field used to belong to a small Caltean clan long before the Horde had arrived here. Their shaman hadn't been present at the famous council. He'd probably never made it.

The Calteans mood had changed. Instinctively, the warriors stood back to back, weapons at the ready.

They seemed to be expecting an invisible enemy to charge at them from the wood. All conversations had stopped. Any wayward travelers had rejoined the ranks.

Warily the caravan moved along, skirting the abandoned field.

The skulls' song followed us for a long time afterward, urging us to leave the spooky opening.

Even when we finally re-entered the safety of the woods, the clan didn't regain its cheerful mood. They walked in silence, casting frequent glances back and peering into the falling darkness.

Only when we decided to stop for the night did the tension subside somewhat. Hundreds of campfires shot into the sky in a large forest meadow, filling it with the aromas of food and smoke.

Our stew was ready and poured into wooden bowls which we passed around. In the meantime, Orman reached into the fire and produced a bird baked in clay. An appetizing juice oozed from the cracks in it. Orman had baked the bird feathers and all; now he was breaking up the clay which came off together with skin revealing the tender piping-hot meat underneath.

A heady aroma hung over the fire.

Shorve crouched next to me. "Did you notice?"

he whispered.

"That someone is following us?" I said without lifting my eyes from my food. "I did."

"Yeah. I noticed it this morning. They might catch up with us tomorrow. You know who it is?"

"No idea. They're disguised really well. I didn't dare get down any lower. They've been following us since yesterday morning in small groups. Twice they disturbed the birds. I think they know we've noticed them. You're right, they'll probably catch up with us by midday tomorrow."

"I'd love to know who it is," he mouthed.

"They're definitely sentient. Had they been animals or Nocteans, they would have already declared themselves."

I didn't like it. We had another hard day in front of us. Our pursuers had been following us since the very next day after our battle with Vapree.

I remembered some advice from a survival expert I'd seen on the Net. According to him, in order to find your bearings in a forest, you needed to find an elevated spot like a cliff, hill or a tree.

Or Boris' back, I added mentally.

Those who followed us seemed to know everything about my skills. I could bet my life they were players. Rogues, most likely, or someone with excellent stealthing skills.

Still, even they couldn't have foreseen

everything, like the birds they'd disturbed. Even though all I could see was a smattering of tiny black dots, I was pretty sure our pursuit was rather big: a very large creature or even a group.

Closer to the evening I went on another recon just for my own peace of mind. Everything was quiet; then some birds took to the wing again.

This was no coincidence. We were being followed.

The next day, my suspicions were confirmed. Our pursuers were catching up with us. Shorve noticed them too.

I didn't want to alert the others. A panicking tribe was the last thing we needed.

We informed the warriors. Common tribespeople didn't need to know.

Droy increased our speed. Luckily, the terrain allowed us to walk faster. We planned on reaching the cliffs by the seashore which offered us an excellent foothold for confronting any unwanted guests.

The night passed uneventfully. Closer to midday, we finally reached the seashore.

The sea was raging, throwing tall gray waves against a lone black cliff on top of which towered an old lighthouse built with huge slabs of stone. Like a fairytale giant it stood proud over the furious surf which attempted to swallow it whole.

Next to it, I realized my own insignificance

unworthy of the elements' wrath. The sea was beautiful. It raised the winds to such a crescendo that we couldn't hear each other over their roar. Mountainous waves broke against the cliffs, shooting cascades of spray into the air. The breeze sprinkled our faces with brine.

Immediately our clothes turned wet; our hands and faces were covered in a fine sprinkling of salt.

We'd made it.

The corridor of cliffs welcomed us, calm and silent, its high vaulted roof dripping brine on our heads. The mere sight of it was breathtaking. It must have taken the sea many centuries to have cut this narrow passage through these cliffs which now resembled the insides of a giant snake or dragon.

Strangely enough, the passage was well lit inside. Sunrays seeped through the many cracks covering the rock ceiling, illuminating the walls that glistened with water.

"Part of the group will stay here," Droy told his captains when the last cart of our caravan had disappeared into the passage. "We'll post the archers on the clifftops. The foot soldiers will defend the passage. I don't think we'll need the cavalry here. Bevan the Raven and his men will meet the enemy on the other side."

"*If* the enemy makes it to the other side,"

Badwar growled. "Which I doubt."

The others met his words with predatory smiles on their bearded faces.

"Take up your positions!" Droy snapped.

Our army shifted into action.

Four hundred warriors — more than half of our little army — stayed by the cliffs outside to cover our retreat.

Our upgrading to "blue" gear was already in full swing by then. Admittedly, it was taking longer than our initial swap to "green". Making rare-class items took more time and demanded higher skill levels.

That's not to even mention the fact that our Masters had to work on the go. You can't do much without a proper workshop. Still, they'd been doing their best. At least we had plenty of materials courtesy of the Ennan treasury.

So now, a blue-and-green army stood in the enemy's path.

"Can't see a thing in this fog," Droy whispered, peeking from behind a large boulder.

Indeed, despite the proximity of the sea the entire area in front of the cliffs was covered in an unnaturally white mist.

"I think it's them casting it," I whispered.

Droy almost choked with surprise. He stuck his head above the boulder and began casting angry glares around.

"Get down," I told him. "You won't see anything like that."

"What are we going to do?" he asked.

"Nothing yet. Tell everyone to keep their heads down and pretend we haven't noticed anything. Pass it on down the line. Judging by their behavior, they're not local. They're players — either Light or Dark."

Droy nodded. "In that case, let's wait till they attack."

"Exactly."

I was about to add something else when Shorve's hand lay on my shoulder.

I looked at him. Shorve put his finger to his lips and nodded in the direction of the fog.

I took a wary look over the boulder. Oh. He was right. The white haze was thinning out.

"Sir Olgerd! Mr. Ivanenko! How are you?"

I wearily rolled my eyes. Not that voice again. Just when I thought I'd finally gotten rid of him.

I stood up. "I'm fine, Tanor, thank you, how are you?"

"I'd like to talk to you, Sir Olgerd. Could you tell your cutthroats to hold their fire, please?"

"Depends what you've come here with," I shouted back, never forgetting for one moment the guy was the Steel Shirts' scout.

I turned to Droy. "If you smell a rat, just

shoot."

He flashed me a bloodthirsty grin.

I vaulted over the boulder and stood at the foot of the cliff. All my little arsenal was ready: the Fix Box fully charged, the summoning charms ready for activation, the little mirror snuggled in my left hand.

A wave of quiet cheers ran over the Caltean ranks as I activated all the buffs.

In the meantime, the fog had retreated, revealing the slim Alven figure of my arch enemy.

As I walked closer, I managed to work out the fog's nature. The Shroud of Death, how appropriate. Definitely a Necro spell. Which was excellent, considering my friendly footing with that particular class.

Tanor hadn't changed one bit. Still the same squeaky-clean self, delicate and sophisticated. His face did bear the signs of fatigue, though. No wonder: trekking across No-Man's Lands was a bit different from prancing around in the Citadel.

He flashed me a pearly smile. "You've changed a lot."

"You haven't," I replied, stopping a few feet away from him. "I'm listening. The sooner we get this over with, the better. We have too many things to do."

Tanor cast a quick glance behind my back. "Of course. You're the leader of a whole nation now, aren't you?"

He sounded dead serious. How weird. Was it my imagination or was he sucking up to me?

I ignored his question. "Do I understand correctly you're here to deliver more threats and ultimatums? I'm afraid, you'll be wasting your time."

He waved his hands at me. "Not at all! Why would I do something like that?"

I chuckled. "Why wouldn't you? It wouldn't be the first time."

He shrugged. "You made the right decision leaving Ennan City. Still, why did you do it?"

He seemed to be avoiding the subject. Had he come here with the proverbial carrot?

"What do you mean, why?" I said. "I'm not mad, you know, having to battle two allied armies and the Noctean horde to boot. My warriors' lives are too important to me."

"Of course," he said with a knowing smile. "That's why you refused to sacrifice your NPCs in order to activate the obelisk. We couldn't work out why you did it. Our analysts' conclusion was that you'd simply failed to locate the obelisk, so you just left."

"Are you surprised?"

"Oh no, not at all. You decided to keep the clan instead. This strategy has a much bigger potential in the long run."

He didn't understand, did he? Never mind. It

---

was better that way. Let him think whatever he wanted. His underestimation of me worked to my advantage.

"So the city is yours now?" I asked.

His face darkened. "Yeah, sort of. Today at least. Tomorrow, I don't know. We'll see."

"Why haven't you activated the obelisk, then?"

"Let's put it this way: we won't be gaining a lot from it."

Whatever that was supposed to mean. "Aha. I see."

"Now, about the matter at hand. Sir Olgerd, I have the power to offer you a peace treaty. An alliance, if you wish."

So that's what it was, then. I'd thought it would come to this.

Of course: they didn't have enough resources to come after me, did they? They had them all tied up in their little scramble for Twilight Castle. While in the meantime, I could afford to level up my own resources at leisure.

So you want to have your cake and eat it, Sir Tanor? Very well.

I smiled to him. "Sounds good. A peace treaty to begin with, and then we'll see. Wasn't it Cicero who said that a bad peace is better than a good war? Are you happy with my reply?"

He beamed. "Absolutely! More than happy," he

heaved a sigh of relief.

* * *

"Congratulations, my friend," I lay my hand on Droy's shoulders.

He stood listlessly in front of a large log house. A tear rolled down his cheek.

It looked like my Droy the Fang used to be an important landowner in this part of the world. Before the Nocteans had come, that is. The house was a beauty. The barns. The outhouses. A large cattle yard. Everything still in good shape, virtually untouched.

"Thank you, my friend," Droy looked up at me with his open, grateful gaze. "That night, the skies took my best friends but in their mercy they sent you instead! You gave me my old house back! And not just mine! You gave us our homes back!"

He showed me his farm and his household, telling me how he planned to improve them. He and I, we had so much in common. He was just a man like myself, someone who loved his home and his family.

Boris soared on the air currents, enjoying his flight over the valley. What a beautiful place. Silver Mountains! Like a towering rocky stockade, they shielded the valley from the northern winds. A giant lake glistened below amid the lush green of endless gardens and groves.

"So what do you think, kiddo? Do you like the Calteans' home? Do you think Sveta and Christa might like it here too?"

Sensing my mood, Boris opened his powerful beak and shattered the skies with his triumphant aquiline cry.

We landed on top of the hill. I threw my arms around Boris' muscular neck, then activated the summoning charm.

I gave one last studying look at the valley below. Lots of work to do. Not now, though. Later.

I focused on the Log Out button. You can't imagine how happy I was to press it.

A Short Epilogue

DARKNESS. Boundless and intangible. Infinite.

It feels scary and comforting at the same time. Nameless it is, limitless and unending, holding the whole world within its embrace.

It has no face nor soul. Still, it's not empty. Because I'm there.

I don't yet know who I am. I can neither sense nor see myself. I don't feel anything. Still, I can think... therefore I am.

Wait a sec. I know that expression. It's been around for centuries.

Centuries? Does that mean there's more to the world than this darkness?

Of course. Now I remember. It's *time*.

My thoughts begin forming a chain, gradually bringing more memories out of my subconscious.

Obediently darkness succumbs to them and steps back.

My awakening hurt. The dull throbbing in my temples echoed down my neck and shoulders in sharp, piercing pulses. Impaled on thousands of little icy spikes, my frozen, numb body refused to come out of its hibernation.

The cumbersome leaden quilt of mental fog lay heavy on my weak awakening mind. Like a young blade of grass reaching for the sun, my brain strained its every cell trying to resurface from the darkness enveloping my subconscious.

Finally it shot out, its fiery flower blossoming within my mind and filling my body with joyful life.

Slowly I tried to part my eyelids. A thick cloudy film prevented me from seeing clearly. I blinked a few times but the obstacle wouldn't go.

Mechanically I raised my right hand to wipe my eyes. My fingers hit something. Their numb nerves refused to send signals to the brain, thus not allowing me to identify the obstacle.

After several fruitless attempts to remove the annoying item, my arm felt unbearably heavy. I summoned up all my strength and tried to hoist myself onto one elbow. A dull pain spread over my limp body. It didn't work.

I needed some rest. A heavy feverish slumber came over me.

I awoke from a bright warm light seeping through my shut eyelids. My ears felt blocked.

Without opening my eyes, I tried to move my fingers and toes.

They seemed to be okay.

The unpleasant throbbing pain was gone. Sensitivity had returned to my fingers.

I could hear voices coming through the rubbery silence. The familiar beeping of a life support machine. A door opened, then closed, letting in the sound of approaching footsteps.

This felt like a hospital bed. No wonder. How long had I spent in the capsule, several months?

Why was it so cold? Did they keep me in the fridge?

Something warm, soft and gentle lay on my cheek. It felt good. My unyielding lips began to stretch into a smile.

My eyelids parted. Through the cloudy haze in front of my eyes I made out the vague, blurred outline of a human face.

The soft, warm touch moved to my other cheek.

It was a hand. A very small one.

Then I heard a voice. So dear it was, so familiar and so warm.

"Daddy? Are you back now?"

End of Book Four

About the Author

Alexey Osadchuk was born in 1979 in the Ukraine. In the late 1990s his family moved to the south of Spain where they still live today.

Alexey was an avid reader from an early age, devouring adventure novels by Edgar Rice Burroughs, Jack London and Arthur Conan Doyle.

In 2010 he wrote his first fantasy novel which was immediately accepted by one of Russia's leading publishing houses Alpha Book.

He also used to be a passionate online gamer which prompted him to write the story of a man who joins an MMORPG game hoping to raise money for his daughter's heart surgery. In 2013, the first book of *Mirror World* was published by EKSMO, Russia's largest publishing house. The original Russian series now counts four novels which have been translated into English.

Want to be the first to know about our latest LitRPG,
sci fi and fantasy titles from your favorite authors?

Subscribe to our **NEW RELEASES** newsletter:
http://eepurl.com/b7niIL

Thank you for reading *The Twilight Obelisk!*
If you like what you've read, check out other LitRPG
novels published by Magic Dome Books:

An NPC's Path LitRPG series by Pavel Kornev:
The Dead Rogue

Level Up series by Dan Sugralinov:
Re-Start

**The Way of the Shaman LitRPG series
by Vasily Mahanenko:**
Survival Quest
The Kartoss Gambit
The Secret of the Dark Forest
The Phantom Castle
The Karmadont Chess Set
Shaman's Revenge
Clans War

Dark Paladin LitRPG series by Vasily Mahanenko:
The Beginning
The Quest
Restart

Galactogon LitRPG series by Vasily Mahanenko:
Start the Game!

**The Bard from Barliona LitRPG series
by Eugenia Dmitrieva and Vasily Mahanenko:**
The Renegades

The Neuro LitRPG series by Andrei Livadny:
The Crystal Sphere
The Curse of Rion Castle
The Reapers

***The Expansion (The History of the Galaxy)* series
by A. Livadny:**
Blind Punch
The Shadow of Earth

Point Apocalypse *(a near-future action thriller)*
by Alex Bobl

***The Sublime Electricity* series by Pavel Kornev**
The Illustrious
The Heartless
The Fallen
The Dormant

You're in Game!
(LitRPG Stories from Bestselling Authors)

You're in Game-2!
(More LitRPG stories set in your favorite worlds)

***The Game Master* series by A. Bobl and A.
Levitsky:**
The Lag

***The Naked Demon* by Sherrie L.**
(a paranormal romance)

More books and series are coming out soon!

In order to have new books of the series translated faster, we need your help and support! Please consider leaving a review or spread the word by recommending *The Twilight Obelisk* to your friends and posting the link on social media. The more people buy the book, the sooner we'll be able to make new translations available.

Thank you!

Till next time!